Praise for
Elizabeth Rymer Patterson
and *Bonners' Fairy*

The Legend Begins

BOOK ONE

Although mainly an avid reader of historical fiction and non-fiction, I read the *Bonners' Fairy* series because my daughter is the Author. I was absolutely amazed how they grabbed and held my interest from start to finish. They were a wonderful escape from the distressing events that normally occupy my thoughts in today's world. A refreshing change and a great read. Press on my daughter!

—*Gerald L. Rymer, Wisconsin*

Bonners' Fairy has become one of my favorite books ever. I urge everyone to explore what this work of imagination has to offer. I await more words of wonder and magic from the author of *Bonners' Fairy* in the future. An inspiring read.

—*LLH*

I loved your book! It was such a fun read! I can't wait to see what happens to Haley and Henry in the next one!

While Patterson's book is juvenile fiction, it was a refreshing look back at a time in my life when things were simpler—that of being 15 again. And yet, I think there is a fine line between fantasy and reality sometimes, something as adults, we need to embrace more often.

The world of *Bonners' Fairy* was a treat into which to escape. It is the first book in Patterson's planned series. I can't wait for book two!

—*Pat Walker, author of* Dance of the Electric Hummingbird

Bonners' Fairy, by Elizabeth Patterson, has been one of the most entertaining books I've had the gift of reading. At no time did I find it slow. The book was a page-turner from the very beginning.

Charming, imaginative, and the only thing that could possibly make it better is the release of the next book soon. Very impressive.
—*Robert White*

I read the book, and I loved it. My favorite part was when Haley and Henry first got into Roan. I loved all the characters and the way you described things; you made me really want to taste rainbow dew. Anyway, I love the book. I think that a lot of people are going to like it too.

P.S. I loved the note that you wrote me in the book.
—*Jessica Kirk, age 11*

This fascinating tale tells of Haley and Henry and their childhood escapades into the land of the fairies to save Zeb from the obsidian stone of Molock.

I thoroughly enjoyed this tale and eagerly await to hear more from our young heroes!
—*Sherwin Bydens, award-winning producer, professional actor*

I met Elizabeth at a book signing and was delighted to get her book. I had no idea how fun it would be to read! I thought it would be more of a tween book, but it appealed as an adult as well.

I would highly recommend it for all ages. What a fun tale of adventure and intrigue! Great book!
—*Gina Geldbach-Hall, author of* Firegal . . . Rising from the Ashes

A whimsical and uplifting fairytale for the future. A colorful and magical story of hope for all generations. It is a very comforting read for one's imagination that will leave you wanting more. A story to read and share with the whole family.
—*Sean Crawford*

Children of all ages will enjoy this story, for it is a compelling story of good over evil and courage and love over fear and hate.

A New Kind of Battle is the second book in a series by Elizabeth Rymer Patterson. Her first was a spell-binding and wonderful story I couldn't put down. *A New Kind of Battle* is just as wonderful, and again, I couldn't put it down. Elizabeth is a fantastic storyteller with characters so vivid and awesome that you are drawn into their world and lives. I can't wait for book three. I have known Elizabeth for years and never knew she had this kind of talent and imagination. I have a new respect and love for her. Keep writing, Elizabeth; you are amazing.

—Sally Meyer, South Lake Tahoe, CA

Just when Haley and her twin brother Henry return from their amazing adventure in Roan, a land of fairies, Sersha, their dear friend and fairy princess, returns to the human world with news of trouble. Haley and Henry set off immediately to the breathtaking and enchanted world to help explain the dangerous and mysterious happenings in the normally peaceful realm. Things that seem to come so easily for humans aren't so easy for fairies, and now, with the help of Haley and Henry, they have to learn how to live with the beautiful chaos that emotions can bring.

Bonners' Fairy: A New Kind of Battle sweeps you off into an enchanted world of fairies that can change size with a snap, witches on broomsticks, mermaids with beautiful shimmering tails, and creatures beyond imagination. Patterson's intricate details paint the picture of the captivating world of Roan so well that you feel as though you are flying through the air with Haley, taking in the breathtaking sights or talking to the Bocan Fish at Julius Caesar's house. It makes you believe that fairytales can be true and wish on that falling star that you can explore the world with your own eyes. Bonners' Fairy: *A New Kind of Battle* takes you to that world.

—Wendy Lee, Gardnerville, NV

Patterson does it again, *Sailing Toward Destiny,* bringing childhood characters to life and showing us how the bonds of love and friendship can conquer the most difficult of challenges. She displays how a scary and impossible journey to find and kill Medusa can be accomplished with the help of friends and loved ones. It's a great book and a must read series; can't wait for the next one!

—Wendy Martin, South Lake Tahoe, CA

I really like the *Bonners' Fairy* books. They are exciting, very good stories, and I really get into them. I'll keep spreading the word on your books!

—*Rain Allsenberrie, Nevada*

This series is magical! I became lost in this fantasy world and didn't want to put the books down. Elizabeth has a way of captivating the reader. I was entranced by the entire series and cannot wait till the next one comes out!

—*Dena LeGross, Nevada*

I finished the first book of the *Bonners' Fairy* series. It was quite the read! Elizabeth Patterson wrote her first book in a way that causes the reader to want more. She is a very creative individual and I enjoy her storytelling. I cannot wait to read the rest of the series!

—*Addison Poulin, Maine*

Bonners' Fairy

THE LEGEND BEGINS

Elizabeth Rymer Patterson

Published by
Elizabeth Rymer Patterson

Production Team
Patricia Beaulieu, Literary Agent, book division manager, and editor;
Nancy Ratkiewich, book production, njr productions; Juliette Burns, cover
designer; David Patterson, author photographer Elizabeth Rymer Patterson

For general information on other products and services, please visit the
website: https://www.bonnersfairy.com/

ISBN: 979-8-9897207-0-5 Paperback
ISBN: 979-8-9897207-1-2 eBook

LCCN: 2011910172

Printed in the United States of America

Dedication

Thanks to my husband, David,
for his continued support.

Contents

Acknowledgments

Gratitude and love goes to my husband, David, for unwavering support throughout this journey.

I extend heartfelt thanks to Trish Beaulieu, not only my Literary Agent but also my editor and proofer. Your invaluable contributions have played a pivotal role in shaping this work.

Special acknowledgment goes to Nancy Ratkiewich, the driving force behind the book's production, who handled the layout and formatting with utmost precision. Your dedication is vital to the readers who are engaging with this material.

A sincere shout-out to Juliette Burns, the creative mind behind the captivating cover design. Your imaginative prowess has exceeded all expectations, adding a unique and compelling dimension to the project.

Most of all, I thank the Lord. Without Him, this story would never have evolved into such an adventure.

Our story begins during the nineteenth century.

The sequence of events during that time period

have relevance to what occurs in the present time.

In the course of the story, we will jump from

one time period to the next and back again,

to fully appreciate the character's journey.

Chapter One

THE BEGINNING OF A LEGEND

It was the month of April 1806. William Clark and Meriwether Lewis had just returned from their long expedition out west. Half of Missouri was crammed into St. Louis to hear of their adventures.

The local mercantile buzzed with activity, as ladies admired the latest fabrics from Paris, while the children longingly eyed the candy barrels. William Bonner, the proprietor, breathed easier as his eldest son Zeb rode up on his bay mare. Zeb would now be able to help him with the hordes of customers.

Lewis and Clark's expedition inspired many with their long trek west. Even a newspaperman from Philadelphia was in town.

Zeb, his heart beating fast, was most excited. He and his new wife Sarah had been seriously considering heading west. Many young couples had already gone, with visions of gold in their heads, but Zeb wasn't interested in gold. His family was quite well off because of the mercantile and farm, which he worked in the morning hours. Zeb and Sarah craved adventure. In the spring they would get itchy feet, with a desire to travel, which stayed with them unfulfilled all season. They had grown up together, running in the fields and exploring where the roads would take them. Inseparable since they were children, they married on Christmas Day.

Zeb was twenty years old, tall and muscular. His dark brown hair complimented the twinkle in his deep blue eyes. Sarah had been a tomboy, who grew into a stunning beauty. She was sixteen years old, five feet tall and petite, with thick dark hair falling to her waist. She was sweet, kind and loved by everyone. Zeb adored her and had always been very protective. Many suitors wanted to court her, but Sarah's eyes sparkled only for Zeb.

He stepped behind the counter and for the next four hours, waited on customers without a break; selling everything from peppermint candy, muskrat and beaver pelts, to horse grain and one saddle. By closing time, he was exhausted. After locking up, he led his horse out of the small stable behind the mercantile.

The sun was just setting, and the sky was dark blue with pale purple hues. The smell of home baked bread drifted down the street as Zeb turned south and headed for home.

That night Zeb and Sarah talked for a long time about their desire to hit the road, to find adventure and a new home in the Wild West. She looked into his eyes.

"I want to go," Sarah said. "I really truly want to go. We can make it anywhere as long as we're together."

Zeb held her tight in his arms. "I love you so much. I'll tell Father in the morning and help my brothers finish putting in the crops, and we'll leave soon."

Over the next few weeks, Zeb helped with the crops and prepared the covered wagon. He purchased many tools and supplies they would need when they began building their cabin. Sarah stayed busy packing and finished the quilt she had been making.

Soon the day came to leave. After many hugs and tears, they tied four cows to the back of the wagon, loaded the chickens and climbed aboard, waving goodbye as they headed down the road. Zeb's heart raced. They had dreamed of going west since they were small kids, and now they were finally on their way.

The first couple of weeks they traveled many miles, the road was wide and well maintained. However, the further into the wilderness they went, the more difficult and time consuming the trip became. The heavy wagon had to be unloaded many times after getting stuck in the mud. Then there were the rivers to cross. On a few occasions, Zeb had to build rafts big enough to fit the wagon, in order to cross deep water, then scout for narrow places for the animals to swim across.

The journey took much longer than they anticipated, but Zeb and Sarah never lost heart. They enjoyed the blue skies and colorful sunsets. Even the pounding rain didn't dampen their spirits. When they arrived in what is now South Dakota, they had their first encounter with wild Indians. Sarah had never seen Indians before. Her heart pounded, and she was nervous. However, she was more curious than anything else. She heard stories about how Indians killed people and took their scalps, but never believed them. She was taught not to listen to gossip or to judge others by rumors and hearsay. It was the good Lord's place to judge, not hers.

They spotted them, as they were about to cross a small creek. Zeb told her to quickly get in the back of the wagon. They slowly began crossing the creek, when one Indian rode toward them, while the others stayed behind watching. Sarah peeked through a crack in the canvas.

He was naked from the waist up and was a fierce looking man with long shining black hair. The scar across his cheek was evidence he had seen many battles, but his jaw was firm as he rode tall and straight upon his horse—a man to be respected.

Sarah was afraid, but at the same time, fascinated, and she thought he was handsome.

Zeb got off the wagon and she watched as the pair walked to its rear. She held her breath, not daring to make a sound. Neither man could speak the other's language, but communication was not an issue, as the Indian gestured toward the animals. Zeb understood exactly what he wanted and they left the creek minus one cow.

"Better to lose a cow than your scalp," said Zeb with a slap of the reins.

For the next twenty months, they crossed many rivers and went over mountains with much difficulty, until finally, sometime in September, they arrived at a raging river. Sarah could tell by Zeb's frown they would never find a place where the animals could cross safely. She was weary and wasn't looking forward to waiting for days while Zeb built another raft.

Sighing, he scratched his thick beard. Turning to Sarah, he announced they reached the end of their journey and would homestead here.

She gave him a soft smile and nodded.

About a quarter mile behind them, they crossed a grassy meadow full of small knolls, bushes and ponds,which were surrounded entirely by tall rocky bluffs covered with dense thickets of pines, maples, and birch. A winding narrow creek babbled at its base.

They turned the wagon around and crossed the meadow. As they arrived at the creek, they knew this would be the perfect place to build their home.

Zeb decided the top of the bluff would be the perfect spot. He hiked to the top as Sarah stood, stretching out the kinks in her legs, watching her husband ascend.

At the top, he turned and surveyed the beautiful view.

"It's perfect!" he yelled, grinning from ear to ear.

Sarah smiled back and waved then turned toward the wagon. She would be glad when they finally had a shelter up. She was tired of living out of the wagon.

The next morning they were up at sunrise. Zeb scaled the bluff and started cutting down trees. The area was covered in many years' worth of fallen trees, leaves, brush, and pine needles; it would take a lot of work to clear.

A week later, with Sarah's help, they had a clear spot and enough pines to begin building. They constructed a makeshift shelter for the animals and built a small smokehouse, then finally began the outside structure of the cabin.

The first flakes of snow began to fall just as they were filling in the last cracks between the logs with sod. It had taken them a full three weeks to complete.

Hand in hand they admired their hard work.

Large soft flakes began to cover Sarah's hair. She never looked more beautiful.

They kept themselves busy during the following cold months. Sarah had her sewing and mending, and Zeb would venture out to hunt. The land was plentiful with rabbit, elk, and deer; they would have more than enough smoked meat to keep their stomachs full.

Finally when the warmer weather arrived, Sarah began her spring house cleaning, while Zeb tilled up a spot for the garden.

By the end of May, the garden was in, and within a few weeks seedlings began to appear. While Sarah was busy keeping house, Zeb surveyed the property in search for a good place to put in a cistern. He picked a spot about twenty yards from the cabin.

The cistern took an unusually long time to construct. He kept running into problems while digging. His shovel kept breaking, taking away valuable time for repairs, not to mention the torch kept going out. He was beginning to wonder if this was a bad spot.

Sarah went to the cistern several times a day to check on him. He was always late for meals and often worked late into the night. Finally, he finished and began to fill the cistern with water from the creek, but that wasn't the end of his troubles. Zeb had the cistern half full when it caved in. The water was contaminated. Frustrated, he threw down the bucket and sat on the ground. He would have to find a new place to dig.

A month later, a new cistern was complete and none too soon. Sarah was going to have a baby. Zeb never liked her hauling water from the creek and was glad he was finished.

He planted an oak tree by the caved in cistern for some strange reason, which Sarah thought was funny, since so many trees already surrounded them. He told her it was to mark the beginning of their home together.

The months went by quickly. Zeb finished a fine two-story stable to the left of the house, while Sarah harvested and canned vegetables from the garden as she grew bigger and happier. She was always singing and humming these days, her cheeks grew rosier than ever.

The weather began to turn cold and every morning the ground was thick with frost.

Zeb spent his days chopping wood, he watched as the leaves began to turn color and fall to the ground. He finished a huge woodpile just as it started to snow. They were comfortable and snug in their cabin as winter set in. Christmas came and they celebrated their wedding anniversary during a snowstorm that lasted over a week.

At the end of December, Sarah gave birth to a beautiful baby girl. She had mounds of dark brown hair and her father's bright blue eyes. They named her Rose Marie after Sarah's grandmother, but they called her Rosie. Zeb adored her. She was the sweetest baby and hardly ever cried. She was always smiling and cooing, the first time she laughed was truly a delight. He was so proud to have such a beautiful wife and daughter.

That spring, Sarah announced she was going to have another baby, so Zeb decided to add an addition to the house. He was overjoyed.

One evening, he told Sarah he had a surprise for her and disappeared for several hours, right after supper. When he returned, she asked him where he had gone, but he just winked and gave her cheek a pinch.

"It's a surprise. You'll see," he answered.

For weeks Zeb would leave the house right after supper and would return hours later, always without an explanation. Finally one evening, he came home with a big grin on his face.

"Hold out your hand and close your eyes." Sarah did as Zeb said. "No peeking now."

"I'm not," she said, excitedly. She felt something light placed in her hand.

"Okay, you can open them."

She looked down, and in her hand was a beautiful red stone. It sparkled in the firelight.

"Oh, how pretty!" she exclaimed, with delight. "It looks like a ruby. Where did you get it?" she asked, her eyes shining.

"I found it buried under some rocks while I was clearing brush for the new room. It's a gift to celebrate our new baby."

"It's just beautiful!" she exclaimed. "I love it!"

She went to her chest of drawers, and took out a small-carved wooden box. Lifting the lid, she removed a long silver chain her mother had given her.

"I'll attach it to this chain and wear it next to my heart always," she said, kissing him tenderly on the cheek.

At the beginning of summer they met their first neighbors. Roger and Velma Whiting were homesteading about a half-mile away. They spent quite a bit of time with them, helping them with their cabin and cistern.

Sarah had another girl in December. Susan was the spitting image of her big sister. There had never been prouder parents.

As the next six years passed, more and more couples and families came west. Some went on, but others stayed to homestead and soon the countryside was peppered with cabins.

Their nearest neighbor was still a half-mile away. Everyone was friendly and would gather together to help put up barns, stables, and cabins. Some took up farming in the valleys and glens, one didn't have far to go to hear the laughter of children and happy families. It was quickly becoming a wonderful little community. There was something about it. It was almost as if there was love and humor in the countryside.

Some of the women got together and decided it would be a great idea to have a get together, a festival of sorts, to celebrate their new homes and discuss building a school. Since Zeb and Sarah were the first to settle there, they were elected to organize and run the meeting. Zeb and some of the other men decided to unveil the brand new ferry they just finished building, to top off the celebration. The ferry was what one might call a glorified raft, but a bit more sophisticated. It was constructed with freshly cut lumber and had a small paddle wheel and it was larger than your typical raft.

It was their first autumn festival and everyone was excited. There were about thirty-two families and everyone was coming. They decided to have horseshoe tournaments and games for the children. Sarah organized a baking contest and a quilt show.

The day of the festival came. The men gathered early and drove their wagons, loaded down with tables and bales of hay, which they placed under the few oaks and maples that grew there, roughly a mile up from Zeb's place. Two hundred yards away roared the mighty river.

Families started showing up soon after. The tables were laden with all sorts of desserts for the baking contest. There were chocolate, white, and yellow cakes, and an assortment of pies–mincemeat, blueberry, pumpkin, and apple, even a few pecan.

Fire pits were dug, and turkeys and pigs were put on the spit. There were loads of casseroles, corn on the cob and squash dishes. The aromas were incredible.

Someone brought a wagon loaded with bright orange pumpkins and decorated the eating area. The bales of hay were used for sitting. Bushel baskets full of apples, squash and potatoes were on display for sale. A couple of men brought their fiddles, so there was music and dancing. The children chased family dogs through the fallen leaves and played tag and hide and seek. The quilt show and baking contest were a big success. Zeb was one of the judges. Sarah took second place for her quilt, and Mrs. Wilson who lived just down from the Bonners, took first place for her mincemeat pie. The kids had gunny sack races and tug of war.

After eating, the adults gathered together for the meeting. It was decided that the building of the new school would commence immediately and everyone agreed that these festival grounds would make a fine park. That idea was later dismissed because of the possibility of flooding. Construction would begin the following week, roughly two miles from the river, on top of one of the bluffs.

The women were excited. They discussed making the curtains and planning where flower beds and the playground would go. They adjourned the meeting after setting the date for the next gathering. They would then choose the name for their town.

Everyone ambled over to the riverbank, where Zeb and the other men unveiled the new ferry. There was much applause and everyone had to take their turn walking on board. It had taken them two months to complete, but everyone gave Zeb the credit for its design.

It was a sturdy craft and sure to withstand the power of the river. Sarah and the girls stood by grinning and clapping. Rosie and Susan, six and seven years old, were proud as they could be. They adored their father.

There was a bite in the air as wagons were loaded up and people rode toward home. There were rosy cheeks and cold noses; by the time

Zeb and Sarah traveled the short distance home, the girls had fallen asleep under the pile of quilts in the wagon.

Zeb looked down with love at his sleeping children, a feeling of contentment rose up in him. After they carried the girls into the house, Zeb went to bed down the horses and feed the animals, while Sarah helped the girls get dressed for bed.

The next morning was bright and sunny. There was a layer of frost on the pumpkins left in the garden and the autumn leaves were brilliant orange, red, and yellow, falling fast from the trees. By nine thirty, the temperature had risen to sixty degrees and the girls played outside. They were miniature tomboys just like their mother had been. Their hair was always messed up and dirt seemed to grow on their faces, but they were the prettiest little girls one ever laid eyes on, even when they couldn't keep their dresses clean. They ran through the forest and glens, and could climb a tree as well as any boy their age.

Sarah worked in the garden digging up the last of the potatoes.

Zeb left before dawn to go help Mr. Wilson fix his plow. He was good at repairing wagons and plows, he was always helping someone.

Susan and Rosie went down to the bottom of the bluff and played in the creek. They were busy looking for gold to surprise their parents, when a snow-white rabbit came tearing across the creek with Mr. Wilson's dog hot on its trail. They looked at each other and took off after them. The girls loved rabbits and were terribly afraid the dog would kill it. They chased him for a while but quickly lost sight of him. Hunting around for a bit, they were about to give up when Rosie spotted a dog track in the dirt and off they ran. Twenty minutes later, they were at the bank of the river. They saw the beautiful ferry and forgot all about the rabbit. Climbing aboard, they admired the great job their father did and enjoyed the floating sensation.

Back in the garden, Sarah stopped suddenly. A strange feeling came over her and she dropped the shovel, listening. All she could hear was the wind blowing through the trees. Fear crept over her when she realized she could no longer hear the girls. She called out to them but got only silence. Pictures of the raging river loomed into her mind. A feeling of dread poured over her. Sarah ran down the bluff to the meadow floor. The river was only a half-mile away, but it seemed like she was running in slow motion. She jumped over the creek, calling out the girl's names as she went.

Susan grabbed one of the ropes securing the ferry to a tree branch that came loose during the night. She whacked the rope like the reins on a horse.

"Yah! Yah!" she yelled.

Both girls were laughing, jumping up and down, and having such a good time pretending; they didn't see the strain being put on the other rope. With Rosie's next jump it snapped. Neither child realized what had just happened. The ferry slowly began to move away from the bank, heading down stream. The current was strong and it didn't take long before they were moving toward the middle of the river. They passed a large boulder that stuck out of the water and knew they were in trouble. Rosie looked around to see if there was anything she could do. Susan saw the fear in her sister's eyes and the realization that neither one of them could swim made her start to cry.

Sarah ran hard. She seemed to sense exactly where to go and headed up river. Flying over the bank, she spotted the girls on the ferry a short distance downstream in the middle of the torrent. She screamed out their names, running along the bank, jumping over rocks and underbrush. She could hear them crying.

"Mama! Mama!"

Tripping over a large root, Sarah fell. She looked up to see Susan's outstretched arms. Sarah screamed louder.

"Susan! Rosie!"

The ferry kept slamming into the rocks jutting out of the water. Each time they hit one, they would lose their balance and fall. Sarah kept screaming as she ran along the bank.

Up the river, Zeb and Mr. Wilson were on their way back to the Bonner cabin when they heard Sarah's screams. They looked at each other, slapped the horses, and took off toward the river.

Sarah looked down stream and saw, with horror, a huge jagged boulder right in the path of the ferry. Without a moment's hesitation, she dove into the water screaming, "No!"

Immediately, the current took her and quickly swept her past the ferry. The craft was larger and heavier, it didn't move as fast. She swam hard, but was having trouble making any headway.

Zeb and Mr. Wilson skidded to a halt at the top of the bank and jumped off their horses. They watched, in horror, as the ferry crashed into the jagged rock, spilling the girls into the water.

Sarah heard Zeb call out and looked over at him. Tears streamed down her face. She called out his name. Now exhausted and frozen from the cold water, she knew she wasn't going to make it. All she could do was stretch out her hand to him.

"I love you!" she cried.

Zeb heard the words and looked at his beautiful wife. He cried out to her and ran along the bank, but couldn't catch up to her because of the rocks. He ran down stream, looking for a place to get down calling, "Sarah! Sarah!"

She and the girls disappeared around a sharp bend in the river.

Zeb searched for them for days, but all he found was the beautiful ruby necklace he gave Sarah, snagged on a thorn bush at the top of the bank. Often he would sit for hours, staring out at the water with a blank expression, breaking the silence with his sobs. He never stopped mourning them and had a private funeral for his family.

Neighbors came by to try and comfort him, bringing food, but Zeb was inconsolable. Several times a day, his wails would echo down the valley. The sound seemed to travel for miles. Everyone felt so bad for him and wished there was something they could do to ease his sorrow.

After weeks and weeks of this, Mr. Wilson and some of the other men got together and decided to force Zeb out of the cabin, away from there. When they arrived, they found the door standing open. There was a mournful silence as they searched the place, but came up empty. They figured he must be down at the river and took off in that direction. They searched up and down the bank for at least a mile, but couldn't find him. The men decided to come back the next day and try again. The following day provided no new clues. Zeb was still nowhere to be found. They waited another week and searched again, but to no avail. A month later, the cabin was covered in snow and the searching ceased. Everyone decided Zeb had gone off somewhere and died of a broken heart.

That winter, during one of their meetings, they named the town after Zeb. They called it Bonners Ferry, after the wonderful family that discovered this beautiful place. Plus, they never wanted anyone to forget the tragic circumstances of their deaths.

The following autumn, it was decided the annual festival would be held on top of the bluff, several miles from the river. The day after the second festival, a long mournful wailing echoed through the valley below the Bonner cabin. Word spread quickly that Zeb must still be alive and Mr. Wilson volunteered to go investigate. Three days later, they found Mr. Wilson wandering the edge of the Bonner property. He was all scratched up, shoeless, and covered with dried mud. He was incoherent, muttering something about big hairy monsters. He was terrified to have anyone but his wife around him and kept fighting off invisible creatures. He never came out of it.

One year later, one of the Haven children, two farms over from Bonners, disappeared. He was last seen crossing the old festival grounds, heading toward the river to do some fishing. He was fourteen and old enough to handle himself. Half of the town thought he fell in the river and drowned, while the other half were convinced Zeb Bonner's ghost came back from the dead and drowned him. They decided he tried to drown Mr. Wilson too. Every year around the time of the autumn festival, people reported hearing a long, loud wailing echoing through the valley. They tended to steer well away from the Bonner property during festival time and families kept a close eye on their children. Rumor had it, the Bonner homestead was haunted or cursed. Superstitions grew and so did the legend of Bonners Ferry.

Chapter Two

A NEW ADVENTURE

Present Day

Henry woke up early. This was going to be an exciting day. It was the first day of summer and a moving day. He sat up in bed and searched for his slippers. Putting on his robe, he walked over to his sister's bed.

"Haley, wake up!" Haley was Henry's fifteen year old twin sister.

She opened her blue eyes and smiled. "Today's the day!" she said excitedly.

"Yes," replied Henry. "Finally!"

Their father, Paul purchased a large estate in Northwest Idaho, deep in the mountains somewhere. He had gotten it for a "steal." Apparently, the previous owner was an eccentric old man that died some twenty years ago. Since then, the estate had been sitting empty and unattended.

Paul couldn't believe what a great deal he made. He was never good at haggling, but the real estate agent seemed easy to deal with and accepted Paul's first offer without a fuss.

"Well, what's wrong with the place?" said the twins' mother, Carol.

She was almost insistent something must be wrong with it, but Paul assured her everything was on the up and up, he inspected every inch himself before making the decision.

Henry and Haley didn't care. They were dying to get there and explore. They both loved adventure and the outdoors.

Haley grabbed her robe, after a stop at the bathroom, she went to the kitchen; while Henry let Casey, their Labrador, outside. He could hear someone rummaging around in the kitchen. He turned the corner and saw his mother with her head buried in a box.

"Whatcha' looking for, Mom?"

"Morning, honey. I'm trying to find the paper plates. Could you help me? Dad brought home breakfast."

He climbed over several packed boxes to help in the search.

Haley came into the kitchen. "Umm . . . what smells good?"

"Take out," said Henry, grinning.

"I found them!" Carol yelled from the dining room, just as Paul walked in from the garage.

"Morning, Daddy," said Haley.

"Good morning, sweetie," he replied, giving her a peck on the cheek. "Morning, son," he said, roughing up Henry's hair.

"Morning, Dad," Henry replied, grinning and rolling his eyes.

Paul was a gentle man. He was six foot three, slender, with dark brown hair. He and Carol, a happily married couple, just celebrated their eighteenth wedding anniversary. They were a close-knit family that did everything together.

The Miles family could never afford a vacation and the move to Idaho was to be their first big outing anywhere. They never had much money because Paul had been in college the past eight years and was only able to take part time jobs. He graduated at the beginning of May. It was the most exciting thing to happen to the Miles family up to that point. Two weeks after graduation, they found out about the estate.

Paul had been going to Creston, British Columbia for three weeks each year, for the last four years, studying under one of the most well-known architects in Canada, Dr. John Malcolm, who recognized Paul's talent after talking to him during a seminar in Spokane. He was impressed with the younger man's mathematical ability and knowledge of the works of Frank Lloyd Wright, among others, and Paul was ecstatic when Dr. Malcolm offered him an apprenticeship upon graduation.

Now, everything was finally coming together. He would be able to give his family everything he'd always wanted and the advance the company gave him was quite generous. They used most of the money on the purchase of the house and furniture. The estate was just a stone's throw away from Creston and he wouldn't have far to commute every day.

Carol emerged with the paper plates and they each sat on a box and ate. After breakfast, Paul went out to check under the hood, while Carol walked through the mostly empty house. A moving company had been arranged to haul their belongings and would arrive any minute to pick up what was left.

The twins stood in the small bedroom they had been forced to share for as long as they could remember. Both were lost in different memories when Paul called that they needed to hit the road.

"Come on. It's time to go meet our own rooms," said Henry.

They wished their house had more than two bedrooms for years.

Haley smiled and took Henry's arm. Together, they walked out, calling Casey after them.

They waited in the van for their parents.

In the house, Carol came out of the bathroom to find Paul standing in the living room doorway, looking around the empty room.

"We've gone through a lot together in this house," said Carol, with tears in her eyes.

"We sure have," he sighed. "And now we have our future waiting for us and a life we've looked forward to for so long."

They put their arms around each other, taking one last look around. Paul put the key down on the kitchen counter and they left the house for the last time.

Twenty minutes later, they got on the interstate heading east toward Idaho. The entire trip to Bonners Ferry would only take roughly six or seven hours, according to Paul.

The excited chatter died down about an hour later. Casey was comfortably sprawled out on the folded down rear seat, while Carol was busy with the map and Haley was dozing.

Henry was mesmerized by the passing city. He hadn't realized how big it was until now.

An hour later, they turned off the interstate and headed north. The four-lane highway turned into two lanes over rolling hills. There weren't many trees yet, but the grass was green and there were puffy white clouds in the bright blue sky.

Henry was elated. He longed to get out of the city. All his life, he had only been able to see mountains and forests on TV. Now he was actually going to be living there.

Paul talked often about how scenic the drive was through Northwestern Idaho. Henry imagined himself being there in the mountains, hiking and exploring the forests and valleys. He couldn't wait to get there.

They pulled into a rest area a couple hours later, getting out to stretch and use the restroom. Carol brought out some sandwiches she'd made along with oranges, chips, and sodas.

They sat at a picnic table near the van and ate a quiet lunch. Everyone seemed to be in his or her own little world, thinking about the estate and what the place would be like.

Paul was thinking about all the unpacking they would have to do, while Carol was imagining putting things away in the cupboards and arranging furniture.

Haley was dreaming about her own room and where her bed might go.

They finished lunch and continued the climb into the mountains.

The twins watched the giant pines fly by. They could barely see anything, the trees were so thick. They climbed up and down, twisting and turning, round and round, like they were going in circles half the time.

Their eyes were full of wonder and the excitement was starting to build again as they got closer to their turn off. They had been on the road for what seemed like ages, when finally Paul said excitedly, "There's our turn!"

Everybody craned their necks, looking ahead. There was a small sign that said, Rush River Road. They slowed and turned left onto a narrow paved road. It looked barely wide enough to fit one vehicle, let alone two. Henry wondered what they would do if they met another car.

"Is this the driveway?" he asked.

"No," Paul answered. "It's just up the road, a little way on the right."

Five minutes later, the twins were starting to get impatient, waiting for the turn.

"I don't remember the turn off, being so far," said Paul, anxiously.

"Are you sure we took the right road?" Carol asked.

"Not anymore," he replied, with a worried look.

"Maybe we should turn around," she said.

Paul scanned the sides of the road to see if they could manage a turn. As they rounded the next curve, he saw the driveway entrance.

"There it is!"

The twins sighed with relief. Everyone sat on the edge of their seat and kept their eyes glued ahead.

Paul turned right, onto Blue Bell Glen. It was a one lane, dirt drive that looked like it hadn't been used in years, starting out wide, but gradually getting smaller and smaller. Branches and bushes scraped the sides of the van as they drove forward.

"It gets a little rough here," said Paul, with a quick reassuring glance at Carol.

The van bobbed up and down as he tried to maneuver around the potholes and tree roots in the road.

"It's a good thing we had new shocks put on," he said, with a nervous chuckle as they came close to bottoming out, while crossing a small creek with no bridge.

"We'll always have these little creeks in the spring," he said quickly, when he saw Carol frowning. "It's just run off from the snow. I'm told it never gets any bigger than this."

Carol didn't say anything, but the pursing of her lips said it all.

Just as she decided to comment on the creek, a clearing emerged into view. The driveway widened here and went from dirt to cobblestone, curving to the right. The estate loomed into view. Everybody held their breath. No one but Paul was prepared for its size.

"It's huge!" exclaimed Haley, excitedly.

"Whoa," said Henry. "It looks like a tree is growing right out of the roof!"

They pulled up in front of a large arched doorway and shut off the van.

The estate was completely surrounded by huge oak trees with a weeping willow swaying in the breeze on the right and an old wooden mailbox sat atop a four foot rock wall surrounding the property. An open meadow was visible beyond the wall with more weeping willows and tall grasses, leading downhill and out of sight. A small creek meandered its way along the border of the meadow and disappeared behind a knoll, carpeted with clover. Behind it was a forest of trees they couldn't see beyond. To their left, a small grove of birch surrounded an old building that looked like a stable of some sort. The estate's outer walls were easily two stories high.

Carol frantically dug through the pile of trash and maps at her feet, for her purse. She pulled out a skeleton key they got from the real estate agent. Paul smiled at the excitement on her face, with elevated anticipation they got out and walked up to the door.

Large, old-fashioned lanterns hung on each side of the arched entrance. She inserted the key and turned it, but nothing happened.

"Here let me try," said Paul, taking the key.

After several turns he looked at Carol. "Don't tell me they gave us the wrong key!" he exclaimed, with a note of disgust.

"Can I try?" Haley asked.

Paul handed her the key. She inserted it into the hole, turned it once, and heard the lock click. Everyone looked at her with surprise. She shrugged her shoulders and pushed on one of the heavy doors, it slowly swung forward. They stood there amazed. The doors opened into a large courtyard. Ahead on the right, thick stone steps led up to a walkway that ran on top of the ivy covered walls. Straight ahead was another arched doorway that led to the rest of the estate and in the middle of the courtyard stood an old oak tree. Its branches were so thick and high, you could step onto the roof if you dared climb it. Its trunk was massive and the twins noticed how easily accessible the lower branches were.

Haley especially enjoyed the walk through the courtyard. The sun was warm and the smell of wildflowers was strong. Patches of tall weeds blew gently in the breeze as sweet songbirds twittered out their beautiful melodies. Butterflies flit from flower to flower and the sound of buzzing honeybees could be heard close by. Passing the big tree, they discovered an old cistern covered in thorns and briars. It had an old wooden cover and the rusty cast iron pump handle looked like it hadn't been used in a hundred years. Haley could have stayed in the courtyard for hours, listening and smelling the sweet scent of lily of the valley, admiring the pretty little spot covered in violets.

"This is just a lovely spot," Carol remarked.

"I agree," said Haley. "I could stay out here all day."

"Yes, well, we will have plenty to do as soon as the movers show up, so let's keep moving," said Paul, with a smile.

Entering the second arched doorway was like walking through a small tunnel. A wide grin spread across Paul's face as he opened the wooden door and watched their mouths all drop open at the same time. They entered a large foyer and straight ahead was a grand marble staircase leading up to a balcony adorned with polished oak rails in the center of the room. The balcony led to a hallway toward the left and right, and a huge lead crystal chandelier hung, sparkling in the afternoon sun, filtering through the wide upper floor windows.

"Oh my goodness!" Carol exclaimed. "I had no idea it was this beautiful!"

To their immediate left was a long corridor. A bit further into the foyer, there were large open rooms on the left and right, with doors on either side of the staircase leading to the kitchen. The floor was black marble and the walls were covered with beautiful tapestries.

"You would never have known from the outside, how modern and beautiful it is in here," exclaimed Carol, looking around in awe. "How am I ever going to keep this place clean?"

"You should have seen it before," said Paul. "There were layers of dust and cobwebs everywhere, but don't you worry about a thing. I have a surprise for you. I hired a housekeeper weeks ago to clean the place up."

No sooner had he spoken, when out of the kitchen came a short woman with graying hair and a kind face.

"Hello, Estelle. Everyone, this is Estelle Grimsworth. Estelle, this is my wife, Carol."

"How do you do, Mrs. Miles," she said, with a curtsy.

"Estelle is very familiar with the estate," Paul continued. "She was employed here for many years by the late Mr. Johnson."

He turned toward the twins.

"And these are our children, Henry and Haley."

The twins were quiet, and looked at Estelle curiously.

"Mr. Miles, Miss Miles," she replied, with a curtsy and smile.

"Now, Mr. Miles," she said, turning to Paul. "Dinner is cooking and shall be ready in a half an hour. The parlor in the west wing has fresh linens for you and young Mr. Miles . . . and for you and the missus . . . " she continued, glancing at Haley oddly. "The east wing is ready as well."

Estelle was a plump little woman with a soft high voice and bright eyes. Haley liked her at once.

"Miss Miles," she continued, taking Carol by the hand. "I think you will find the kitchen is in order. Mr. Miles has instructed that I do all the cooking and cleaning. I hope that meets with your approval."

Carol looked over her shoulder with a sort of bemused, bewildered look as Estelle ushered her through the swinging door into the kitchen.

"I think I'll go to the den and make some calls," said Paul. "Why don't you two do a little exploring and pick out your bedrooms. Oh and don't forget, dinner is in half an hour," he said over his shoulder.

Looking at his sister, Henry asked with excitement, "Can you believe this?"

"Barely," she whispered.

"Come on," he said, grabbing her by the arm. "Let's check it out."

They climbed the grand staircase, admiring the extremely large paintings that lined the walls of the balcony. At the top, the corridor ran to the left and the right. They decided to go left. It was like touring a museum. The corridor was lined with deep crimson carpet and tapestries hung all along it. They passed two doors on the left and two on the right as they headed for the large wooden door at the end of the corridor first.

Henry peeked in to find a very bright and sunny spiral stairway full of windows. "This looks like a tower!" he exclaimed.

They quickly climbed to the top, passing a door along the way. A few seconds later, they stood at the top.

Henry pushed open the door, and Haley drew in a loud breath.

"Oh my gosh!"

It was a huge, round room with windows for walls from the floor to the ceiling.

"This is my room!" she whispered, excitedly.

But most amazing, was the incredible view. They discovered they were, indeed, in one of two towers. This was the west tower. They could see for miles and miles. Looking out the left side, they could see the estate was situated on the edge of a bluff. It gradually sloped downhill to the valley floor. Looking right, they could see open meadows and glens. It was almost like a park, with lots of open spaces. Further out, they could see the small brook that ran parallel with the rock wall. It curved to the left and went down around the backside of the tower to the base of the bluff.

Haley gave Henry a strange smile.

"I could stay up here forever, it's so beautiful."

"I know what you mean. I have a feeling that other door we saw on the way up is probably another bedroom. Let's go take a look."

They descended the stairs and entered another bedroom with the same set up as Haley's room. Henry decided this would be his room. So the twins claimed the west tower and went toward the kitchen. They talked excitedly about the second floor west tower during dinner with their parents. Paul and Carol were delighted at their enthusiasm and after dinner it didn't take long for everyone to find their way around. They discovered there were six bedrooms, four bathrooms, a formal dining room, a library, den, and a family room with a fireplace so big you could stand in it. Some of the rooms were furnished.

Paul and Carol approved of the twins taking the west tower for their own. They themselves chose the east tower, top bedroom. They could look out their tower windows and see each other. Carol and Haley thought this was great fun. Carol decided to use the lower bedroom of the east tower for her studio. She was a talented painter and supplemented their income selling her paintings at the local flea markets the past few years.

Landscapes were her specialty. She could paint a picture so realistic you felt you could almost step right into it.

The movers arrived soon after dinner and the family spent the remainder of the evening showing them where to put everything. Paul was especially appreciative he didn't have to lug furniture for three bedrooms, up the tower steps.

Carol was ecstatic when the truck with the new living and dining room furniture pulled in. The dark mahogany dining table and chairs looked fantastic against the deep, crimson carpets.

"I feel like we've just won the lottery!" she exclaimed, looking around at their new home. "And I can hardly wait to get a garden in the courtyard. Haley can finally plant the flower garden she's always wanted and Henry can explore to his heart's content. It's like a dream, isn't it, honey?" she said, looking into Paul's eyes.

Looking at his beautiful wife, he didn't answer and he didn't have to. Carol knew what he was feeling because she felt it, too. He put his arm around her and they ascended the staircase toward the east tower.

Chapter Three

EXPLORING THE UNKNOWN

The next morning the twins slept in and by the time they got up, it was ten o'clock and raining out. They knew they wouldn't be able to do any exploring of the grounds or beyond. They went down to the kitchen to see what they could find for a late breakfast.

Carol had every kitchen box unpacked, with all her dishes strewn about and piled everywhere. She and Estelle were up to their knees in newspaper and cardboard. They looked quite comical and the twins started laughing.

"What are you two laughing at?" Carol smiled.

Estelle looked at Carol and started to giggle. Carol looked at her and began to laugh. Both their faces were completely covered with ink from the newspaper.

Estelle walked over to an old fashioned hutch and fetched a plate full of pastries, fresh strawberries and melons.

"Now, Mr. Miles, Miss Miles, I trust you won't be getting up this late every day. There's plenty of work to do."

Carol nodded in agreement.

"Now, you two hurry along and eat your breakfast," she continued, ushering them over to a rather large wooden table in the corner. They moved aside some of the dishes piled there and ate. Estelle promptly brought them two glasses and a metal pitcher full of ice-cold milk. With a nod of approval, she turned and went back to helping Carol make sense of the mess.

When he finished breakfast, Henry went into the family room where Paul was struggling to pull the plastic and cardboard off the new sofa.

"Need a hand?"

"I'll say," replied Paul.

They spent the rest of the morning unpacking and arranging the new furniture.

"You know, your mom will be in here before long and she'll have us move everything a half dozen times before she's satisfied."

No sooner had he finished his sentence, Carol came in. For the next hour, they moved and rearranged all the furniture. In the end, everything looked just right. She was happy everything fit in the right places and the guys were happy to be finished.

In the meantime, Haley unpacked her room and arranged everything the way she wanted it. She would stop every once in a while and look out one of the many windows. It was such a breathtaking view even in the rain.

She could see the bluff drop below her and the small brook winding its way down, out of sight. Small patches of mist rose here and there. It was like looking out at little clouds. She had never seen anything like it before and the sound of so many birds singing was mesmerizing. It was a continuous concert from sun up to sun down.

She finished arranging and stood back to admire her new room. Extremely pleased, she felt a little like a princess in her tower bedroom. She went downstairs to find Henry and found everyone in the family room finishing up.

"How do you like it?" asked Carol, turning to Haley.

"It looks fabulous!" she exclaimed, plopping down on the new lazy boy. "I need a breather."

"Me too," Henry agreed, sitting on the sofa.

Just then, Estelle came in with a pitcher of lemonade and some glasses.

"Oh, great, thank you, Estelle. You read my mind," said Carol, getting up to help.

"It is my pleasure, Mrs. Miles," Estelle replied, going back into the kitchen.

Carol turned to Haley. "I'm going into town for seeds. You want to come along?"

"Yes!" Haley exclaimed. "I can't wait to plant my flowers."

An hour later, they climbed into the van and drove toward Bonners Ferry. As this was their first time to town, Carol was hoping they wouldn't get lost.

Paul told them it wasn't much of a town and they may not be able to find everything they wanted. He said it had a gas station and an old-fashioned country store that sold hunting licenses, bait, and groceries, which Carol couldn't wait to see. There was a small post office with a park next door and a diner-combination tavern. Bonners Ferry was so small it didn't have a school. All the kids went to school in the larger neighboring town of Moyie Springs.

Carol wasn't used to driving on roads so bumpy and narrow and it took them longer to get to the main road than they remembered. When they got to the spot where the water went over the road they stopped, watching it for a moment.

"We can still cross, right?" Haley asked, nervously.

The water level had risen a bit and was moving faster.

"Piece of cake," Carol replied.

She looked calm on the outside but gripped the wheel more firmly than usual. She revved up the engine, the van lurched forward, and they plowed on through.

"See . . . a piece of cake," she sighed, with relief.

Neither of them realized they were never in any danger. The water was not nearly deep enough to cause problems. It started to get darker and they could hear the distant rumble of thunder. They looked at each other pleased. A good thunderstorm was something they both loved. They used to sit together in front of the living room window back home, sipping hot chocolate and listening to the cracks of thunder, watching the rain. It was at times like these, Haley felt closest to her mother and they developed a tight bond.

Carol was a strong woman. For the past eight years, Haley watched her mother take on challenges like fixing the broken pipe in the crawl space under the house and changing the distributor cap on the car. Things their father would have normally done. The twins seldom saw him as they grew up, with him being in college and working part-time. She admired her mother's will power and determination; she hoped she would grow up to be like her.

"I just love a spring rain," said Carol, with a sigh.

"Me too," Haley replied as they approached the main road.

"Now remember where we turn," said Carol.

Haley turned to look for some kind of marker. There was nothing she could see to indicate their turn off, except for the Blue Bell Glen sign, which was almost hidden by branches. It could easily be missed if you weren't watching for it.

"I know, we'll just write down the mileage from here and we'll have no problem," said Carol.

"That's a great idea!"

They couldn't find any paper, so Carol wrote down the mileage on a napkin they found in the glove compartment. They turned onto the main road and immediately went uphill. Bonners Ferry was only four miles from their turn-off, but since they had never been there before and the road was so winding, they took their time. It was really raining hard now, and they didn't see one car during the entire drive. It made Haley feel a little uneasy. Finally, as they rounded a curve, ahead on the right, they could see the country store and diner sharing a gravel parking lot. On the left was the gas station and post office, which was small indeed.

"The post office is so small; it reminds me of a playhouse I had when I was a kid," Carol remarked.

"That's the post office? How tiny."

They pulled into the store parking lot. There was a brand new Cadillac parked there and several old beaters, including one rusty truck. The old, faded sign, which hung over the door, said Owens Country Store. They parked and ran for the door, not noticing the two women staring out the window. As they entered, they could hear the soft jingling of bells and the sound of a crackling fire coming from a pot-bellied wood stove standing to the right of the counter. Haley headed toward it. The mountain rain made it damp and a bit chilly. She found the fire warm and comforting. It made her feel sleepy and she wished she was back in her tower, snug in her bed.

Carol looked over at the two women. "Good afternoon," she said to them cheerfully.

The older woman replied with a nod of her head, but the younger woman, looked her up and down suspiciously. "I'm wondering, do you carry vegetable and flower seeds?" she asked.

They're in the back," the old woman replied, pointing toward the rear of the store.

"Thank you," said Carol. With a glance at Haley, they made their way toward the back. The seed rack was loaded with packets and they began to go through them.

"Oh . . . check out these beautiful tomatoes," said Carol.

Haley smiled as she went through the flower packets. She shared her mother's passion for gardening and was happy to see her so excited just looking at the tomatoes. Their garden back home wasn't very big, as they didn't have a lot of time to spend on it. She was glad her father finally graduated. They would both be able to do all the gardening they wanted together.

After picking out what they wanted, they checked out the rest of the store. The aisles were narrow and loaded with goods. They went up one aisle and down the next, amazed at the variety of products. There were two parts to the store. The right half was used entirely for food; everything from meat and dairy, bread, vegetables, and canned goods, to a small frozen food section. The left side of the store was household goods; cleaning supplies, dishes, pots and pans, brooms, light bulbs, etc., anything one would need.

Carol was delighted to find a small stool at the end of each aisle, to help reach the top shelves. The simplicity of this old store brought back childhood memories and she was thoroughly enjoying herself. Halfway down the last aisle on the left, the scent of incense hung thick in the air.

A dimly lit light bulb hung inside a door, revealing another room with a straw covered floor. There were gunnysacks full of planting corn and wheat. Used farm equipment lined the walls as dust particles floated through the air. It gave Haley the creeps.

"Where in the world would anyone do any farming around here?" Carol wondered, out loud.

As they neared the end of the aisle, they could hear the two women talking in low voices. Haley heard the words, *wailing sound,* which made her ears perk up.

"Yep," said the old woman.

"Started up about dusk. Almost sounded like a woman screamin'," she continued. "Wrong time of the year, too."

That got Carol's attention, she stopped examining the box of fabric softener in her hand and listened.

"That's when I heard it too," said the other woman. "At dusk. I hope there are no accidents or *missing children* this year. I'm not going to let my boys outta my sight for the next few days."

This was too much for Carol. She stepped around the corner, startling the two women.

"Excuse me, I didn't mean to eavesdrop, but I couldn't help overhearing. What did you mean by *missing children?*"

The older woman cleared her throat and offered her hand.

"Sorry, didn't know you was listenin'. Didn't mean to scare ya. Name's Clara Owens."

"Carol Miles," she replied, shaking the woman's hand. "And this is my daughter, Haley."

"Hi," Haley replied, smiling politely.

"This here's Judy Seers," Clara motioned toward the other woman.

Judy was smartly dressed in the latest fashion and wore too much makeup. She looked Carol up and down and gave her an insincere, thin smile. It immediately made Haley dislike her.

"You just moved into the old Johnson place, right?" Clara asked.

"Yes."

"Welcome to Bonners Ferry," she said, with a smile.

Haley liked this woman. She seemed to be a down to earth person. Heavyset, with silver-gray hair pulled back into a loose bun. She reminded Haley a little of Estelle and wondered if they were related.

"What did you mean *missing children?*" Carol repeated.

"Oh," said Clara. Lowering her voice, she spoke in almost a whisper. She looked at Haley. "Folks don't like to talk too loud 'bout that round here. You ain't heard the Legend of Bonners Ferry?"

"Legend? No."

"Folks say that the forest is haunted. Zeb Bonner, who was the founder of this town around two hundred years ago, lost his wife and little daughters in a horrible accident. They drowned in the Kootenai, just a little down river from your place."

Carol put her hand to her mouth.

"Around the same time every year, for a few days, folks hear wailin' and moanin' comin' from the place where they drowned, and every year, bad things happen round that time."

"What bad things?" Carol asked, concerned.

"Well, 'bout four years ago, a kid from Moyie Springs went into the forest to investigate the wailin' and never came back. And the year after that, Jake Simmons shot himself with a shotgun. A shotgun. How do ya shoot yerself with a shotgun?" Clara wondered out loud. After a brief pause, she continued. "Anyway, there seems to be somethin' happenin' every few years. They say it's Zeb Bonner, mournin' the death of his family, his sorrow so great that supernatural forces cause bad things to happen. Even old man Johnson himself went inta the forest an' nobody seen him for three days. Came out alive, but in a daze. Kept babblin' 'bout fairies and monsters. Never was the same after that. Couple months later, they found him dead on the banks of the Kootenai. His face was all twisted up in pain and he was covered in deep scratches. It was like somethin' tried to tear him to pieces. They say he went mad after he came out of the forest. Always talkin' to himself, goin' in and out of the forest and down to the river. People say he saw the ghosts of Bonner's wife and kids and it drove him mad."

Carol's face went pale. Haley stood there, rooted to the spot, afraid to move.

All of a sudden, Clara started laughing hysterically, slapping her knee. Judy stood there with a smug look on her face.

"I'm sorry, I really had ya there!" she laughed, a tear rolling down her cheek. "Quite a legend, huh?" she said, still laughing, holding her stomach.

Carol gave her a half-hearted smile. "Yeah, you had me there for a minute."

Haley was embarrassed.

Judy started for the door. "I gotta run," she laughed. "Ike will be back from Spokane by now and I'll need to get the cook movin' as usual. It's so hard to get good help these days," she said, with a note of sarcasm.

"Cook?" Carol asked.

"She's Ike Seers' wife," Clara replied, as if Carol should know who Ike Seers was.

After paying for their purchases, Carol and Haley headed for the door.

"Nice meetin' you folks," said Clara, with a chuckle as they walked out.

"They must be rich," said Haley, as they drove.

"Who? The Seers'?"

"Yes."

"Maybe. Mrs. Seers sure was dressed in some rather fine clothes. I wonder where she lives. It would be nice if we were neighbors."

Haley frowned. "I didn't like her."

"Why not?"

"She seemed like a rich snob."

"Haley, I'm surprised at you. You know better than to judge a person on your first meeting."

"I know, but she seemed that way to me."

Carol hid a small smile. Haley was usually a good judge of character.

"I can't wait to get these seeds in the ground," said Carol. "It's too wet to do it now, but hopefully it will dry out in the next couple of days."

"Yeah," said Haley, looking down at her flower packets, but her mind was on the conversation back at the store. She couldn't wait to tell Henry about it. "Do you think any of that legend was true?" she asked.

"No. It's just a spooky little story to amuse the tourists that pass through," answered Carol, with a chuckle.

By the time they got to Blue Bell Glen, the rain let up. They plowed right across the stream without slowing down; when they got home, Estelle had dinner on the table and they had just enough time to wash up and sit down.

As Paul read the paper during dinner, Henry was engrossed in a rerun of *Gilligan's Island,* so Haley didn't get to mention the visit to the store. As they finished dinner, Carol announced she wanted all the unpacked boxes broken down and out of the twins' tower before bed. The twins took the boxes out through the side kitchen door. It was so dark; they could barely see the outline of the garage. The rain clouds moved on and the moon was cresting the treetops. Shadows danced across the courtyard wall in the light breeze. As they dumped the cardboard, Henry stopped abruptly.

"What?" Haley asked.

"Shh."

She stopped and listened. "I don't hear anything."

Suddenly, far off, a wailing sound made the hair stand up on her arms.

"Did you hear that?" he whispered.

"Yes."

Henry crept toward the back of the estate. Following, Haley remembered Clara's story and was about to tell him about it, when the sound came again. They reached the base of the west tower and stood staring out at the dark valley. It was completely dark now and the moon, higher and brighter, lit up the hills. Light mists were slowly rising, blanketing the valley floor, like the set of a horror movie. They stood cocking their heads, straining to hear the slightest sound. There, it came again, from the right. Suddenly, a long screech, almost a scream, echoed through the valley. The sound startled them both. With their backs against the tower, they stood rooted to the spot.

"Let's go get a flashlight and come back out," suggested Henry.

"I don't think I want to," whispered Haley. She was unnerved. The whole afternoon had been creepy. They stood listening, but the only sound now were the crickets, croaking frogs, and an occasional bird call. Haley suddenly remembered the store and quickly related the story to Henry.

"Wow," said Henry when she finished. "Do you think any of it is true?"

"I didn't until now," she replied. "We thought it was all a joke, but there really is *a wailing.*"

"Unless it's someone trying to scare us. Let's check it out in the morning," said Henry. "I'm dying to see what's out there."

"Me too."

They walked back through the kitchen and went in to say good night to their parents, then went up to bed.

Haley and Henry got up early the next morning. They could hear Estelle bustling around the kitchen as they came downstairs. Henry told her they were going exploring and she made up a little knapsack to take with them while they ate breakfast.

"Mind you, take care while crossin' the valley floor, especially down by the river," Estelle said, handing them the knapsack. Henry wondered how she knew where they were going.

The sun was peeking over the mountains and the sky was peppered with large, puffy white clouds. Water dripped from the trees and began to evaporate. It was already starting to get warm. They walked to the edge of the bluff and looked out over the valley. The morning pockets of fog began to burn off quickly and everything was bright and green. They walked along the bluff for a bit before they spotted an old path leading downward through the trees. It didn't look like it had been used in years. Weeds covered most of it with an occasional old root sticking out for them to trip over. Trees and thick brush lined the narrow, twisting path. Low branches tore at their clothes, making their decent slow and laborious, while the sun beat down on the back of their necks. The forest was nice and shady with sunbeams filtering their way through the canopy, like small spotlights. Every once in a while they would step off the path into the cool of the shade, but the mosquitoes would drive them out after a few seconds.

"How miserable," remarked Haley, irritated. "We should have brought some mosquito spray."

The smell of pine was strong as they continued down the hill. Despite the scratches, heat, and mosquitoes, the twins were enjoying themselves. Exploring was their passion. At the bottom they stopped to catch their breath. The small creek at the base of the bluff was inviting. After splashing water on their faces and at each other, they discovered three well-worn paths. One went left, one right, and the other straight ahead. They took the path leading into the meadow. There weren't many trees here and it looked fairly level. Tall, scraggly bushes were everywhere with an occasional tree. There were piles of dried up old trunks and branches stripped clean of bark, like they had been lying there forever.

"This place must have flooded at one time," said Henry.

There were great open patches, filled with yellow flowers and clover. They spotted a small pool of water as they rounded a large group of bushes. A couple of ducks suddenly took off, which surprised them both. After about ten minutes of walking, they discovered it was like going through a maze. They would go around a large area of bushes to find a pool of water blocking their path then would have to turn around and go back the way they came. There were knolls everywhere.

Tons of grasshoppers jumped in every direction, getting out of their way as they went, while crickets sang and frogs continued their croaking chorus. The valley was full of wildlife. All types of birds and ducks, Haley even spotted what they thought was a woodchuck. As they neared the top of the next knoll, they saw another small creek. The banks were lined with weeping willows and wildflowers grew everywhere. Haley squealed with delight. Her two favorite things, weeping willows and wildflowers. When they reached the creek, they took off their shoes and socks, sat on a fallen log, and dangled their feet in the water.

"Cold!" said Haley.

"Feels good," Henry said, with a sigh.

He opened the knapsack. Haley peeked into the bag and pulled out two fresh peaches and a couple of energy bars. Henry pulled out two of the four boxed juices and a can of mosquito spray. They looked at each other and laughed.

"Wish we would have known about that earlier," said Haley, with a big smile. "Estelle sure is great."

"It's like having a grandmother living with us," Henry added.

Haley ate her peach and applied some of the mosquito spray to her arms, while Henry polished off his peach, one of the energy bars, and drained a juice box. When they were finished eating and cooling off, they put on their shoes, crossed the creek, and headed over the next knoll. At the top, they spotted a grove of poplars and could hear the roar of water ahead. They hurried down and arrived at a high bank. Looking down, the rushing water sparkled and they were captivated.

"Wow," was all Henry could say.

Haley was silent. She felt this place was wondrous, almost magical.

The river was wide, and shallow in spots, full of rocks and jagged boulders. A little further downstream, the water deepened and moved slower.

"This must be the Kootnai!" Henry yelled, over the roar.

"Do you think we can cross it?" Haley yelled back.

He studied the river for a minute.

"Yeah, no problem! It's very wide, but it doesn't look that deep over there!" he yelled, pointing upstream.

"Look, the bank isn't as steep there. It's moving fast though, so you'll have to keep hold of my hand while we climb down and cross."

"Okay," said Haley, unsure about it.

Holding hands, they reached the bottom and began to cross. It was as Henry said. The water was rapid, but only ankle deep. It was cold and slippery.

"This river was a lot deeper here at one time," Henry said, pointing. "Look how high the banks are."

A path ran along the bottom edge of the river. They walked for a couple miles along the water's edge. The water got deeper and calmer as they went. They stopped along the way when they spotted a fish or shiny rocks. Small streams split off from the main river here and there, disappearing and twisting their way out of sight. They came upon little pools and watched swarms of tadpoles swim around, darting to and from the weeds, while small crayfish lay in wait. After a while, Haley became tired and they stopped to rest. Henry looked at his watch.

"Whoa!"

"What?"

"It's one o'clock already!"

"You're kidding!"

"Nope. I guess we better start back, especially if we want to explore what's up top."

"Let's go," said Haley, standing up, refreshed.

They turned and began looking for a path back up. After about ten minutes, they found one and climbed up. Henry reached the top first and stood there, staring. The distant mountain looked so huge from here. It was so beautiful. They could see it from their tower, but it seemed so far away.

"Jeez, I wonder how far we've walked?" Henry asked.

"At least a couple of miles," Haley answered.

As they stood there, Henrys attention was drawn from the mountain to an even more unusual sight. There, in front of them, was a field. The knolls were bigger on this side of the river and the field grew right over them as far as the eye could see. There was a great old tree in the middle, but the rest was field.

"Where did this field come from?!" Henry exclaimed. "This is really weird."

"Come on, let's go," said Haley.

The path here was well-worn and much wider.

"This looks like a road," she said.

"Yeah," replied Henry. "It is. They use it for farming."

He still couldn't get over it, a field in the mountains. They followed the road for what seemed like hours until they spotted the place where they crossed.

"You wanna go home?" Henry asked.

"No, let's keep going a little further."

They followed the road for a while, but the river kept drawing their attention. It got calmer and deeper again, there weren't as many boulders. As they came around a large bend in the river, up ahead, they could see a fairly good-sized waterfall with large rapids and many large rocks. The road led away from the river, uphill into a dense birch grove. The twins climbed the twisting, turning road to the top. Looking down the other side, they saw the largest, most beautiful house midway down the hill. It was twice the size of their estate and modern. It had a huge, triple-tiered yard and was completely landscaped.

The upper tier was like a dream come true for Haley. There were many flower beds, with the most colorful blooms. The large middle tier had a wonderful in-ground swimming pool with a fountain in the middle, surrounded by a nice patio area with several covered tables. Lawn chairs were placed neatly around an outdoor covered bar, beyond that was a tennis court. The most unusual thing about this yard was an old fashioned carousel right next to the house. It looked like it hadn't been used for some time. The paint looked faded and the poles were rusty. The lower tier contained more flower beds, benches, and small water features. It was plain to see, everything had been done professionally and was kept well-manicured. Haley imagined the people who lived here were extremely wealthy and entertained often.

The road they were standing on led down to a paved parking area and driveway that disappeared around the back of the house. Beyond the house they could see a silo, a barn, and a stable on the right side of the driveway. Across from that sat green open pastures dotted with trees and a shallow creek winding its way through it. Henry counted five horses.

The twins stood there, amazed.

"Look!" Henry exclaimed, pointing. "There's our house!"

Haley looked and sure enough, there it was. She could make out the tops of the towers. "Well, at least now we know where we are for sure," she replied. They stood there for a moment, letting it sink in.

Haley started toward the house.

"Come on, nobody seems to be home. Let's go check it out," she said, eyeing the flower beds.

Henry hesitated and looked troubled. "I don't think we should. We're probably trespassing."

"Yer trespassin' all right!" thundered a loud voice behind them.

The twins spun around and saw two boys on bicycles.

"You can get shot for trespassin' round here!" he continued, in a snotty voice.

He looked like one of those bully types. He had messy hayseed yellow hair with a dirty face and a filthy shirt stained with melted popsicle; he was extremely overweight. His companion looked like the same sorry mess; however, he was as skinny as a rail with the same hayseed yellow hair. He stared at them silently.

"We just moved—" Haley began, when the mean fat kid interrupted her.

"I know who you are!" he replied. "Now get off our property!"

"Let's go," said Henry, but now Haley was mad.

"We didn't know we were trespassing . . . there aren't any signs posted."

"Signs?"

"Yes," she answered, mocking him in the same snotty voice. "Signs . . . no trespassing signs . . . you know, a post made of wood with a piece of metal at the top with writing on it."

"We don't need no signs round here. Everybody knows this is the Seers' property. I'm Ike Jr. and this is my brother, Ernie."

"Sears?" Haley wondered out loud.

"Yeah . . . Seers."

"You mean you own Sears?" she asked, astonished.

"No!" Ike answered. "My father is Ike Seers."

Haley looked at him in disgust.

"Where you from? Nowhere USA?" he sneered.

"No, we just bought the property across the valley," she answered proudly.

"That dump?" Ike replied, with his nose up in the air.

"It's not a dump!" Haley snapped back, glaring at him.

"Yes it is! It's a piece of crap! You better keep your lights on at night or you'll be sorry!" he snickered. "What are you talking about?" Henry butted in, annoyed.

"Everybody knows old man Bonner built that house hundreds of years ago. He was rich, and buried his treasure somewhere down by the river, but then his family was murdered and he disappeared. Now, everybody who moves into that house gets killed in accidents or disappears, and . . ." He paused for effect. "Every few years, some stupid kid disappears on *your* side of the river. They say, it's old man Bonner's ghost getting revenge for his murdered kids. Everybody knows those kids are buried on your property and you can hear them wailin' at night, trying to get out and breathe."

The twins stood there silent while Ike continued.

"Old man Johnson went mad because he found some of Bonner's treasure and stole it from where it was buried, then took it back to that dump you live in and hid it. When Bonner's ghost found it missin', he came and drove old man Johnson mad. He went around talkin' to himself all the time, goin' in and out of the forest and down to the river. Finally, a few months later they found him dead, just a little way up the bank. He had mud all over him and he was all cut up. Somethin' tried to tear him to pieces."

Ike paused again, enjoying the stunned looks on their faces.

"Looked like something tried to grab him down at the water's edge, 'cause you could see marks in the bank, like he tried to claw his way up. Whatever had him must have lost its grip, 'cause he made it up the bank but he bled to death right there. That's why nobody's lived in your house since he died, because it's haunted."

"That's not the way I heard it," Haley retorted. "The women at the store told me and my mom the real story yesterday." Haley suddenly remembered that the young woman at the store said her husband's name was Ike. "You said your name was Ike Jr.?" she asked.

"Yeah? So what?"

"I met your mother yesterday at the store and she told me a completely different story. And then, laughed about it when she was through, because it was all a big joke!" she replied triumphantly. "You're a liar."

Ike made a move toward Haley as if he was going to hit her.

"Don't even think about it!" Henry spoke out, loudly.

Ike looked at Henry and backed down quickly. Henry was several inches taller and looked much tougher.

"I've heard enough of this garbage. Let's go," said Henry.

The twins walked past the Seers' boys defiantly and headed back to where they crossed the river. They could hear Ike Jr. cat calling and teasing behind them, telling them they better beware.

Henry broke the silence as they crossed the river. "You know that whole thing is a crock."

"Yes, I know," she replied. "We should check out Bonners Ferry on the Internet. This town is around two hundred years old and I'll bet it says something about the legend."

"You know what I want to do?" Henry asked. "Even though most of what he said was bologna, I think it would be fun to look around for treasure. After all, our place is around two hundred years old, too. Maybe there really is a treasure."

"Yeah, let's hunt around and see what we can find when we get home. What do you think that wailing really was last night?" Haley asked.

"Oh, it's probably just some animal we've never heard before. I heard somewhere that a mountain lion sounds like a woman screaming. It could have been a mountain lion."

"Then why do you suppose the women at the store would tell such a story?"

"To keep little kids from going into the forest and down by the river. It's not a safe place for a little kid to go wandering around by himself," Henry answered.

"Yeah, sounds like a grown-up."

Chapter Four

ANOTHER WORLD

1975

Ike Seers was an adventurous young man. After his parents died in a tragic fire, he came to live with his grandparents in Bonners Ferry when he was five years old. His grandparents were poor and made a meager living growing and selling potatoes. They were kind, simple folk. In their eighties, they'd been living on the farm all their lives. Grandpa taught Ike about farming, which he detested.

Ike spent his childhood running barefoot through the forests and meadows. He knew every inch of the hills and mountains surrounding the farm. His dream was to get rich and live in style, with all the comforts that came with it. His only tie with the outside world was school and his Grandpa's old radio, which he loved listening to at every opportunity. His other passion was building things. He was inventive, but usually none of his contraptions worked. Ike still had high hopes of someday inventing something that worked he could sell. He especially liked his neighbor across the valley, Mr. Johnson. Once in a while, Mr. Johnson would invite him in and he would get to watch the television or browse through Mr. Johnson's vast library. He loved reading the adventures of Tom Sawyer. All in all, he had plenty of things to occupy his time, but still, his most favorite thing was being in the hills, valleys, and forests.

He spent most of his summer vacations exploring and would come home tired and hungry. Grandpa and Grandma always had plenty in the way of food, but Ike being a growing boy, he always seemed to go away from the table still hungry. When it came to food he was a walking stomach, which earned him the nickname Skinny Seers at school. The kids always teased him because he ate everything he could get his hands on.

He didn't have any friends, mostly because he was so poor and wore ragged clothes full of patches. He fancied a pretty little blonde girl a year younger than him, but she teased him right along with everyone else.

Ike also had a habit of talking to himself, which earned him his other nickname *Iko the Psycho*. He usually ignored it, as he may have been skinny, he was also tall, and no one was ever a threat to him physically. It was just such a day, at morning recess the kids were taunting and teasing him, he grew tired of listening to it.

"Psycho! Psycho! Iko the Psycho!" they chanted.

Ike decided he'd had enough. He didn't return to class with the others. He was seventeen years old now and he figured he was old enough to leave school without getting into too much trouble. Grandpa and Grandma surely wouldn't approve, but he didn't care and he entered the forest. It would be a long walk home, but he was used to long distances. A beautiful spring day, it took a couple hours for him to reach an old dirt road that led to a calm, deep pond.

Local kids had been going there for years to swim. It was a mile from Ike's home and right now it was deserted. He was hot and tired; the water was inviting. Its banks were lined with bright orange tiger lilies, cattails, and tall reeds. They swayed in a gentle breeze as he came over the small knoll to the path leading to the water's edge. Ike stopped halfway down to watch an eagle soar overhead. As he looked back at the pond, the tiger lilies, cattails, and reeds became perfectly still. There wasn't a sound or breath of wind. A sunbeam shone through the quiet forest trees into the middle of the swimming hole. A peculiar feeling came over him and he watched as the calm water slowly began to churn and spin as if an invisible giant spoon was stirring the surface. Slowly at first, then faster and faster. All of a sudden, in a sparkling burst, a tower of shiny glitter appeared. It floated from the center of the whirlpool straight into the air, towering twelve feet. It swirled and sparkled like diamonds, in all the colors of the rainbow. He gazed at the scene, dazzled by its beauty, and felt himself drawn toward it. Ike felt like he was in some colorful, hazy, lazy dream. He had to get to it. He needed to touch it before it was gone.

Ike entered the water. With each step, he went deeper and deeper until he was up to his waist. He was a few yards away from it. Ike reached his hand toward the swirling mass, as he did, the pond suddenly became a violent cyclone. He lost his footing and was quickly sucked into the vortex and yanked under the surface. The shock of cold rushing water filling his nose and ears snapped him out of his trance. He wanted to shout for help. A strong unknown force was pulling him deeper and deeper. His eyes were open and he could see the same sparkling glitter swirling around him, shining like the sun. Ike thought to himself, he must be drowning. It didn't feel bad and he wasn't afraid. Even the water didn't feel cold anymore. He tried to think about whether or not he was breathing. It seemed like he had been underwater for at least ten minutes, yet he wasn't struggling for air. Then he felt himself being pushed, as if something had hold of his feet and was gently thrusting him upward into warmer, gentler water. He could see light above, but not as bright as before. Ike was released and left to float below the surface. He quickly swam upward and into the sunlight. Looking around he expected to see the swimming hole, but at once he realized he was somewhere else. He was still in a pond, but a much larger one. He turned in the water to survey his surroundings. It was a stunning park-like scene.

The land around him was green and lush. There were huge, towering trees evenly spaced like they were purposely planted that way. They were perfect, not like what he was used to seeing in the forests at home. These were almost identical, growing straight up, their branches reaching for the sky. Every leaf was in its place, not a crooked branch anywhere. The grass around him was a deep emerald green and freshly cut.

Swimming for the bank, he saw movement out of the corner of his eye, but when he turned to look, there was nothing there. He scrambled up the bank and looked back. The sparkling tower slowly swirled above the water. He felt himself being drawn into that hazy, lazy feeling again and quickly looked away toward the other end of the pond and saw a quick flash of orange.

Peering into the water, he was startled to see the pond was filled with fish. Bright, florescent-colored fish. Some were striped in crimson reds and green, some orange and blue. Suddenly, one of the orange and blue fish shot through the water to the surface. With alarm, Ike realized these fish were huge, at least twenty feet long. He could have easily been swallowed whole. The fish stuck its head out of the water and smiled at him. Ike saw that all the other fish were smiling too. He again wondered if he was dead. This had to be a dream. He couldn't believe his eyes. He stood, dripping on the bank, not knowing what to think.

The fish cleared its throat in a watery gurgling sound and spoke. "You all right?"

Ike stumbled backward, tripping over his own feet. "Y-y-yes."

The fish studied him for a moment. "You're a strange looking human. Not much to you, is there?"

He looked at the fish, dumbstruck.

"That's why we didn't eat you. Nothing but skin and bones," it said, chuckling.

Ike stammered, "Oh."

"Not too intelligent either," it said, still smiling.

Ike finally got over the shock a bit. "W-wh-where am I?" he stuttered.

"You're in Wisen. Land of the giants."

"Giants?"

"You are in the realm of the fairies and giants, boy! You got yanked into a world of wonder and magic. By mistake, I'm sure. You must have a good heart; otherwise, you'd never have made it through."

He looked at the smiling fish in wonder.

"My name is Tibit. I am a bocan fish. My tribe and I clean and eat all the garbage that flows through our territory. You're too skinny to eat. We could have used you for a toothpick, though," he said, laughing as he disappeared back under the water.

Ike watched as the other fish gathered around Tibit. They looked up at him, still smiling. Ike decided he'd better get away from the bank before they changed their minds about eating him. He turned and walked away, wondering what to do. Surveying the horizon, he noticed beams of sparkling glitter dotted here and there like over the pond. Some were over other ponds, and some came right out of the ground. He thought to himself, they must be other entrances. He walked toward the big grove of trees. He wanted to stay and explore, but he kept thinking about how much trouble he was already in for leaving school. Grandpa and Grandma would be worried if he didn't get home at the usual time. He loved them very much and hated disappointing them, especially Grandma.

He walked along the edge of the grove for a while, looking through the trees and feeling a little apprehensive about going into the grove. Up ahead, butterflies fluttered around a patch of huge blue and white flowers. As he drew closer, he realized the butterflies were as big as eagles. Remembering what the bocan fish said about this being the land of the giants, he wondered if everything was giant sized here. As he passed, several fluttered around his head then flew off, going about their business. The flowers, he thought were amazing, with heads the size of wheelbarrows, at least six feet tall. They gave off a strong perfume. Off in the distance, a soft tinkling sound like tiny bells drew his attention.

Stepping into the shade of the towering trees, he marveled at the hundreds of sunbeams shining through the branches, illuminating the grove, in a magical dance in the soft breeze.

An intoxicating scent of roses penetrated his senses, making him feel drowsy. He hurried through the grove, remembering how the glittering tower made him feel.

Stumbling out the other side, he felt like he was about to pass out. Bending over, he took in deep breaths. After a few minutes, his head cleared and he looked up. A field of black-eyed Susans, paved the way to a small grove of trees ahead. Their leaves were a bright, translucent red, like you could see through them. He thought this was odd. The black-eyed Susans stood just about eye level and he found it difficult to see what direction he was going as he made his way through.

The soft tinkling grew louder as he emerged. A red translucent mass carpeted the ground, gleaming in the sun. He gasped in wonder. The ground was littered with tiny little rubies. Looking up, great clumps of rubies hung heavy from the branches. Ike excitedly scooped up a handful.

His heart raced as he turned them in his palm. Thoughts of riches filled his mind. He thought of building a brand new house and buying new equipment for Grandpa as well as new pots and pans for Grandma. A thousand ideas flowed through his brain all at once. With a quick look around, he jammed them in his pockets, expecting to be caught like a kid with his hand in the cookie jar. He squatted to the ground and with both hands, scooped up more. A great pile of red wealth. He filled his pockets until they were bulging.

Suddenly, the ground shook. He froze in fear. It shook again. He quickly took cover in the field, behind the vast flowers. The shaking became more violent. Something was coming. He continued to back up, hiding behind the flowers, when, over the hill, came a giant! It looked almost human except for the leaves and twigs growing out of its head and chest. Moss grew where its eyebrows should have been, and it stood almost fifteen feet tall, wearing a massive vest of large leaves. Two wide leathery belts with large silver buckles held up its britches, and its arms were long and hairy, hanging past its knees.

The giant looked so comical, Ike would have laughed, except for the terrifying fear radiating through him. He peered out from behind the flowers. It carried some kind of pack on its back full of odd looking tools. He recognized a large pick, a mallet, and a weird looking tool with a long wooden handle that looked like an old- fashioned umbrella on the end. It stopped at the base of one of the ruby trees and pulled out the tool with the long wooden handle; sure enough, it opened into a rather large umbrella. Tucking the handle firmly into the back of its britches, it took the mallet and swung it, smacking the base of the tree with a thunderous blow.

Rubies began to fall, bouncing off the umbrella like little hailstones. Again and again, the giant struck the tree until every ruby had fallen. Moving through the entire grove, it emptied each tree of its payload. When finished, it stood back and looked up at the bare branches, waiting. After a few moments, to Ike's amazement, tiny pink buds began to appear. First, on one tree, then the next. It was like watching popcorn pop. He smiled. It was a delightful spectacle; forgetting about the danger, he giggled.

Immediately, the giant turned its foliage-covered head and looked almost directly at the spot where Ike stood hidden. The giant took a step toward the flowery field, sniffing the air, when the cry of a bird in the distance diverted its attention. As it turned toward the sound, Ike seized the opportunity and tore through the flowers as quietly as he could, disappearing over a small hill. He ran like he had a pack of hounds hot on his trail and didn't stop until he almost went over a cliff, skidding to a halt just in time. He turned around. The giant was nowhere in sight. His heart hammered in his chest until he thought it would burst. Twenty feet below was a running brook of water and to his right was a waterfall. Finally relaxed, he got up and carefully made his way down the steep, rocky embankment and began to wade across the brook.

The rocks were slippery, and before he could catch himself, he lost his balance, and down he went. Ike spotted a shiny blue object by his knee. Reaching into the water, he pulled out a beautiful stone. It changed from one blue to another as he turned it in his hand. He remembered seeing similar stones like this in one of the books in old man Johnson's library. It was called a sapphire and was worth a lot of money. This one was close to the size of a small plum and unusual. Ike stood up, jammed the gem into his back pocket, and began scanning the brook for more.

Again, he thought about how much money these gems might be worth, what he could buy, and how happy Grandpa and Grandma would be. Ike began wondering how he was going to find his way out of here. He was so preoccupied; he didn't notice the creatures emerging from behind the trees on the opposite bank.

The hair on the back of Ike's neck stood on end and he got the feeling he was being watched. He quickly looked up and saw half a dozen creatures emerging from the trees.

They had bronze skin and wore long silky flowing garments made from rose petals, girdled with golden and silver sashes. Each creature had long, shining hair; some golden, some auburn, some jet-black, and some silver, white. All had small delicate noses, rosy cheeks, and pointed ears; their skin was flecked with that same sparkling glitter. Their silky garments seemed to change color with the slightest movement.

Ike stood in the middle of the brook, frozen in fear. One of the creatures took a step forward, and a great pair of wings fanned out behind it. They were pearlescent gossamer wings in pastel colors also flecked with glitter. They were the most magnificent creatures Ike had ever seen. He thought for a moment they must be angels, then quickly dismissed that idea because of the pointed ears. They must be the fairies Tibit mentioned.

The creature in the front kept fanning its wings then suddenly moved through the air at incredible speed, landing a yard away. Ike took a step back. It was a female with a radiant face, towering over him by at least a foot. Her eyes were deep green speckled with brown and her pupils were black, a bit larger than those of a human. Upon her long auburn hair was a small silver crown, adorned with emeralds and pearls. Smiling down at him, an essence of gentle compassion permeated his heart. He felt her tenderness and affection like a wave of warm air. Joy and gladness surrounded him, and he felt he was about to cry at any moment. When she spoke, it was melodic, with every word a different melody.

"My name is Sersha. I am the Princess of Roan and guardian of this realm. We have been watching you since you arrived. What is your name?"

"Ike," he answered softly.

"Welcome to the fairy world, Ike. One of my brothers will accompany you while you are here. This is a wonderful magical world, but it is also full of dangers you are unaware of."

"What are you? Are you a fairy?"

As he spoke, another group flew over and landed next to her. This was a male. He was taller with a rugged face and much larger wings. He had golden hair, and his pale blue eyes seemed to look right through him.

"Yes, you are correct," she answered. "We are of the Manwan race. We have been the guardians of this realm for a thousand years. This is my brother, Valian. He will accompany you while you are here."

Valian bowed slightly in acknowledgment. Ike looked from Valian to Sersha.

"I don't know exactly how it is that I came to be here. I mean, I know *how*, but I don't know how it was possible. I don't know how to get home. I mean . . . the way I got in had giant fish that wanted to eat me and—"

"Don't worry. Valian will take you where you need to go; however, I must warn you. You must promise to keep this land and everything in it a secret or you will never be allowed to leave."

"Oh . . . sure," Ike replied. "I promise."

"You must give us your solemn oath; you will never speak of it. In return, we will allow you to keep what's in your pocket," she said, glancing down.

Ike's face turned red, and he couldn't think of anything to say except, "I-I swear, I won't tell a soul." All the while, he thought of how he didn't want to lose his chance to buy the things he'd always wanted.

"Very well. Valian, please see to this young man's safe passage back to his world."

With a nod of his head, Valian lifted Ike like he was light as a feather, flying up over the waterfall and across the land. Ike was thrilled, watching the countryside fly by. They skimmed the treetops, going over vast forests and fields of giant flowers. He thought he spotted the giant but he couldn't be sure, as they were flying so fast. Valian dove down steep cliffs and skimmed the water of a lake, making ripples as they went. Before long, he spotted a tower of glitter, shining up ahead. It was on a long white sandy beach surrounded by tall shady palms. He had never seen a real palm tree before. They set down a few feet from the sparkling tower.

"Thank you, sir," said Ike, looking at his magnificent host, nervously.

"It was my pleasure. Don't forget your promise," Valian said, with a smile, but his eyes were piercing and seemed to give a warning of their own.

"I won't. I promise, I won't."

Valian nodded his head and watched as Ike turned and faced the glittering tower. With his heart pounding, Ike stepped into the swirling mass. Immediately, he was sucked down. His journey back was exactly the same as his arrival. He came out in a different place, but knew at once where he was, in the middle of his Grandpa's potato field, about a mile from the house. He was standing next to an old tree Grandpa had been unable to remove from the field.

Ike stood there trying to make sense of everything that happened to him. It was mind-boggling and he could scarcely believe it. He quickly felt his pocket and was relieved to find the gems still there. He wondered what to do with them. He couldn't tell anyone about them or sell them; otherwise, he would have to explain where he got them. The look in Valian's eyes flashed across his mind. He looked around for a hiding place. There were several boulders and piles of rocks surrounding the dead tree. Pulling a handkerchief from his shirt pocket, he tied them in a bundle and picked out a spot among the rocks. He hid them behind one of the smaller rocks and would come back later with a shovel to bury them. After looking around for any possible prying eyes, he walked toward home.

He thought about his journey along the way and how he wanted to go back for more jewels. If he brought a pail or sack, he could fill it up and be a rich man. His mind began scheming on how he could maybe sneak back in and out before anyone knew he was there, but then he remembered Sersha saying they'd been watching him since the moment he arrived. Well, they did let him keep what was in his pocket. Maybe they wouldn't mind as long as he continued to keep it secret. Maybe he could go every weekend and get a whole pile of jewels.

His mind raced. Wouldn't the kids at school be jealous when he became rich? They wouldn't dare tease him anymore. They would get what they deserved. He smiled to himself. It was at this point Ike started to change.

Valian watched as Ike jumped into the glittering tower. He promptly took flight, arriving a short time later in the outskirts of Roan. He met up with Sersha at a little cottage nestled in a cozy, hidden hollow next to an enchanting waterfall. A large waterwheel creaked and groaned outside the cottage as it slowly turned. A crone ran the place. She was old and bent over, with a head of straggly, white hair. She looked like she could turn you to stone with her frightful face full of warts, but she made the best food in the outskirts.

Valian landed and walked over the cobblestone courtyard, joining Sersha at a covered table. A scruffy looking brownie with a pointed little hat and dirty apron came over with a tray laden with an assortment of small cakes and a goblet with a refreshing orange flavored drink brewing inside.

"Rainbow dew?" the brownie asked.

"Please and thank you," smiled Valian.

"Well, what do you think?" he asked, helping himself to a powdered pink cake. "He seemed like a nice young lad," he added.

"I don't know," Sersha answered.

Several others from the scouting party arrived and joined them.

"There's something about him," she continued. "I can't quite put my finger on it. I think we need to call an assembly with the royal lords and ladies of the realm, get their opinions, then decide what to do," she concluded.

The others nodded their heads in agreement. They finished their cakes and rainbow dew, then took flight.

There were many varieties of Manwan fairies. Sersha and Valian were of the Woodland tribe; like many of the various species, they were able to change their appearance and size. As they entered the borders of Roan, in the blink of an eye and a sudden sparkle of glitter, they changed from seven feet tall to seven inches. Roan was a beautiful, enchanted city nestled high in the trees. As they flew toward the palace, dozens of fairies darted to and fro from tree to tree. There were matchbox-sized homes and shops tucked away in the crooks and branches of the great trees. Most were made from tree bark. Some of the more well-to-do families had homes made from stone and brick, and their doors stood open, welcoming the gentle breeze and fresh air inside.

One of the challenges of living in trees was that sunshine had difficulty penetrating the thick canopy of leaves covering much of the city. Many of the tiny houses were lit up by dozens of candles shining through gem-covered windows. It was a dazzling sight, especially at night. Every inch of the forest floor was covered in flowers of every variety. Enchanted light posts and lanterns were everywhere, keeping the flowers fed with much needed light, giving the forest a magical glow.

They flew at a swift pace, dodging between the trees until the palace came into view. It was stunning, glittering and shining like the sun. It was a grand sight, with many towers and turrets.

Swooping down to the palace courtyard, they went inside. A meeting was called in one of the many grand ballrooms, usually used for parties and celebrations.

Lords and ladies gathered together around large, white marble tables. Tall pedestals adorned with great bowls stood around the room, filled with rubies, diamonds, emeralds, and sapphires, representing the four elements. Diamonds symbolized water, rubies signified fire, emeralds denoted the earth, and sapphires characterized the air.

When everyone was seated, the queen entered. She was stunning in a white and yellow gown made of fine silks that billowed in the breeze as she walked. She wore rings of gold and diamonds, upon her head rested a golden crown inlaid with the bluest of sapphires. Her very presence and beauty demanded respect. She stood at the head of the table and waited until the room quieted.

"My daughter, Sersha, has brought news of a young man entering our world. His name is Ike Seers and he comes from Bonners Ferry," she announced.

The assembly erupted in excitement and alarm.

"Quiet. Quiet down, please," she continued, with a wave of her hand.

A hush came over the room.

"As everyone is aware, we've been hard put in contending with our current situation."

There were nods of agreement from the crowd.

"Sersha and Valian have suggested keeping a close eye open for this young man. They have reminded us that it takes a pure heart for a human to enter our world and this young man may just be the one we have hoped for."

There was more whispering among the assembly and the queen waited until they quieted down before continuing.

"I must propose the question to all of you. We need everyone's thoughts and opinions on the matter. Do you think young Mr. Seers may assist us?"

There was much discussion about his arrival and the fact that he left with pocketfuls of gems. Some didn't see anything wrong concerning the gems, but others found him suspicious. An agreement couldn't be made and they decided on a vote.

"All in favor of giving the boy a chance, say I," said the queen.

Only a few responded.

"Opposed?"

Most everyone spoke up. A large fairy with bulging muscles rose in the air.

"I think the boy needs more observation before we rule on this matter. How do we know we can trust him?" The response was overwhelming, with most in agreement.

"The majority rules," replied the queen. "I will assign guardians to observe the boy in his own world. Rotate shifts and report back to me. This assembly is adjourned."

The assembly dispersed in small groups while the guardians stayed behind to discuss who would go and when.

For the next few days, Ike was consumed with thoughts of returning for more gems. Grandpa, it seemed, had other ideas. He had Ike working from dawn until dusk, helping with the spring planting. By the time the weekend was over, Ike hadn't had any free time to do anything.

The following week dragged by like time stood still. Ike was thrilled this was the last week of school. He imagined collecting gems all summer and couldn't wait until he would be able to spend them.

The last day of school came. He was the first one out the door, high-tailing it over the hills to the swimming hole. He was disappointed when he arrived and found there was no tower of swirling glitter.

He tried to remember exactly how it happened.

"It must be too late in the day," he said to himself. It was more around one in the afternoon when the tower first appeared. He would come back the next day at the same time.

He was up before dawn, sneaking out before Grandpa got up and put him to work. Practically running the entire way, he arrived at the swimming hole out of breath. Almost six hours later, the water began to swirl, as the familiar glittery particles rose high into the air. He jumped into the pond. He was quickly spiraled downward, when suddenly, he remembered the giant fish. Looking up, he realized there was no way he could go back. He braced himself. Being a good swimmer, he would give it all he had. He would fight them tooth and nail if he had to. The water became warm, and he felt the familiar gentle push from underneath. Frantically, with all his strength he swam upward and almost leaped onto the bank. He turned and looked back in the water. Not a single fish was in sight, and he wondered where they went.

Heading toward the giant trees, he quickly made his way under their shady cover. Things had changed slightly. There were patches of giant blue bells now lining the edge of the wood, with huge purple heads. Giant toadstools grew around the trunks of the trees in the oddest shapes and colors.

He ran through the wood, stopping at the edge of the field. Peering out, he checked to see that the giant wasn't there. Satisfied, he darted out, running through the black- eyed Susan field and over to the ruby trees, looking over his shoulder as he went. He looked all over the ground but only saw four or five rubies. Looking up, he saw the branches still had little pink buds, but no rubies. He picked up the few rubies he could find, wondering where the rest had gone. He scanned the horizon, trying to spot a glittering tower before he was caught.

To his right, in the distance, he saw flashes of glittering color. He could make it to that tower in no time at all. It wavered in the breeze, next to the base of a tall cliff. He crossed a small glen covered with daisies and huge butterflies, then into a dense growth of large cowslips that grew along the base of the cliff. Hugging the wall, he remained mostly hidden. He darted from flower to flower, keeping an eye out for the giant.

On the left side of the glen grew a large border hedge behind several mounds, covered in yellow and green toadstools, lined with bluebells. Dozens of dragonflies buzzed around a small opening in the mounds. Flower laden branches hung low, over the mounds, dropping pink petals like snowflakes. He had no idea dragonflies lived in mounds. He thought of checking it out, but decided he better get out of here before he was discovered.

Approaching the sparkling tower, he was startled to see the entrance to a cave in the side of the cliff. He almost missed it, had it not been for the shining, red mass he saw spilling out of its mouth. At once he knew they were rubies. *So, this is where they all disappeared to,* he thought, approaching the entrance. At that moment, the ground shook. He spun around. Looking to the left, then right, he expected to see the giant. There was nothing there, but the ground kept shaking, faster and faster, like a stampede. It got stronger and closer as he ran toward the tower.

To his horror, he saw running toward him from the other side of the glade, a terrifying creature. It was so hideous, he thought he might collapse in terror. Standing at least ten feet in height, it was almost bald except for a few tufts of hair on its bumpy head. It had large beady black eyes and a face that resembled a pig. Sharp, curved tusks protruded upward out of the corners of its mouth. It was drooling and squealing the most hair-raising sound. Muscles bulged under its iron breastplate and a wide belt held up torn green britches, but most terrifying, it was dragging a huge brown club covered in spikes. Its hooves were thunderous as it approached. Ike came out of his fright, making a dash for the tower and jumped. As he was sucked down, he thought he saw the creature swing its club.

Suddenly, he was thrust into a large thorn bush. He was dangling half in and half out, covered in deep cuts and scratches. His trousers were ripped and he was bleeding all over. Painfully, he slowly worked his way out of the bush and looked around. He was on top of a large bluff above his farm, roughly ten miles away. He slowly limped toward home. When he got to the river, he cleaned himself up as best he could. Grandma was going to have a fit about his torn clothes and he wondered how he would explain his appearance. It took him what seemed forever to get to the dead oak in the potato field where he deposited the few rubies he'd found into his handkerchief. When he finally got home, he found Grandma sitting at the table. Her head was hung as if sleeping. She looked up when he came in and he could see she'd been crying.

"What happened to you?" she asked.

Ike mumbled something about falling out of a tree and into a thorn bush. She got up and ushered him to the table, pulling his shirt open in the process.

"Tsk, tsk, tsk," she clucked at him, looking at his scratched-up back and arms. She hurried to find some antiseptic. He watched her digging through the drawer and asked what was wrong. She stopped with her back to him. "Grandpa has gone home."

She paused for a moment and then began digging again.

After she came back to the table, she explained she went to call Grandpa to lunch and found him sitting in his old rocker outside the shed, looking out over the valley. He looked so peaceful and content, sitting there with his eyes closed; she thought he was sleeping. He wasn't. They had a funeral for Grandpa and buried him on the little hill behind the house under an apple tree. It was one of Grandpa's favorite spots. No one came, just Grandma and Ike.

Ike didn't go back to Roan or even think about it for weeks. Even though Grandpa always made him work and seemed hard on him at times, he loved him very much. Grandpa was the only father he could remember.

About a month later, he was back at the old swimming hole, waiting for the tower to appear, but it never did. He even jumped into the middle of the pond, trying to make the tower appear, but to no avail. He went back to the thorn bush he fell into on his second return, but nothing. Days turned to weeks, weeks to months, and months to years, but no tower ever appeared.

Grandma passed away a few weeks before Ike's twenty-third birthday and he buried her next to Grandpa under the apple tree. A day later, he drove Grandpa's old pick up to Spokane with the gems and sold them for a considerable amount of money, explaining that he inherited them from his grandparents. Afterward, he went right out and purchased the fanciest car he could find and drove home in style, leaving the old pick up behind.

Back at Bonners Ferry, he made up a story that he sold one of his inventions for a lot of money, which seemed to satisfy the locals. The pretty little girl that used to tease him in school took a sudden shine to him and they were married after a brief courtship. He never told anyone about the fairy world, in hopes that someday he would be able to get back in somehow. He still had plenty of money from the sale of the gems and he tore down Grandpa and Grandma's house to build a huge fancy place. The potato field, he neglected and it became weed infested. The tools and equipment became rusty and forgotten. Later, he leased the farmland to a neighbor for a considerable amount every season.

Ike became interested in the legend of Bonners Ferry and studied the stories and rumors that developed over the years. He found it fascinating and believed there was treasure buried on old man Johnson's property.

Over the past two centuries, many different families lived on the property and they all seemed to have had an over-abundance of money. Originally, the land housed only a small cabin, but additions were added on over time until it became a large estate. It was rumored, the courtyard wall had been put up so prying eyes couldn't see what was going on inside. Nobody would be able to see the owners burying their treasures in the walls and there were rumors of hidden passages.

When old man Johnson was found dead a few years later, Ike seized the opportunity to search the grounds. There was never any worry about being caught, as most of the locals were convinced the estate was cursed and stayed well away. He was over there almost every day, for weeks at a time, searching. Going through rooms, knocking on walls, and looking for secret passages. He even took a sledgehammer to the outer courtyard wall.

Eventually, he gave up on the house and searched the stable. Up in the attic he discovered old boxes and trunks; in the back on a dusty old shelf, he found a diary. It was an extremely worn simple black leather bound book with the binding worn and falling apart. The diary revealed there was a map. The description was vague, but it did use the word *portals* in the entry. He got excited. He just knew the map had to be real. If he could find it, he would be able to get back into fairy world at last.

Just when he decided to the search the estate again, the property was sold. He just about threw a fit. How was he going to search again, with people living there? And worse, what if one of them found the map? He was beside himself. He would have to keep a close eye on his new neighbors somehow. The day came when they arrived–a couple with two children. Ike thought about going over and introducing himself but decided against it. He would put a bug in the ears of his two sons, so they would keep an eye on them. That wouldn't be so conspicuous. Kids always make friends quickly, so he suggested rather strongly that they go introduce themselves, sooner rather than later. A couple days later, Ike's sons ran into Henry and Haley looking down at their house.

Sersha and Valian took the first watch and flew directly to the human world. All shifts watched for a little over a week as Ike worked with his Grandpa on the farm from sun up to sun down. Ike worked hard, without any free time until after dark. Most fairies were impressed with his devotion to his family and his stamina. Others felt sorry he had to work so hard and reap so little. Most reported back to the queen that he seemed like a decent and well balanced boy, however, Sersha and Valian seemed to think they needed a little more time to be absolutely sure. Sersha had a feeling she couldn't overcome.

The next morning, they watched as Ike left the house just before dawn. They watched him wait by the swimming hole and jump in when the time was right. They saw him exit the bocan fish pool and run through the wood, across the field to the ruby trees.

They exchanged glances as he picked up the few rubies on the ground and headed for the nearest glittering tower. With sadness, they saw Ike spot the boar troll, jump into the tower and disappear. The boar troll skidded to a halt, almost losing hold of its spiked club, falling into the sparkling tower.

It was a viscous boar troll. Luckily, it hadn't seen Ike. It turned and ran off in the other direction. Valian had a solemn look on his face as he turned to Sersha.

"I guess your hunch was right."

She nodded sadly. "We'd best get the news to mother," she replied.

They slowly flew back to Roan to report the bad news. All the lords and ladies of the assembly were saddened to hear the story and wondered what they would do now. The queen looked at them all with such kindness and love.

"One will come," she said.

With a nod of her crowned head, she fanned her beautiful wings and was escorted out the door. The rest of the assembly dispersed and went about their business with hope in their hearts that truly someone would come.

Chapter Five

WONDERS AND MAGIC

1813

Zeb wandered aimlessly for days, in mourning for his lost love and beautiful daughters. After his mock funeral, he realized he'd never find them. He sat at the edge of the river with his head resting on his arms. He was exhausted, emotionally and physically. He sat there for a long time and finally drifted off to sleep.

As he lay on the bank, Sersha appeared suddenly and stood over him. Her long auburn hair blew in the wind. Compassion and pity radiated from her green eyes. She knew Zeb. He accidentally discovered the fairy world while digging his first cistern. He became good friends with the fairies and visited them often. The fairies enjoyed Zeb's humor and kind heart. They even gave him a gift for being such a trusted friend. It was a beautiful red ruby, which Zeb promptly gave to Sarah as a gift. Sersha gazed down at Zeb. After a moment, she turned to see Valian walking through the tall grass toward her. He looked down at the sleeping man.

"The poor soul, it will take him a long time to heal from this," he said.

"Yes." Sersha agreed. "How did you find out?"

"I was in the sacred chamber and saw it through the luminous sphere. What a tragic event."

"He needs to be cared for," said Sersha. "He is unable to think clearly and must be looked after for a while. We need to check with mother to see if we may bring—"

"She's already consented," Valian interrupted. "She saw it too and is quite distressed. That is why I have come."

He passed his hand over the exhausted man. A light shower of glitter fell over Zeb's body and melted like snowflakes.

"That should keep him asleep for a good long while," he said.

Valian reached down and picked Zeb up. The three took to the air. They flew as if following an invisible trail, up over the trees, across ponds and meadows. The wind picked up, creating a spinning column of dust and leaves. They flew into the whirlwind and disappeared.

They continued their flight over lush green fields, through valleys, glens, dells, and hollows. Finally, they came to rest in a cozy little dell just inside the borders of the Roan realm.

The city was at least fifty miles away, giving Zeb peace and quiet.

The queen, upon seeing the horrible events that happened to Zeb's family, ordered the construction of a small cottage. Valian carried Zeb inside. There was a bedroom next to a small bathroom and a large living area with a kitchen. It was quite cozy, with a fireplace in the middle of the main wall. The builders put a charm on the cottage. The outside walls were immediately covered with ivy and surrounded by lilacs and flower beds. The yard was well manicured and a grove of aspens grew in the front. Valian took Zeb into the bedroom and gently laid him on a puffed up featherbed. Sersha came in and opened the shuttered window to let in the fresh air. After they were satisfied he would be comfortable, they walked into the kitchen, waved a hand and charmed the room. A large ice chest in the kitchen immediately filled with food. The table was suddenly covered with loaves of fresh baked bread, bowls of fruit, and an assortment of nutmeats.

After a look around the room, they departed and flew back to Roan, where they could keep an eye on Zeb through the luminous sphere. The luminous sphere was a large unbreakable glass ball that illuminated the four colors of the elements; white, blue, red, and green in light faded colors. When they looked into it, the fairies could observe everything going on in their world and the human world with a wave of the hand.

It was a most sacred object and was kept in a special room in the palace, only accessible to a few.

Ten hours later, Zeb woke up. It was just getting dark. Someone came in and lit the lamps in the bathroom and kitchen. A hot tub of bath water was ready with a clean towel and fresh bar of soap. He sat up and looked out the window at the fading day. The sky was purple and the clouds bright pink, with hues of red around the edges. He knew instantly he was in the fairy world, but couldn't remember how he got there. His stomach was growling as he got up, but he was still tired. Walking into the kitchen, he saw the food on the table and realized how hungry he was. He tore off a chunk of bread and started eating. He spotted a fresh dish of butter, and he tore off another chunk of bread. Pulling some grapes off their vines, he popped one in his mouth. It was the sweetest grape he'd ever eaten. He looked around the room. It was modest and cozy, with an overstuffed sofa and a rocking chair by the fireplace. There was a pedestal table with a lamp on top and a large, braided rug in the middle of the floor. He spotted the ice chest and looked inside. It was full of the foods he loved. Eggs, cheese, a large platter of ham, and a pitcher of ice-cold milk—just to name a few. He took out a couple of thick slices of ham and made a sandwich. The milk tasted so good he polished off almost half the pitcher.

A fire was crackling in the hearth, and he sat down in the rocker to eat. A thick quilt hung over the back of the rocker. He covered his lap and finished his sandwich. He spotted a bowl of cherries and sat spitting the pits into the fire. His mind began to ponder his loss as he slowly rocked. Tears filled his eyes, and he wept softly. Finally, the emotions drained him of what little strength he had left and he fell asleep by the fire.

Back in Roan, Sersha, Valian, and the queen shook their heads sadly at the sight.

He awoke the next morning at sunrise, stretched and got up. His body was stiff as he hobbled to the bathroom. There was still a steaming tub of hot water waiting for him. He smiled to himself thinking, *the fairies don't miss a thing.* He took a bath and trimmed his beard. Emerging from the front door, he felt refreshed, but in his mind, he was broken. Again, he wondered how he got there and what he would do now.

The morning was bright with a blue sky and popcorn clouds. Birds were celebrating it with a chorus of song, and the ground sparkled with dew glistening in the coolness of dawn. A small herd of goats was wandering through the aspens, and he saw a pair of peacocks pecking at the ground outside one of the small flower beds. The little brook babbled, tumbling over smooth stones. He could see a snow-capped mountain behind the aspen grove, its peak brilliantly shining with snow. He admired the brilliant blooms of the flowers and slowly inhaled the fragrance of roses, which grew on a trellis bordering one of the gardens. He smiled at the thought of how Sarah would have loved this place and wished he told her about fairy world and brought her here. Maybe they could have lived out their days without the dangers of the human world.

Zeb looked around for a sign of a fairy but none came. He went back into the cottage and found the kitchen cupboards stocked with dishes, pots, and pans. He made himself a stack of flapjacks and prepared some more of the ham. After breakfast, feeling a little better, he decided the dishes could wait, he would go out and see the lay of the land, not knowing exactly where he was in the fairy world. He didn't recognize this place. He had never done much exploring when he visited the fairies, being so busy chatting with them all. He remembered one time coming in after dark and finding them dancing around a big fire. They jumped and leapt into the air, shouting with glee. Some sang songs, while others would appear and disappear in a snap of glittering color. They were celebrating the new moon. Even a few pixies were invited. Zeb knew there were strange and wondrous creatures in fairy world, but he had never seen a pixie before. They were much the same size as fairies, but they weren't covered in glitter and didn't have wings. This particular species had brown skin and wore small green pointed hats. Some wore clothes made from the smooth flesh of trees and leaves, while others wore nothing.

Zeb sat and watched the celebration, which lasted long into the night. At one point, the fairies cried out for a story. Zeb was a master at story telling. The fairies especially liked to listen to human fairy tales, they would giggle with delight and scream in fits of laughter. He always had a jolly time at every visit.

Zeb made up his mind to reach the mountain by noon and headed off in that direction. He crossed the aspen grove and went north. The ground was still wet with dew and his steps were silent. He traveled several miles in the first hour, crossing crystal clear brooks, sparkling with flecks of gold, through green valleys and flower-filled glades. He stopped for a rest at the top of a deep gorge. Trees flanked its walls, seemingly growing out of solid rock. At the bottom was a fast running river. His mind wandered back to the raging current that took the lives of his family and he quickly turned away.

Unbeknownst to Zeb, as he wandered over a rolling hill full of sunflowers, he left the realm of Roan and entered the Woodland realm. It was just as beautiful but wasn't as well ordered or maintained. The fairies had much to look after and didn't get to spend a lot of time in any one realm. A small forest stood before him, full of fallen logs and dead brush, which looked like it would be extremely difficult to navigate. Another species of woodland fairy lived in this forest and preferred to let fallen logs lie. They weren't as friendly as Manwan fairies and didn't care for strangers. The woodland forest was also full of charms and enchantments to keep out intruders.

As Zeb neared the forest edge, he became nervous and thought it best to go around. Woodland fairies peered out at him from behind massive trunks and fallen logs, ready to bring swift retribution if he entered, however, they recognized him as being a frequent visitor to the Manwan's and let him pass by. He continued northward and soon found himself wandering in a thicket of tall weeds. There were many paths leading through and he wondered who made them. He walked for what seemed like hours before he came to the edge. Stepping out, he paused in front of a wide swamp. Dragonflies dove toward the still surface, causing the water bugs to scatter in every direction. Tall reeds and cattails grew along the bank in large clusters and the lily pads covering half the swamp, floated gently in the light breeze. The scene was tranquil and he felt a bit sleepy as the warm sun beat down on him. Suddenly, he was startled by a splash. He blinked his eyes a couple times and saw tiny ripples move across the water.

"Must have been a fish," he said to himself.

He gazed at the spot where the ripples began, and soon he saw movement just under the surface. *Must be a big one,* he thought, wishing he had a fishing pole and bait. A fresh catfish for supper made his mouth water.

There was another movement. As he shaded his eyes to see better, a patch of slimy greenish gray fur or hair broke the surface, rising slowly. Slightly alarmed, he stepped back behind the thicket line, just enough to hide himself and watched the slimy patch move slowly through the water. It began to rise out of the water–a slimy, muddy head. The creature had a long hooked nose and a gaping mouth full of tiny sharp unevenly spaced and crooked teeth, long strands of weeds and muddy slime hung from its corners. Its eyes were as black as coal and extremely sunken in, with thick bushy eyebrows that grew together. Water dripped from its long, stringy gray hair with bald patches here and there, like great chunks of hair had been ripped out and replaced with scabs. A few long, stiff hairs grew out of its face. It was the most hideous looking hag. Slime and mud dripped off her shoulders as she stood. She snatched a large dragonfly that got a little too close right out of mid-air and devoured it, chewing loudly.

Zeb stood as still as a statue, watching as she scanned the area for something else to eat. She stopped and slowly turned her head toward him, sniffing the air, looking directly toward where he stood hidden. Sinking back into the water, she slowly glided toward the bank.

"Come over here, young man, so I can get a better look at you," she croaked at him.

Hesitantly, he came out from his hiding spot but didn't move any closer. Her arm came out of the water and she motioned him to come a little closer. She had long, bony fingers and skinny arms. Her saggy skin hung under her arms, flapping as she moved.

"Who are you? What are you?" he asked.

At the second question the old hag leered at him and snorted in anger.

"Can't you tell? I'm a beautiful fairy," she cackled at him. "I was the most beautiful, ravishing, and respected lady in the palace of Roan. Then that pompous queen decided to banish my sister and me to live like vermin for no good reason."

Zeb looked at the old hag curiously. "Your sister?" "Yes. My sister was doomed to live out her days trapped in a willow just over the next hill. She wasn't as beautiful as me," she croaked, leering at him as she smoothed her hair. "The queen even clipped our wings!" she screeched, while turning her back to show the humps protruding slightly from the slime and mud. "Now I'm forced to live in this miserable swamp, eating bugs and fish, with no family to comfort me. A little like you, eh?" She sneered slightly.

"What do you know of my family?" asked Zeb, his heart skipping a beat.

"I have my ways," she answered, giving him an innocent look. "They're not dead," she continued, swimming out into the water a little way, with a hideous grin on her face.

"What do you mean, they're not dead?!" he shouted at her. "I saw them drown myself! I was there!" he cried, in anguish.

"Nope. They came here through the portal in my swamp. I grabbed them and pulled them through myself." She cackled proudly. "I plucked them, one by one, out of your world and into mine," she continued, grinning again. "Then the moss trolls came and dragged them away, kicking and screaming through the swamps."

Zeb was shaking all over with anger and excitement at the possibility of his family still being alive. "Where did they take them? Which way did they go?" he shouted at her.

"Come here and I'll show you," she replied.

"No! Which way did they go?"

"I'm not sure," she croaked, looking around with a snicker.

Her hand came out of the water, grasping a human arm. Tearing off a chunk of flesh, she munched and cackled at him through mouthfuls. Horrified, he stumbled backward and started to run.

"They went north to the mountain! No, they went south to the seas! It doesn't matter! You'll never live long enough to find them!" she screamed. Lowering herself into the water, her face grimaced into a dreadful frown as she descended into the depths.

Zeb ran. The old hag's words echoing in his head. *Still alive . . . taken by moss trolls through the swamps.* His mind spun. *You'll never live long enough to find them . . .* He slowed, breathing heavily. *The hag eating from a human arm.* He shuddered at the thought. He clung to the idea she was telling the truth and he would find his family alive.

For miles, he half-walked and half-ran until he reached the cottage, exhausted. He went in and collapsed on the bed. After he calmed down, he forced himself to get up and went into the kitchen. He was surprised to see the dishes were all cleaned and put away, and a new tray, with fresh bread and fruit sat on the table. He pondered the hag's words as he ate. Tomorrow he would set off in search of his family. After his bath he went to bed.

He left at sunrise and kept an eye out for the fairies as he walked, hoping to thank them and tell them everything the swamp hag said. He traveled all day without seeing anyone. No family, no fairies. Toward dusk, he arrived back at the cottage tired and discouraged. After eating, he sat by the fire. He was sure they were alive, out there somewhere. Fairy world, unknown to Zeb, was vast. A world in itself with tens of thousands of realms. He dozed and dreamed of his lovely Sarah, the way they laughed and walked hand in hand, exploring the new land, and he was still with her. Upon waking, he had a strange feeling and turned to see Sersha and Valian sitting at the table.

"Boy, am I glad to see you two! I was beginning to wonder if I'd ever see you," he said, getting up.

"We are very sorry for your loss, Zeb," said Sersha.

"They will truly be missed," Valian added.

"They're still alive!" he exclaimed, with excitement.

They looked at each other then back at Zeb.

"We saw it happen," replied Sersha, with a sad look.

"No . . . no," he continued, relating everything the hag told him.

"We weren't aware the swamp hag had such a portal. That entrance was supposed to have been sealed more than a thousand years ago. How could she have possibly opened it?" Sersha wondered aloud.

"I don't know," answered Valian. "Before she was banished, she had access to all the portals. When she saw she was about to be caught in her treachery, she must have opened it. I wonder how many others she's opened."

"If we had known, your family would have been taken under our protection immediately. We're so sorry, Zeb," said Sersha.

"It's all right. At least I know they're alive and they're here somewhere. I'm going to continue to search for them if takes me the rest of my life."

Sersha sat thinking for a while. The room was silent, except for the crackle of the fire. It was getting dark outside by the time she spoke.

"We will aid you as much as we can. I will accompany you myself."

Valian rose in protest. "You can't take on this burden alone. You must—"

"I won't be alone," she interrupted. "I will take you with me. It is dreadfully important we help him find his family. You know of the many dangers he will face. He must have our protection."

Valian smiled and nodded his head. "Very good," he replied, satisfied.

Sersha turned to Zeb.

"We'll start in the morning. I have a feeling, finding your family is going to be extremely difficult. We may not find them for a long time. Moss trolls are vicious, but clever. There are a million places they could be and they won't be out in the open where they can be easily spotted. If the old hag was telling the truth, the moss trolls will have them imprisoned in a thick wood or perhaps a cave and may even live underground. It may be against my better judgment, but I think we'll need to use an elixir."

Valian gave Sersha a look of warning.

"He will need it to keep up his strength," Sersha continued. "If this takes as long as I fear. He'd never make it. Besides, Zeb is a trusted friend. I don't think we have anything to worry about."

Valian didn't look convinced, but he agreed.

"What is this elixir?" Zeb asked.

Sersha pondered a moment before answering.

"After a fairy comes of age, we shed our wings once a year. Some of our power and immortality is shed with them. It was discovered centuries ago that an elixir could be made which has healing powers. It also bestows strength and continued life and youth for the partaker. It can produce wings," she went on. "You will need it to keep you going in the long journey ahead. Sir Valian is quite right in being apprehensive. It can be a dangerous thing in the wrong hands and used for evil purposes. I have heard tales of its abuse in other realms. There is one realm in particular where fairies don't go. It is a dark and dreadful place, guarded by creatures so horrible, trespassers have been driven mad. An evil presence resides there, in the very rocks and ground that surrounds it."

"What is it?" Zeb asked. "Where did it come from?"

"It has been here from the beginning," she answered. "What it is, no one knows. We call it Molock the Merciless. It is the lord of decay and death. It represents all the fires of hell and darkness. Its evil penetrates the very air. It is malicious and cunning; it hates the freedom of the world. It is a despiser of light; it curses the sun and can barely tolerate the moon and stars. There are those who have seen into its realm and it is terrifying to the mind." Zeb looked at her speechless.

"Anyway," she continued. "We'll need to get the elixir. We'll be back in the morning."

"Wait!" he cried. "If this elixir will keep me healthy and alive, what about my family? Won't they get older? And what if it does take years? I'll be young and they'll be old!"

"I wouldn't worry about that," Sersha answered.

"Moss trolls don't kill their prisoners, they enslave them. They have their own way of extending life and they wouldn't let a chance to have a human slave slip through their fingers by dying of old age."

Zeb breathed a sigh of relief. He was terrified for them, yet relieved they wouldn't grow old and die before he could find them.

Sersha and Valian bid him good night and flew off into the twilight.

The next morning, they arrived back at the cottage just after sun up. Sersha produced a tiny, brass stein with a mother-of-pearl handle and a jewel-encrusted lid. Zeb opened the little container and a putrid smell filled the air.

"Phew!" Zeb said, wrinkling his nose. "Drink it, quickly," Sersha urged.

He held his nose and downed the potion in one swallow. His grimace turned to a smile. It didn't taste anything like it smelled. It had an almost peachy flavor.

"That will last you for about a month," she remarked.

Suddenly, Zeb felt funny. His whole body felt as if it was buzzing and the skin on his back started to get warm. He was dizzy and began to sweat. His back felt like it was on fire.

"What's happening?" he panted, bending over.

"Oh, you're fine. I forgot to tell you, you're growing wings," said Sersha.

"Wings?" he gasped.

"You'll need them to keep up," answered Valian, with a smile.

"Oh," Zeb replied, breathing a little easier.

"You'll need to remove your shirt," said Valian, helping Zeb get his arm out of a sleeve.

Zeb was still hunched over. Suddenly, humps on both sides of his back appeared under his skin. They grew in length quickly. All at once, something that resembled a wing protruded through his skin, wet and deformed looking. Slowly they unfolded like a blooming flower. They were translucent, in pastel colors and expanded to their fullest, soft and wet.

"Now, just stay here in the sun and let them dry," instructed Valian.

"Wow!" exclaimed Zeb excitedly. "This is great!"

"Don't get used to them," Sersha interjected. "They're just temporary," she added with an amused look. "As long as you take the elixir regularly, you shouldn't have to go through the process of re-growing them."

"Wow," he said again. "How do they work?" he asked, looking over his shoulder, admiring his new wings.

"You just think about flying. Picture it in your mind," she answered. "See your wings, and that will get them started. To go forward, lean forward slightly. To steer left, move your right shoulder forward. To steer right, move your left shoulder forward. To hover, straighten your body. When you want to stop, move both your shoulders back to lower to the ground, and just point your toes. Once you touch the ground, your wings will stop. To fold your wings, just think of folding them, and they'll close," she finished.

"Gee," replied Zeb, looking bewildered. "I don't know if I can remember all that."

"You'll get the hang of it," said Valian.

Valian and Sersha watched Zeb, full of smiles. He was so comical, fanning his wings, but the look on his face, full of wonder, made them both laugh.

"Will I be able to change size too?" he asked hopefully.

"Yes, but we'll go over that later," answered Sersha. "First, I think you need to practice your flying."

Valian examined Zeb's wings, making sure there were no defects and that they were completely dry.

"They look good," said Valian. "Are you ready?"

"I think so," he answered excitedly.

He closed his eyes and started thinking about flying, seeing his wings. Slowly, he rose in the air.

"Just practice taking flight and landing first!" Sersha yelled.

He wobbled in every direction, trying to get control.

They watched half with concern and half delight as he struggled.

"Okay, come back down!" Sersha yelled. "Remember, straighten to hover and point your toes to lower!"

Zeb was elated as he landed. Up he went again, laughing with delight.

He practiced for about a half hour before everyone felt comfortable with his technique.

The trio flew for days over mountains, valleys, and vast oceans spanning hundreds of miles through gorges with sheer granite walls, sparkling deep lakes, and thick forests. Days turned to months. Everyone was totally discouraged. Confidence was low, and spirits dampened. They saw no sign that would indicate Zeb's family had been there. The queen finally called Valian and Sersha back to Roan. There were matters that needed attending, and she could no longer spare them.

Zeb decided to go back to the cottage and rest up before going out again. When he arrived, the kitchen was again stocked with fresh bread and fruit, the ice chest was full. He spent three days recuperating before leaving again.

A month later, he lost his wings. He'd forgotten about getting more elixir before Valian and Sersha left. Now he was stuck, walking a thousand miles away from Roan. They had shown him how to make the elixir, but he had no fairy wings. He walked for weeks before he found some lying in a patch of May apple; unfortunately, it took a dozen to make one dose. He felt drained. He was desperate to find his family but found it difficult to go the distance he could a month ago. He was starting to feel his age. It took him another month to find enough fairy wings to make the elixir. It brought newfound strength and vigor, he traveled at a much faster pace.

Time went by quickly and Zeb saw no sign of his family. He collected wings as he went, replenishing his vitality. He wandered on his own, never finding a trace of his beloved Sarah. Then one day late in the autumn, wandering on the edge of the Spicewood realm, he became nervous. Fear crept into his mind, and he became confused. He began to stumble as he walked. All of a sudden, in the distance, he saw Sarah and both girls! His heart raced. His hands got all sweaty. He called out to them as he ran along the border of the realm. They stood there facing his direction, looking the same as when he saw them last. They seemed to be looking past him and didn't respond to his calls. He stepped across the Spicewood border and into the realm. The moment he crossed; his family vanished before him. He skidded to a halt, turning in all directions, trying to spot them. He called out in desperation but saw and heard nothing. Rubbing his eyes, he wondered if he imagined it. He'd struggled for so long to find them, maybe his mind was playing tricks on him.

Looking around, the fear again entered his mind. He didn't know why he felt so uneasy and noticed it seemed darker than it did a few moments ago. He felt a sudden urge to go forward. He walked for miles and cursed the rough terrain. It was extremely rocky and tree roots stuck out everywhere. There were fallen logs too numerous to count and thick underbrush. He was drawn forward, not understanding why. At one point, he could swear he saw Sarah again in the distance standing still, gazing past him, then she disappeared.

He continued wandering. Days passed. The only thing that sustained him was the elixir. He only had one dose left and hadn't bothered looking for wings. He didn't seem to care anymore. He trudged on and on, catching glimpses of Sarah and the girls every so often. It continually got darker, the further he went. The feeling of fear wouldn't let up and he no longer seemed to be able to control himself. He felt lost and desperate. His mind continually played tricks on him. His desire to hold Sarah in his arms tormented him. He called out to her in tortured anguish.

At one point, as he walked along the top of a small ravine, he slipped on the dry, dusty pea-sized rocks and fell ten feet to the bottom, spilling the entire contents of his elixir and spraining his left ankle in the process. Fortunately, the elixir in his system healed him at once. A few days later, his wings fell off. He left them behind and continued forward.

The terrain grew steadily worse. The skies were darker and he couldn't remember if it was day or night. A growing dread filled his brain.

One cold gray morning, through a dense fog, a shallow marsh emerged into view. It was covered with tall weeds and grasses, thick with mud. His footsteps made sucking sounds as he walked. Swamp flies were everywhere, which he continued to swat. Leeches began to attach themselves to his legs.

It was a miserable place that got hotter every day. It didn't seem like autumn, it felt more like a hot day in July. The air got thicker and it was harder to breathe. He kept seeing movement out of the corner of his eye, but when he turned to look there would be nothing. He hadn't seen any animals or heard any birds. Each step became more tedious and dreadful, while the hair on his arms and the back of his neck were constantly standing on end.

Once out of the swamp, he picked off the leeches and rubbed his weed cut, bug bit arms with mud. Over the next bare dirt hill were pools of bubbling black muck. All around, pitch-black stones jutted out of the ground like jagged pieces of sharp glass and the smell was putrid.

His eyes watered and the inside of his nose burned. Dead trees stood around like petrified skeletons. One large tree was covered in huge, long-dead black leaves hanging still in the dead silence. The only sound was the thick *glug! glug!* of the pools. Here and there, flames shot out of the ooze. Zeb thought he must be in hell.

He began to make his way around the boiling masses, when suddenly, the black leaves in the great tree began to flutter madly as if a strong gust of wind had begun to blow. They began to drop off; before hitting the ground, to his horror, they shot into the air in any angry jumble of confusion.

Zeb ducked and flung his arms over his head, trying to fend them off. They were huge ferocious looking bats with tiny sharp fangs. They swirled above his head, then shot into different directions and disappeared into the thick layer of fog that blocked out the sky. He cowered there for a bit, making sure they were gone, then slowly continued to make his way, dripping with sweat.

He came upon a huge cave at the base of a dead mountain, like an ancient extinct volcano. Inside, the walls gave off a dark red glow, an eerie light to show the way.

His mind wasn't his own any longer. He was being drawn forward, through deep caverns and long narrow passages. He had no emotion, no fear. He moved like a human robot being led to his doom. He came upon a creature so horrifying; one look would have made most people go mad. Its form changed constantly. It was the face of death and destruction. It was the great evil the fairies warned him about. Zeb, on his knees, was bent to its evil devices.

Chapter Six

BONNER HISTORY

The twins arrived home just in time for a delicious dinner. Estelle had prepared a lovely beef roast with all the trimmings—potatoes, gravy, corn, and a fresh apple pie à la mode for dessert.

They chatted about meeting the snotty Seers' boys and the legend of Bonners Ferry while they ate. Paul related the real story of Zeb Bonner's tragic loss and how there was no treasure, just legend and folklore.

After dinner, the twins decided to search every nook and cranny of the west tower, but of course, didn't find anything. They were up early the next morning, looking high and low.

They spent most of the summer searching the grounds and exploring the woods and meadows. One morning in early August, Haley went out to the courtyard to pull weeds in her flower garden. She hummed as she crawled on her hands and knees, going from bed to bed, pausing every so often to listen to the birds and breathe in the sweet fragrance.

As Haley neared the east wall, she noticed several rocks she missed when preparing the area for planting. The first few rocks moved easily, but several were mostly buried. She went to the little shed her father built for her gardening tools and came back with a shovel.

A short time later, Haley was pulling and heaving at a fairly good size rock. When she was finally able to roll it aside, she discovered a wooden board buried underneath.

Clearing some of the dirt away revealed a trap door with a rusty iron ring for a handle.

She pulled at it excitedly, but it wouldn't budge. She ran to get Henry, knowing in her heart this just had to be where the treasure was buried.

She dashed up the tower stairs and burst into Henrys room, panting. "Come quick!" she gasped. "Hurry!"

"What?" he asked. "I found it!"

"Found what?"

"You *know!*"

Henry's eyes got big. The twins flew down the grand staircase like their feet were on fire. When they got to the spot, Henry couldn't contain his excitement.

"This has got to be it!" he said, excitedly.

Furiously, they began to clear the dirt from around the edges. Together they lifted the heavy door and peered into a dark hole filled with floating dust.

"Wait," whispered Haley, running to the shed.

A moment later she was back with a flashlight. Stone steps became clear as she shined the light inside. They slowly descended, entering a small room, filled with old cobwebs. The room was empty except for a single door to the left. Henry pulled on the handle. It took all his might, but finally the door opened, creaking with age.

Haley shined the light inside. It was another, larger room. An old-fashioned kerosene lantern hung from the back of the door. She shined the light around the room, revealing a long wooden box with two smaller boxes on either side.

"Those look like coffins," she whispered.

"They are," Henry agreed, his voice shaking. "Let's open one."

"I don't think we should."

"Come on, it can't hurt to take a look," he pleaded.

After a pause, she agreed. Henry lifted the lid off one of the small coffins. With apprehension, they looked inside.

"It's empty," he said.

After they looked in the other small coffin and found it empty they held their breath as they lifted the lid on the larger one. Inside was a beautiful old garment with a high collar embroidered in delicate beadwork and lace with long sleeves that puffed out at the shoulders.

"Oh my God!" Haley exclaimed, lifting the dress out of the coffin.

Henry grabbed the flashlight and examined the rest of the inside.

"Hey look," he said, lifting out a small-carved wood box and a rolled up piece of parchment. "It's a map!" he exclaimed, unrolling it.

"Look at this," Haley whispered, holding up a red stone, attached to a silver chain. "It's a ruby," she whispered.

She took it to the stair doorway and held it up to the sunlight pouring in from above. She examined the dress again.

"I wonder who these coffins were for?" she asked.

"Obviously, they were for the Bonners," Henry answered, looking up from the map.

"Huh?"

"Don't you get it? Zeb Bonner made them for his family, but he never found their bodies, so he buried the empty coffins with these mementos. Look at this map."

She glanced at the map. It looked like an entire layout of the mountains and valleys surrounding the estate. Three faded X's were barely visible, pointing out three locations.

"Oh, my goodness," Haley whispered.

Henry nodded at her.

"I bet those are the places where he buried his treasure," she stated, with delight. "Yes, and look, the initials Z.E.B. Zeb Bonner! I wonder what the E stands for."

"I'll bet we could find out," said Henry. "There's a monument in town."

"Let's go see!" Haley said, excitedly.

They ran up the steps into the bright sunshine.

"We can't tell mom and dad about this," Henry panted, as they covered the trap door with dirt. "It has to be a secret. When we find the treasure, we'll surprise them!"

"Yeah," Haley agreed. "They'll freak!"

Just after lunch, they set out for town. By now, they knew the countryside well, taking shortcuts over the hills. They emerged from the forest at the post office and entered the wayside park. It had an outhouse and a couple picnic tables. To the right in the center of the park, stood a tarnished bronze statue of a man leaning on a long handled axe.

The plaque at the bottom read:

In memory of Zebulan Elias Bonner, founder of Bonners Ferry.
His strength and courage laid the foundation for all.
A leader whose dedication and commitment was
the cornerstone of this community.
Erected 1915.

"Zebulan Elias Bonner," Haley whispered.

Henry pulled out the map and examined it again.

"Well, that settles it. Those were the coffins for his wife and children and this map belonged to him. I'll bet you a million dollars; these X's are the spots where he buried his treasure. Look! There's an X on the Seers' property," he groaned. "There's one by that old swimmin' hole we found earlier this summer. And *look!* There is one on our property! Next to the oak tree in our courtyard! Come on, let's get back!" Henry said, excitedly.

As they turned from the statue, a man came out of the post office. He was tall and lanky, with hayseed yellow hair, dressed in a polo shirt, pressed slacks, and loafers. He spotted the twins and walked toward them.

"Hello kids," he said, smiling. "I don't think we've met. I'm Ike Seers, Senior. You're the Miles children aren't you?"

Haley didn't like this man. His smile was insincere. She opened her mouth to reply, but he didn't give her a chance.

"It's Henry and Haley?"

"Yes, we . . ."

"Yes, my boys mentioned meeting you. You moved into the old Johnson place, right? They spoke very highly of you."

His eyes traveled over them, making Haley uncomfortable. He spotted the edge of the map, poking out from behind Henry's back.

"What've you got there, son?" he asked, with interest.

"Oh nothing," Henry replied, stuttering a little. "Just some homework–research on the town."

Ike took a step nearer. "Oh, may I see?" Ike asked.

"Um . . . ah . . . well, we really need to get going. Mom's expecting us, don't want to be late," he answered quickly as he and Haley started to hurry past.

Ike reached out and grabbed his arm. Henry clutched the map tightly in his hand.

"I really must come by and introduce myself to your parents. I hear your father is an architect?"

He let go of Henry's arm.

"Y–yes," Henry stammered.

"Well, good. Maybe finally something can be done to fix up that old place," he replied, rather sarcastically.

"Yes, um . . . thank you," said Henry, backing away.

Turning, he quickly joined Haley a few yards away. They glanced back as they headed toward home. Mr. Seers was still standing there, watching them with a sinister look in his eyes.

They went back into the forest at a quick pace, glancing over their shoulders.

"Man, he gave me the creeps," said Haley, as they ascended the first hill.

"Yeah, he sure was weird. Did you see how he tried to grab the map?"

They stopped for a rest when they got to the river, dipping their feet in the cold water.

"What do you say we check out the swimming hole on our way back?" Henry asked.

"Sure," she answered. "I'm a little baffled by the location on the map."

A short time later, they arrived at the swimming hole and walked around the edge. Not seeing any obvious clues, they sat on the bank, looking at the map.

"There aren't many clues on this map," Henry finally spoke. "I have no idea where the spot could be. It doesn't make any sense."

"Well, the map was made centuries ago," replied Haley. "The landscape has probably changed."

Henry looked at his watch. "Man, time sure flies. It's almost noon. We'd better get home. I'm getting hungry."

They continued their trek home, climbing the last bluff in front of the courtyard. As they reached the top, they saw a strange car parked in the circular drive.

"That's the Seers' car," whispered Haley. "I saw it in town when we first moved here. It was at Owen's Country Store and it belonged to Mrs. Seers."

They exchanged looks and entered the courtyard. The arched door stood open a crack and they could hear a man's voice. " . . . done such a wonderful job on this place. I never would have guessed from the outside that it was so modern in here."

"Thank you," answered their mother. "That's exactly what I thought when we first arrived. It looks like the previous owners did a lot of renovation. Mr. Johnson must have been a very skillful man," she concluded. "Did you know Mr. Johnson?"

"Yes. Well, I knew *of* him mostly. He was a very wealthy man, but I don't think he had a talented bone in his body. As far as I know, he never did any work around the place. He may have hired out for little jobs, plumbers and such, but I don't believe he did any major construction. Many families have lived here over the years," he continued. "My grandparents told me, that when they were young, a rich family lived here. They did a lot of construction, but as far as they knew, from old records, Zeb Bonner lived here originally in a modest little cabin. Then some gold digger, who struck it rich, bought the property probably twenty years or so later, tore down the original cabin, and built a lot of what you see today. That's what they say anyway."

"It's a sad story, isn't it?" Carol replied, turning toward the kitchen. "Would you like some coffee or maybe some lemonade?" she asked.

"I'd love some."

The twins heard the familiar flap of the swinging kitchen door. They looked at each other. Stepping inside, they snuck up the staircase toward their tower, breathing a sigh of relief when they reached Henry's room.

"What is he doing here?" Haley asked in disgust.

"Snooping," he replied, flopping down on the bed.

"I don't like him," she continued. "There's something *false* about him. And did you see the way he was eyeing you up at the post office? I think he's up to something. What do you think?"

"I don't know what to think," Henry answered, sitting up. "He sure seemed interested in the map. Maybe he knows about it."

"How could he?" Haley asked. "That map has been hidden for nearly two hundred years. He couldn't possibly know about it."

"All the same, I think he knows and he knows about the treasure."

"Then we need to hide that map. Somewhere he'd never find it," she said, with a look of determination.

Henry looked around for a good hiding spot.

"How about here?" he said, lifting his mattress.

"No. It'll get crushed under there."

"How about there?" she said, pointing to a large vase in the corner.

"Yes!" He agreed. "It'll fit perfectly inside. Nobody would ever look there."

He deposited the map inside the large vase. Satisfied it wouldn't be found, they waited until Ike, Sr. left before going downstairs.

They didn't have to wait long. They heard the start of a car engine, peeking out the tower window, they saw the Cadillac pull out of the circular drive and disappear behind the trees.

"Whew," Haley sighed.

"Let's go eat. I'm starving," said Henry.

Haley and Henry went down to the kitchen. Carol was helping Estelle prepare lunch. She looked up when they came in.

"Hi kids! You just missed our neighbor, Mr. Seers. He came by to visit and introduce himself. He was a very nice man."

They exchanged glances.

"Actually, we met him today at the post office," Haley said casually.

"Oh? Funny he didn't mention it. Anyway, he had some interesting history on the house." Carol relayed some of the things he had told her.

"Wow," said Henry when she finished. "That's pretty cool."

"By the way," said Carol, "you two will need to get up early tomorrow. We have to go Moyie Springs in the morning to get you registered for school."

The twins looked at each other in disgust. Neither of them was ready for school nor the thought of having to go to school with the Seers' boys was sickening. They spent the rest of the day watching television, but their thoughts were on school, dreading the first day and what it might bring.

As instructed, they were up early the next morning. After a quick breakfast, they went to Moyie Springs. Bonners Ferry didn't have a school, which meant Henry and Haley would have to ride the bus every day, a thought that didn't thrill them at all. The schoolyard was crowded with children playing as parents came out, dragging whining kids behind them. It was like being in a doctor's office.

The Seers' boys and their mother came out as they pulled up. Mrs. Seers watched as the Miles family got out of their minivan and headed toward the school.

"Good morning," said Carol, as they climbed the steps.

Mrs. Seers nodded at Carol with distaste as she passed, calling to her sons, "Come on! Let's go!"

They piled into the Cadillac and sped off.

The registration process was uneventful, and they were on their way home a half hour later. The twins spent the remainder of the summer trying to find the exact locations of the treasure with no success.

The first day of school arrived all too quickly. They stood at the end of the driveway waiting for the bus. It was late. Haley and Henry climbed aboard and saw the Seers' boys sitting in the back. The bus was half full of chattering children, laughing and throwing wadded up paper balls. The Seers' boys jeered at them as they took their seats in the front and then sat whispering to several other kids as the bus lumbered down the road. The rest of the ride was uneventful, as was the day. It was quite boring and the twins couldn't wait to get home.

The following month was much the same. There was the same taunting on the bus and snotty looks in class. They hadn't made any friends yet. Everybody was always staring at them and whispering, especially toward Haley. She was beside herself, trying to figure out why the other girls avoided her. Henry assured her, they were stuck up and weren't worth the trouble.

One day in early October, the teacher announced that the annual Bonners Ferry festival was drawing near. The town would have the usual picnic, parade, haunted house, and costume party. Just about everyone was going, it would be the best festival ever, with spooky decorations and a bonfire after dark. Haley was excited about it, while Henry couldn't have cared less.

"Oh, I can't wait!" she exclaimed. "I know exactly what I'm going to wear!"

She spent the next couple of weeks in her room trying different hairstyles and make up, putting on her costume. She was sure she would look so beautiful that someone would finally notice her and she'd make some friends.

Mrs. Miles was thrilled also. Every family was to bring a dish to pass and a dessert. The town, of course, would be providing the main dish, roasted pig.

There was an air of excitement brewing around town as decorations went up. There were pumpkins of all sizes, bales of hay, and dried up corn stalks arranged in neat little displays. Orange and black streamers hung everywhere. There were skeletons, ghosts, and bats hung from Owens Country Store. Cobwebs were strung from almost every doorway. Stuffed scarecrows stood at the corners of the post office and witches hung from trees. The wayside park was prepared with picnic tables and fire pits. Ghosts and goblins peeked through the bare branches, looking down on the leaf-covered park in bright red, orange, and yellow leaves.

The day finally came. In the Miles household there was an air of excitement. Carol was busy finishing up in the kitchen, while the rest of the family was getting dressed.

The festival was set to begin at nine a.m., but many families were already in town, setting up. Tablecloths were laid, lawn chairs arranged, blankets were spread, and cars unloaded as people began to arrive. Aside from most adults, the kids were already in costume.

Back at the estate, Henry had put on his costume. He was dressed as Indiana Jones, complete with an open shirt, brown felt hat, fake gun, holster, and whip.

"You look great!" Carol exclaimed when he walked into the kitchen. "You look just like him!"

Paul walked in and smiled. "How's it going Indy?"

"Fine," Henry answered, turning red.

"Where's Haley?" Carol asked.

"Still in her room."

"Here," said Carol, handing Henry and Paul each a dish. "Carry these out to the car for me, will you?"

As they left the kitchen, they stopped and stared as Haley descended the stairs.

She was stunning, wearing a long off white lace gown. Her hair was up in a wraparound bun, with dainty soft curls lying across her shoulders. Around her neck she wore a silver chain with a bright red ruby resting over her heart.

Carol came out of the kitchen, her arms loaded down with tablecloths and utensils. "Haley, where did you get that dress?"

Haley dreamily, flowed down the stairs. "I found it in an old box, in the attic."

"And this necklace?" Carol asked, walking over to look at it.

"That was in the box too."

"This looks like a ruby."

"I think it's fake," Haley sighed.

"What else was in this box?"

"Oh, that was all," Haley answered, with a tender look at her mother.

"Well, you look exquisite, darling. Come, let's get going."

The family chit-chatted on the way to town, while Haley sat, almost as if mesmerized. She seemed to be in her own private little world. Her demeanor was radiant. After they arrived in town and drove around for twenty minutes, they found a place to park. Everyone grabbed an armload of stuff from the van and they picked out a spot under an old maple.

As Haley approached, several people stopped and stared. She could hear bits and pieces of hushed conversation as she walked by.

"Uncanny . . . peculiar . . . "

Paul and Henry spread the blanket, while Carol and Haley took their dishes to the food table. After a bit of staring, people went back to their cooking and arranging the pots, pans, and plates loaded with delicious smelling food. Several women gathered around Carol and she looked like she was enjoying some friendly conversation. Paul helped some of the men rearrange the tables to better suit the area. Children were laughing and playing, throwing Frisbees, and rolling around in the leaves. There was horseshoes, croquet, and of course, the annual tug of war. The day was warm and bright, the gentle wind felt good.

The Moyie Springs school band played and marched in the parade. The Mayor sat on the back of a convertible with Miss Moyie Springs, following the floats and the ever-popular police cars and fire trucks, which made for a grand afternoon.

Many families lay napping with full bellies as the afternoon progressed. The women kept busy cleaning up dishes and putting things away as they watched the children play.

Several girls from school sat with Haley at one of the picnic tables, chatting. They were admiring her costume and the beautiful necklace she wore. She seemed to have suddenly made friends and she was ecstatic.

Henry had even struck up a conversation with some of the guys from his class, one of them, a good-looking young man named Nathan, who dressed as a pirate.

He seemed interested in Haley and questioned Henry about her.

"Well, there's not much to tell," said Henry. "She's my sister."

Nathan lowered his voice. "I don't know if you realize," he said. "But she's a dead ringer for Sarah Bonner."

"What?" Henry asked, startled.

"Yeah! She looks just like her. They could be twins."

"Really?" He asked curiously. "How do you know?"

"There is a picture of the Bonners in the post office. It's just a painting, but the woman in the picture looks identical to your sister. Come on, I'll show you."

They entered the post office and Henry's mouth dropped open.

"Whoa!" he said, at the sight. "I don't believe it. It's Haley!"

"See!"

They went back outside. The sun was beginning to set and people were getting up from their naps. It was a calm evening, but there was a bite in the air.

The bonfire was already lit and crackled loudly. Kids were standing around it, throwing in leaves and sticks, while some of the women were getting the leftovers together.

"Haunted house! Haunted House!" the children began to chant.

There was a wide, winding path that led to an old, abandoned house about a hundred and fifty yards from the park. As the darkening sky turned to twilight, carved pumpkins lit up the path, casting eerie grimaces and smiles into the night.

Witches and ghosts hung from trees and the slight evening breeze made them seem alive.

Small groups of adults and children made their way down the path to the old house. Its candlelit windows glowed like eyes. Haley seemed to have come out of her strange mood earlier in the day and was truly having a good time with her new girlfriends. They walked toward the haunted house together, giggling and screaming when several goblins jumped out from behind the trees to scare them.

Families that were only coming for the bonfire and haunted house began to arrive. People milled around everywhere, gathering around the fire. There were ghosts, goblins, and witches prancing all around.

Henry spotted the Seers' boys as they arrived; dressed in the best, most expensive costumes. Ike Jr. was dressed as Darth Vader, while his brother was a devil in a bright red outfit with horns, a tail, and a fake pitchfork. There were angels, fairies, giant M & M's, vampires, mummies, and Fruit of the Loom guys. It was an enchanting evening.

The haunted house was a huge success. There were enough monsters and boogiemen to scare every eager child and enough candy to make everyone sick. Kids were bobbing for apples, there was also a maze of hay bales to go through, and monsters around every corner.

The hayride was truly exciting, going through the forest. Scary horrible creatures jumped out of nowhere, grabbing arms and ankles, making the girls scream.

Finally, the best costume contest was held. Ike Jr. won of course, much to everyone's dismay and disappointment. They finished out the evening gathered around the bonfire, roasting marshmallows and making s'mores. One by one, people began saying good night and packed up their cars to go home.

The Miles family loaded up their blankets and empty dishes then piled into the van. As they pulled away, Haley noticed the few families still standing around the bonfire and the two fairies that stood watching them as they left. She turned to Henry. She had a funny, uneasy feeling. When she turned back, she saw with surprise, they were gone. The few families were still there, but the fairies were nowhere to be seen. She suddenly felt queer, almost afraid. Images flickered through her mind as she drifted into a strange state of mind as if in a trance. She saw a tiny oak sapling, a raging river, creatures dancing in flames, an old well handle, and an arm sticking out of water. With the images came a flood of emotions, terror, joy, and sadness. She shook her head, completely confused by what was happening to her.

As she and Henry climbed the tower stairs when they got back to the house, she said, "I need to talk to you. Some strange things are happening to me and it's kind of freaking me out."

"I need to tell *you* something, too," said Henry. "Something I found out tonight."

Haley sat on Henry's bed and began to discuss the strange events of the evening. Henry told her about the painting in the post office and the resemblance to Sarah Bonner. Haley explained all the feelings she experienced after putting on the dress and necklace, then the disappearing fairies. They agreed something strange was happening and they weren't sure what to make of it.

Henry turned on his television and after a while, he looked over to see Haley had fallen asleep.

Around midnight, she was awakened by a loud, scratching sound. Sitting up, she looked around. A full moon lit up the valley. A sudden movement caught her eye. She turned and gasped. Sitting on the outside ledge of one of the windows was one of the fairies she had seen in the park as they were leaving the festival. She stood up, scared, yet captivated. The fairy sparkled all over and wore a glittering gown that flowed like the wind on the waves. She smiled, putting Haley at ease a bit. She walked over and opened the window.

"My name is Sersha," it spoke. "You are the image of another who lived here long ago."

"I–I know," replied Haley, softly. "You were at the festival. I saw you looking at me as we left."

The fairy smiled again. "Yes, we felt your presence the moment you put on the necklace."

Haley looked down at the necklace against her heart. "Yes-I-w-w-when I put it on, I felt like I was someone else, looking through my eyes. I felt things and saw things I can't explain."

Sersha nodded, knowingly. "The person who wore that necklace was Sarah Bonner. She was wearing it the day she disappeared in the river, along with her two daughters."

Haley sat down, a distressed look on her face. "Where do you come from and how did you get up here? Fly?"

"I'm sorry," said Sersha. "Let me start from the beginning."

Sersha explained to Haley about the fairy world, telling her about how she was princess and guardian of the realm of Roan. She explained how Sarah and her daughters were swept away and presumed drowned, then how Zeb came to live in fairy world.

Haley was dumbfounded.

"Now, I come to the reason why I came to see you," she continued.

"When Zeb last came to our world, he met a swamp hag who told him that she pulled Sarah and the girls into our world through a portal in her swamp. She also said they were carried off by moss trolls. Zeb spent over a year looking for them and then disappeared, we think, into an evil realm. We believe he was drawn in by an evil presence that resides there. We call it Molock the Merciless. Those who enter its realm usually never return. Those lucky enough to escape from its perilous grip either go mad and die or have to go through extensive therapy. Zeb was a good man, but we're fairly certain Molock turned him into an unrecognizable, wretched soul. He has been bent to do its evil. It is rumored, he has been stalking the fairies. Those he has caught, he has tortured and stripped them of their wings."

"Why?" asked Haley, in horror.

"He needs their wings to survive."

Sersha explained how drinkers of the elixir absorb the immortality of the fairies.

"That is why he is still alive. If he runs out of elixir before the change, which I will explain later, he will become his true age and wither away. He no longer looks for wings that have been shed but hunts down the fairies and rips their wings from them. He needs to be saved as much as the fairies. His heart was once full of love and joy, now all he has is sorrow and despair. His mind is not his own anymore, but there is still hope. He still has a chance. That is why I have come. We need your help."

"How can I help?" Haley asked, astonished.

Just then, Henry snorted and turned in the lazy boy, trying to get into a more comfortable position.

As soon as Sersha was sure he was asleep, she continued. "Our realm, aside from Molock's land and a few others, is one of purity, one of love and peace. We have struggled for thousands of years, trying to find a way to rid ourselves of Molock's evil presence, but we don't know how to fight such evil. None of us are human. We don't understand about such things, nor how to battle against it. You are human. You live in a human world where there is, I'm sorry to say, strife and suffering every day. You've lived with that challenge all your life. Please, you must help us save Zeb."

Haley sat silent. She wanted to help. She felt she had to help, like it was her destiny to save another human being from a tragic end. Maybe they would even find Zeb's family.

She was scared, but she was also eager to understand what happened to her when she put on the necklace and why.

Haley felt connected to Sarah somehow and she knew what she must do. "Yes. I will come. I will do all I can to help."

Sersha smiled and nodded. "Here is what you must do."

Chapter Seven

FANTASY OR REALITY

Haley woke with a start. The previous night floated through her mind like a fading dream. Looking around, she realized she was still in Henry's room. He was still sleeping in a crooked, crunched up position. The clock said it was already ten.

Haley spotted the necklace lying on the bedside table where she left it. Picking it up, she examined it in the morning light. It sparkled so beautifully.

It was almost tranquil. She thought about the festival, making new friends, and about Sersha's visit, wondering if it was real or a dream.

She got up, tiptoed out the door, and went up to her room. She pondered whether she should tell Henry. He would probably think she was out of her mind, saying she was worked up from all the excitement of the day. She never kept secrets from him. They had been as close as two peas in a pod ever since she could remember. Still, this was too important to keep from him. She *had* to tell him. Haley would need Henry's help if she was going to keep her promise to Sersha.

After a late breakfast, much to the dismay of Estelle, Haley asked Henry to take a walk. They strolled in silence through the courtyard and out of the front archway. Haley breathed deeply, enjoying the last breath of fall. The air was always crisp now, the sun being unable to warm things up much, the leaves crunched under their feet as they walked.

"What's on your mind?" Henry asked, looking at her.

She didn't speak right away and he continued to glance at her as they walked. He thought there was something different about her. Something changed. She no longer looked like the child he grew up with and he realized she was quickly becoming a beautiful young woman who looked troubled. He wondered what could have happened to make her look so distressed.

They sat down on a fallen log. A couple of squirrels chased each other through the leaves, round and round the trees they ran, chattering loudly at each other. They could hear a woodpecker off in the distance somewhere. Haley looked at Henry questioningly, blurting out the entire evening's events after he fell asleep. When she was finished, he sat there with a slightly amused look on his face, until he realized she was being serious.

"You're not making this up are you?" Henry asked.

She shook her head. "No, I'm not. When I woke up, I thought it was a dream at first, but now I'm not sure. Everything Sersha told me about the necklace and the effect it has on me makes sense."

Henry sat silent.

"She asked me if I would help. I told her, I would."

Henry looked at her for a moment. "This is extraordinary," he said. "I can hardly believe what you've told me. The very thought of fairies actually being real is incredible! Yet, if it really is true, I gotta see for myself!"

Haley was a little shocked at his reaction. "You believe me then?"

"Well, I want to, but you gotta admit it is a bit . . . mind-blowing."

"I can prove it to you. Sersha said she was going back to get consent from the queen to let us into the fairy world. It's forbidden without permission. When she gets the okay, she said she would send a messenger."

"Great. When will that be?"

"I don't know."

They sat in silence.

A month went by with no sign of Sersha. Bonners Ferry turned into a winter wonderland. It snowed almost every day for a full two weeks.

It piled up and by the end of the storm, they had three and a half feet of new snow. Everything was buried. Pine branches hung heavy with it and were bent over as if bowing to winter's royal majesty.

School had been canceled and the twins were overjoyed. Paul bought them brand new snowshoes and they couldn't wait to try them out. Neither of them used snowshoes before and they were excited.

Estelle cooked them a wonderful hot breakfast of pancakes, bacon, and hash browns. As they headed out of the kitchen, she warned them to watch out for frost pixies. They stopped and turned. She had a twinkle in her eye.

"Frost pixies?"

Estelle's face was full of merriment. She chuckled and turned toward the sink. They looked at each other curiously and entered the foyer.

"Do you think—" Henry began.

"No." they said in unison as they sat down on the bench.

Paul came down the grand staircase.

"Hey, you two," he said with a smile. "Have a great time, but be careful, all right?"

"No problem," said Henry. "It'll be a piece of cake." "I've got loads of work to do," Paul said, walking toward his study. "I wondered when this would happen . . . all this snow . . . " his words echoed behind him as he disappeared through the study door. The twins smiled at each other and began to put on their snowshoes.

Dark, gray skies loomed overhead and it was lightly snowing again. They took to the hillsides with little difficulty. It was quite a workout; however, they didn't go far before they had to stop for a breather. The sky turned darker and it began to snow harder. Big, fat flakes lazily floated around them. The wind began to pick up and clumps of snow started to fall from the heavy branches. They saw many tracks in the white powder, which were quickly disappearing.

"We'd better get back," said Haley. "It looks like this may turn into a blizzard. Come on."

They made their way to the top of a small hill, when suddenly, a wailing sound came on the wind. They turned their faces into the blustery deluge, straining their ears. It came again; a long, mournful sound. Looking at each other, they quickly tramped through the snow toward the sound. Before long, they crossed a dense grove of pine. The wind wasn't as strong here and it was easier to see. The sound was much closer now and they slowly moved ahead. A snowy little glade lay beyond the pines. As they gazed out, to their shock, they saw dozens of tiny flying creatures. They were zipping in and around a fallen tree, chirping like little birds. They seemed excited. The twins could hear their wings beating, like the sound of a hummingbird when it flies close by. They were making such a commotion they didn't notice them as they crept nearer. Still obscured by the pines, they got close enough to get a good look, without being detected. They looked like tiny little fairies, but Haley thought, somehow different. Each one had pure white hair and little pink faces with pointed noses and ears. None of them were wearing any clothes, yet they didn't look nude. Their bodies seemed to be made up of glass or ice with tiny colorful snowflakes etched into their skin and they all had sky blue eyes. The twins exchanged glances. Haley was delighted at the sight of Henry's mouth hanging open.

"See!" she whispered.

They watched the spectacle in wonder. Each little creature would dive down toward the base of the fallen tree and shoot back up in the air, chirping up a storm. A gust of swirling snow blew, scattering the tiny creatures in all directions. That's when the twins saw what the excitement was about. One of them was caught under a branch of the fallen tree.

"We've got to help it," whispered Haley.

They stood up, stiff from their crouched position. Immediately, the creatures shot into the cyclone of snow and disappeared.

"Where'd they go?" Henry shouted, trying to make himself heard over the growing gale.

"I don't know!" Haley shouted back, as she stepped forward.

They crouched down beside the tree. The tiny creature was pinned under a branch and it shook in fear at the giant faces peering down at it.

"Look," said Haley. "It has a broken wing."

She carefully dug away the snow and gently lifted it out from under the branch.

"It's so little," she said, with tenderness.

It was only a few inches tall, but its wings were twice as long, making it look like a frozen butterfly.

"Do you talk?" she asked, softly, but the creature only sat in her hand, shaking. "Come on," she said, "we need to get it warm."

She stood up, and opened her jacket. Henry watched, as she gently put the creature inside her coat, against her heart. "This will keep it warm until we can get inside."

They started for home, taking their time and care to make sure the creature wouldn't be harmed any further.

It was as if night had fallen, the sky turned dark with the storm. They arrived home just after two o'clock, stiff and cold.

"Where have you two been?" Carol demanded, coming out of the kitchen. "I was so worried. We're in the middle of a blizzard! We've been watching it on TV. Your father is out looking for you right now. Didn't you see him?" she asked.

"No," answered Henry, concerned.

"Oh dear," she said, softly.

"When did he leave?"

"About three hours ago. He took the snowmobile out when you didn't come back, after it began to get dark."

The twins began taking off their snowshoes. Haley was extra careful. She thought it was strange she hadn't felt any movement since she put the creature inside her coat.

"I'm just going to take my shoes up to my room," she said. "I'll be right back."

"Me too," said Henry.

"I'll get you some hot chocolate," said Carol, trying to sound cheerful. "Your faces are beet red," she added, walking back into the kitchen.

Up in Haley's room, Henry hunted around for something to put the creature in, while Haley tenderly pulled it from her jacket. It wasn't shaking anymore and seemed to be asleep. Henry found a small fishbowl and grabbed a couple of hand towels. He walked over to the bed, where Haley sat, cradling the tiny creature in her hand. He folded up one of the towels and laid it inside the tank then draped the other one over the top. Haley gently laid the creature inside. Gazing down at it, a look of understanding crossed her face.

"What?" Henry asked, puzzled by her expression.

"Frost pixies?"

"Yeah, maybe. Is this what the fairies looked like?" he asked.

"No. I don't think this is a fairy. It's something else. Sersha was big, bigger than I am. This . . . I don't know what this is. It could be a frost pixie. It's definitely something from the fairy family though, ya gotta admit that."

Henry looked at the sleeping creature.

"I'll bet it is a frost pixie. I'll bet Estelle has known about them for years. Dad said she came from this area and she worked for old Mr. Johnson."

"You're probably right," Haley replied. "Estelle has always seemed to know things, you know, like she's part of something else. I can't describe what I'm trying to say."

"I know what you mean, I've sensed it too."

Just then, they heard the sound of a snowmobile engine.

"He's back," said Henry, relieved. "Come on, let's get downstairs!"

"What about him? Her?" Haley asked.

"We'll cover it up and turn out the light. It's probably exhausted from its ordeal and will sleep for hours."

They turned out the light and went downstairs.

They listened to their dad's adventure of snowmobiling over mugs of hot chocolate and buttered toast.

The twins kept an especially close eye on Estelle that evening, waiting to get a chance to get her alone and question her about frost pixies, however, Estelle turned in early. They dashed back up to Haley's room as soon as the opportunity presented itself. The creature was still fast asleep. They kept watch over it as the storm continued into the wee hours. Around two o'clock in the morning, Henry woke. He thought he heard a noise and looked around the room for the source. Everything looked as it should. Then he remembered the creature and got up to have a look. It was still asleep, but it didn't look the same as before. It was a little paler, as if it lost some of its shine. There it came again, a soft rapping noise. He quickly looked around the room. Haley was asleep on the bed. The storm intensified and all he could see outside the windows was a white twisting blanket of snow and blackness. Massive clumps of snow clung to the ledges and picturesque patterns of snowflake designs crept up the glass. Suddenly, a face appeared in the center window. He caught his breath as he stumbled backward, his eyes wide with fear. A hand appeared out of the white mass and gently rapped on the glass. The creature smiled and motioned him to come over. Heart pumping hard in his chest, he slowly got up and edged his way over to the bed, shaking Haley hard.

"What? What's the matter with you?" Haley asked, slightly annoyed.

Henry was pale, staring at the window like he'd seen a ghost. She turned toward the window. A look of surprise and recognition came over her face.

"Sersha!" she exclaimed excitedly, jumping off the bed. She tried to lift the window but it wouldn't budge. "Henry, help me," she said, desperately.

He went over to the window, but together they couldn't open it. They watched in amazement as Sersha traced the outline of the window with her finger and then nodded to them. Henry lifted the window, which moved like a hot knife through butter, then stood back as she entered the room. Haley shut the window and turned to greet this creature like an old friend.

After a hug, Haley turned to Henry, introducing him to the princess of Roan. He was dumbstruck. He could scarcely believe his eyes and ears. She was the most beautiful creature he had ever seen.

Sersha walked over to the tiny creature sleeping in the fishbowl.

"We have to get this pixie outside," she said, with concern.

"Why?" Haley asked, looking down at the sleeping figure.

"It will die if it stays inside much longer. It's a frost pixie. Its survival depends on the cold. Warm air puts frost pixies into a deep sleep. If it is not taken outside soon it will perish."

"But it has a broken wing," said Haley. "How will it fly?"

"It's not broken," Sersha replied, "their wings change." Seeing Haley's confusion, she continued.

"Have you ever put your face up to a cold window and blown on it?"

"Yes."

"Do you remember when you blew on it, a frosty design began to take shape, like a snowflake?"

"Yes."

"Well, that is how frost pixies are. Their wings continuously transform, from the temperature and wind."

Sersha picked up the slumbering creature and carried it to the window, opened it and placed it on the small ledge. They watched as it stretched and sat up with a yawn.

As soon as it saw their faces looking through the glass, it vanished into the swirling darkness.

"Wow," said Henry, sinking onto the bed. "You're really real. When Haley told me about fairies, I didn't believe her."

"I know," replied Sersha. "That's why they're called *fairy tales,*" she said, smiling.

"Where do they go in the summer?" he asked.

"Hmm?"

"The frost pixies, where do they go?"

"Oh, they hibernate."

"And what do frost pixies do?" Henry asked.

"They make the beautiful designs you see when you look at a snowflake or a frosty windowpane. I believe humans call it Jack Frost. They put the sparkle in winter."

"Wow," he sighed. "Unbelievable."

"Now," began Sersha. "I would have been here sooner, but we have had a difficult time back in Roan. Zeb is worse than ever. He is under Molock's total control; more and more fairies are disappearing. We had one fairy escape. Somehow he made his way out of the evil realm and was picked up by a couple of scouts, then brought back to the palace. It took a lot of treatment and rehabilitation to bring him back. For a while, we didn't think he'd make it. But with time, he was able to tell us the horrors of that realm."

Sersha began to pace as she continued.

"Molock has turned Zeb into a vicious keeper of its torture chamber. It amuses itself by watching him torment those held captive. Not killing its victims but subjecting them to unspeakable horrors. Molock knows that Zeb needs the elixir to stay alive and it allows Zeb just enough to keep him from dying. It's controlling him, molding him into something it can use. I'm afraid whatever it's preparing Zeb for, will be devastating to our world as we know it. We can't wait much longer to take some kind of action, to rise up against it. Are you still willing to help us?"

"Yes," Haley answered. "We must," she continued, looking at Henry.

Henry nodded his head.

"What can we do?" he asked.

"I can't answer that," Sersha said, sadly. "You must find a way."

"Well," Haley spoke up. "We'll rescue him somehow." She didn't sound too convinced, but she was determined. "First, we'll have to get you into fairy world," said Sersha. "I cannot show you the way to get in. It is forbidden, even in the gravest of circumstances, but you already have the tools to guide you."

"We do?" they echoed.

"Yes, you have the necklace and the map."

"How did you—" Henry began.

"The map is only part of it," Sersha interrupted. "Zeb discovered our world and drew the map."

"I thought—" he began again.

"The necklace is the key to getting through the portals."

"What do you mean, key?" Henry was finally able to ask.

"The necklace contains a gem, a precious gem not of your world. It may look like just a ruby to you, but it came from fairy world. It has powers you know nothing about. It contains properties most humans can't handle."

The twins sat, puzzled at what they were hearing. Seeing their bewildered looks, she explained.

"Rubies from your world contain but a minute fraction of power. That power is the reason humans hoard them, collect them, gaze at them, and will even kill for them. There is something in the ruby that gives the possessor a feeling. Most humans can handle it in small measures, but others, it possesses. This ruby is … well … alive. It is imprinted not only with the heart of our world, but also with all the emotion of its previous owner. It harnesses emotion, like courage, love, and a fiery spirit, but it can also emulate anger and malice. That is one of the reasons why our worlds are separated."

The twins sat silent, drinking in every incredible word.

"Once long ago, our two worlds were one. Then the great evil came. It was always there, but it was in bondage. We don't know how it was able to contaminate the world, but its evil presence tore a rift in the earth and it was accidentally ensnared during the split, binding it to a realm in our world. Its presence, in your world caused chaos, hatred, greed, strife, and a host of iniquity. Luckily, it was contained in our world, but not without damage done. That is why the purity and true property of the gem is in fairy world, with only a memory of what it represents in yours. The evil one would have had complete control and mighty power, if it hadn't been for the rift. So you understand? Your gem holds the key to entering our world. It's connected to the fairy world and the real world. You must have felt the effects when you put it on."

Haley nodded. She looked at Sersha then at Henry. Her mind spun with all this information. The realization of the world she knew was a farce. All her life, living every day, consumed with only her own little world, never realizing the truth until now. Knowing it wasn't a safe, perfect world where everyone would live happily ever after. Maybe by helping Sersha in her quest, she and Henry could make a difference. Working together to find a solution, maybe the two worlds could become one again.

They spent the next hour or so talking about Zeb and his family, what had happened to Sarah and the girls, and what happened to his mind and spirit during his quest in finding them.

"What a sad story," said Haley, her eyes full of tears. "It just breaks my heart. If we could find his family, maybe it would snap him out of it. Maybe if he saw them, it would jar his memory. Since the evil one used his despair to manipulate Zeb's mind, seeing them again, just might bring him back. What do you think?"

Henry was busy thinking and didn't say anything.

Sersha agreed with Haley. "I think you're on to something."

"We'll work together," Haley continued. "If we could lure him away somehow, away from Molock—"

"Yes! That's it!" Henry suddenly burst out. "You look just like Sarah!"

"What?" Haley asked.

"Yes! Remember, I told you about it after the festival. You look just like her."

Haley nodded, remembering the story. He began to explain to Sersha.

"I saw a picture of her, I mean a picture of Sarah, at the festival. Nathan told me, Haley looked just like her. He took me into the post office and showed me a painting of Zeb and Sarah!"

"Yes. Yes," Sersha chimed in. "It's true. When I saw you leaving in your vehicle, I was amazed at the resemblance between you and finding the necklace makes it almost uncanny! It's as if it were destiny."

"Yeah," said Henry, giving Haley a curious look.

Once again he looked at his sister like she was a different person, like she was destined for something unusual, something big.

She acted as though she knew she was important, like a hero, or someone who would go down in history as being the one who made a difference, saved the day. He looked proudly at his sister.

He would stick by her, through whatever happened. He didn't realize it, but he himself was changing. He was growing up. He looked at Haley with an almost regal respect. He had a part to play in whatever was going to happen and he seemed moved by it. An excitement was building. They were on the verge of probably the greatest adventure they would ever go on.

"Let's go!" he suddenly spoke, startling them both.

Sersha looked at him curiously and smiled. She thought to herself, they finally found the guidance they needed.

"Okay, we need to get you two to Roan."

The twins exchanged eager looks and gave her their complete attention.

"You found Zeb's map?"

"Yes," Henry answered. "It's hidden in my room."

"Go get it," she said. "Quickly."

He dashed down to his room and returned a moment later with the rolled up parchment.

"This map shows entrances to fairy world," she said, unrolling it.

The twins looked at each other. "What?"

"We thought it was a treasure map," said Haley, embarrassed.

Sersha smiled and continued.

"Sarah's necklace is the key to fairy world. It has a property like a homing device. It illuminates the doorways for whoever wears it. Haley will be able to see the portals and go through with no trouble, however, you won't be able to enter by yourself," she continued, looking at Henry.

His heart sank. Not be able to enter? Sersha saw his alarm and raised her hand.

"Don't worry," she continued. "As long as you're holding Haley's hand, you'll be able to enter with her. You won't be able to see the portal, but you will be able to follow. Now you must understand something. This map is dangerous. It can't fall into the wrong hands," she continued, in the most serious voice. "There was a man, some years ago, who discovered our world quite by accident. His heart became one of deceit and greed, therefore he was banned from fairy world for his thievery. After he was barred, he went about, looking through your home for treasure, at which time he found a diary. The diary told of a map."

The twins gave each other a knowing look.

"It's Ike Seers, isn't it?" Henry asked.

"Yes," replied Sersha, surprised. "How did you know?"

They related how they ran into him at the post office and then his visit to the estate.

"Yes, he is a dangerous man and one not to be trusted. He stole from our world and became a wealthy man, but he wasn't satisfied with what he had. He has become covetous and filled with greed. After he found the diary, he spent a great deal of time searching for the map, but as you can see, he never found it. He has never given up on it, I'm afraid. He knows where a few entrances are, but they were sealed up. He thinks the map shows more portals and it does."

Henry looked at the map. "But it only shows three X's," he replied. "And as you said they were sealed up, so what good is this map?"

"Yes, those are the obvious entrances, but it also shows others."

Sersha turned to Haley, "Put on the necklace."

Haley complied.

"Now look at the map."

Haley's mouth dropped open as she looked at the map. Right before her eyes, twelve more X's appeared.

"Oh my God!" she exclaimed.

"What? What do you see?" Henry demanded, excitedly.

"There's got to be at least a dozen more X's!"

Henry searched the map but couldn't see them.

"You have the key and you have the map," said Sersha. "The sooner you can come, the sooner we can save Zeb."

Haley was a jumble of emotions. She felt sad but excited, afraid yet exhilarated. She was charged and ready to venture into the unknown, not knowing where the journey would take her, nor how it would end.

"When can you leave?" Sersha asked, with anticipation.

"I'm ready right now," said Henry, enthusiastically.

"No," Haley replied. "We have to prepare. And what are we going to do about mom and dad?"

He hadn't thought of that.

"Oh, yeah," he said, looking at Sersha. "What are we going to tell them?"

"Nothing."

They looked at her questioningly.

"Your parents won't know you're gone. We will intervene. Your parent's memories of you can be erased for a time, but there is a danger. You must return within a certain amount of time or their memory of you will be erased permanently."

Seeing their bewildered looks, she explained.

"The longer you are gone, the more difficult it will be to restore their memories. If you wait too long before you return, we won't be able to restore them at all. In fairy world, time passes differently. It slows down. I don't know how to explain it. It's just completely different. Fairy world is a different plain of existence. We age differently. Most creatures, how do I say it, they regenerate. Like when a snake sheds its skin or when you lose a tooth you grow another one. Humans in our world aren't accustomed to the time change, they need help to keep the aging process in check. If you stay long enough, that will change and you will no longer need the help. Zeb has been in our world for over a year and is fast approaching the time when his mortality will change. He will no longer need the elixir to sustain him. His body will change and he will become, for lack of a better word, immortal. When that time comes, who knows what will happen to his mind. In his current state, he may become much worse. He may never be able to be brought back."

The twins were speechless. Their eyes were wide, as Sersha went on.

"Every human that has stayed in our world has been affected in one way or another, but all have had a good heart. So we don't know what will happen to someone like Zeb, who's been corrupted by the evil one."

"Are there many humans in fairy world?" Haley asked.

"Oh yes, more than can be counted. All have completed the change and are now immortal. Zeb was the last one to enter and his transformation will occur soon."

"Wow," exclaimed Henry. "Your world is pretty incredible and you say our two worlds used to be one? I can't imagine what it was like."

"Yes," Sersha replied. "And you know all those fairy tales you heard while growing up?"

The twins nodded.

"All true."

They shook their heads and smiled.

"Well," said Haley, with a deep breath. "We'll leave tomorrow then."

Everyone looked at each other with growing excitement.

"What will we need to bring with us?" Haley asked.

"Whatever you think you'll need," Sersha answered as she walked to the window. "We will be waiting for you on the other side. I know my mother will want to have council with you and call an assembly as soon as you arrive. We'll go over any thoughts and ideas the council has and devise a plan."

"Well, all right then," agreed Henry, slapping his knee.

Sersha bid them good night and opened the window.

"Take great care and we'll see you soon," she said, flying into the white night.

The twins sat and talked for a little while after Sersha left, discussing what it would look like in the fairy world and how their parents would act with their memories wiped clean. Haley finally said good night and went up to her room. She lay in her bed looking at the necklace, thinking about Sarah and what kind of struggle she must be in; trying to get away from her captors and worrying about her daughters. She wondered if Sarah was being treated well.

Haley thought about them leaving in the morning and was excited at the prospect of the upcoming journey. It took her a long time to fall asleep with all those thoughts running through her mind. She drifted into a restless slumber, hiding from unseen pursuers. She dreamed she was falling, then she was trying to save Henry from some horrible creature about to eat him. Haley woke in a cold sweat. Her heart was pounding, a scream fading from her lips. She sat up. It was light out and it stopped snowing. She looked at the clock on her nightstand. It was already eleven o'clock. Disgusted it was so late, she jumped out of bed, quickly got dressed, and went down to Henry's room. He wasn't there. Once downstairs, she stood at the bottom of the grand staircase, listening. Over in the foyer, she spotted a piece of paper on the mahogany table, next to a vase of flowers. Haley picked it up and read it.

Estelle,

Paul and I are driving to Spokane to do a little shopping. The weather report said clear skies today, so hopefully we won't have any trouble. We'll be home sometime around six this evening. Don't bother making us any dinner, we'll eat in town. Enjoy a day off.
Always,
Carol

Haley pondered the note for a moment, looking around the room, listening again. Her mother made no mention of herself or Henry and she wondered if Sersha already wiped their parents' memories. She went into the kitchen to rummage through the fridge for something to eat. She was startled when Estelle emerged from the pantry.

"Well, good mornin' to ya, sleepy head," said Estelle, her arms loaded down with baking supplies.

"Thought I'd whip up a batch of cookies and make a couple of apple pies today, since I have a bit of free time."

"Good morning, Estelle," said Haley. "Have you seen Henry?"

"Yes. He's been up for hours, said you two were going exploring again today. He's been out digging around in the shed. I hope you two will be careful. I've made up a couple packs for you," she said, pulling two backpacks from the broom closet. Inside were juice boxes, jerky, sandwiches, and an assortment of dried fruits.

"This should hold you for a few days," she continued, watching Haley intently. There was apprehension in her voice and she had a most solemn look on her face. "You do be careful and watch your back." She looked Haley straight in the eye. "There will be many dangers."

Haley looked surprised. Then understanding came over her face. "You know?"

Estelle nodded. "I've been there myself a few times. It's a beautiful place. It's magical and wondrous, but also perilous. You must be conscious of everything around you."

"What do you mean?" Haley asked, with concern.

"You are important," Estelle said, in a most serious voice. "The other side is full of strange creatures, not all of them are nice. There are realms that aren't what they seem and it will be treacherous, especially for you." Estelle paused for a moment then continued. "You have been predestined. I saw it the minute you arrived. You look like her."

"Sarah."

"Yes," Estelle replied. "Poor soul, I pray you are successful. Now here, take these out back while I make you up something to eat. You'll need your strength."

She watched Estelle a moment then carried the backpacks out the back door.

Haley saw tools and all kinds of gadgets Henry piled outside the door, mostly camping equipment. He came around the corner of the east tower with his arms loaded down. When he saw Haley, a big grin came over his face.

"Ready to rock?"

Haley couldn't help but smile back. "In a while. Estelle is making us something to eat. She said we'd need our strength."

Henry dropped his armload. "She knows?"

"Yes. She said she's been there a couple times. It's kind of nice that somebody else knows, isn't it?"

"Yeah, she can keep an eye on Mom and Dad."

"I think their memories have already been erased."

"They have," Henry replied. "I saw the note and there are no pictures of us in Dad's study or anywhere in the house."

"Wow. It's weird. Well, come on, let's eat and get this stuff packed so we can get out of here before they come home," Haley said, smiling.

Haley and Henry went back into the kitchen and ate their late breakfast, while Estelle described some of the "other side" as she called it.

The twins spent most of the afternoon packing their gear so it would be manageable then got into their snowsuits and boots. They were putting on their snowshoes, when they heard the unmistakable sound of a car coming up the drive. They waved goodbye to Estelle, who watched them from the window and quickly grabbed their packs, hurrying out of sight.

"They're back early," whispered Henry, as they rounded the west tower. They glanced over toward the drive, which was clearly visible now that the leaves were gone.

To their shock, they immediately recognized the Cadillac pulling up front.

"Ike Seers!" Haley exclaimed, in a loud whisper.

"Come on, let's get out of here before he spots us!" Henry whispered back, his heart racing.

They quickly tramped over the edge of the bluff and down the path leading to the valley floor. Henry felt the inside pocket of his snowsuit for the map, letting out a sigh of relief. They trudged on at a fairly swift pace, but they soon grew tired. The packs were heavy and they had to slow down.

As soon as they reached the second creek, they stopped to rest. Henry took out the map.

"Put on your necklace, and let's have a look."

Haley reached into her snowsuit pocket and pulled out the necklace. It sparkled brilliantly in the bright white of the snow and sunshine. She put it on and at once she saw all the X's invisible to the naked eye.

"I wish I could see them."

"Here you put it on," Haley said, handing him the necklace. "I was never any good at reading maps."

Henry put on the necklace and looked at the map. "I can't see anything," he said, in exasperation, taking it off with a sigh. "You'll have to be the navigator," he said, handing it back.

She put the necklace back on and the hidden X's reappeared. "This is amazing, if I'm reading this right, there's an entrance just at the base of the next hill, you know, right on the edge of the forest."

"That's on Seers' property," Henry moaned.

"Don't worry. He's over at our place, remember?" "Oh, yeah," he answered, embarrassed.

They picked up their packs and plodded on. The bright snow was blinding and crunched under their snowshoes as they walked.

Suddenly, Haley cried out. "I see it!"

"Where?" Henry demanded.

"Over there!" She pointed with excitement.

"I can't see it!"

"Of course, you can't, you're not wearing the necklace. Come on! Oh my gosh! It's beautiful!" she yelled, breathing heavily as she ran.

"What does it look like?"

"It's-it's glittering. It's like a chimney of sparkles, all swirling around!"

They crossed an old farming road. The portal was about a hundred yards ahead.

All of a sudden, a snowmobile screamed into view, airborne over a large snowdrift about a quarter mile to the right, landing on the road.

"It's Seers!" Haley screamed.

"Run! Run!" Henry yelled, grabbing her arm.

They ran hard. Henry dragged Haley, stumbling over his over-sized snowshoes.

The glittering tower swirled faster and faster as if urging them on, warning them of danger. Haley looked back. The snowmobile was just yards away. A hooded man was bent over the handles, like a motorcycle racer, his hood obscuring his face.

"Don't look back!" Henry shrieked.

The driver brought the snowmobile to a skidding halt and dove off, landing a few feet behind them.

"Run!" Henry yelled, in panic.

Haley tripped and together they flew through the air, landing with a thud, sliding down a small embankment and right into the glittering tower.

Chapter Eight

A LAND OF WONDER

"Ahhhh!" Down, down they went. The twins fell together in a mass of bright shining glitter, tumbling over one another. They were astounded by the fact they seemed to be falling in slow motion. They watched the glitter fly by them in great swirling waves.

"It's so bright in here!" Haley yelled as Henry gripped her arm tight.

Henry felt terrified yet exhilarated at the same time. They continued to fall for what seemed like an eternity, as if riding an elevator, falling, yet floating.

"I can see an opening," Henry yelled.

"I see it!"

He looked up at the entrance to the portal with unease. It looked like a long tunnel, with a tiny white speck at the top. He couldn't see anyone and hoped the portal sealed itself before Ike, Sr. could dive in after them.

A brilliant green color slowly grew closer and together they burst through at the other end, landing in a patch of soft grass.

They sat, stunned at the dazzling view. They landed beside the top of a fairly good-sized waterfall. Water cascaded gently over many tiers, into a deep pool at the bottom.

It was twilight. Great, gnarled trees with long, twisting branches hung over the water as if standing guard. Gaps in the surrounding trees revealed rolling hills and great mountains towered in the distance. There were trees great and small, lining the banks up the stream and large boulders jutted out of the water. Songbirds were tucking their heads under their wings, settling down for the night. An occasional few last minute chirps could be heard, bidding the light of day farewell. It was serene and silent. Weeping willows gently swayed in the soft breeze. The leaves and golden branches of birch and aspen kept time in the darkening purple blue sky.

"Unbelievable," Henry whispered.

The moon came out and lit up the countryside in incandescent patches of light. Stars appeared, twinkling brightly.

"Stunning," Haley whispered. "I wonder if it's like this in heaven."

It was more of a statement than a question. The vista seemed to sing. It was harmonious around them, in the trees and in the water.

"This reminds me of when Dorothy first got to munchkin land," Henry said, with delight.

"What do you think we should do now?" Haley asked, as they took off their snowshoes.

"I don't know. Sersha said she would meet us. I wonder where she is."

"Well, let's walk up stream and see what's there. Maybe we'll run into her," Haley suggested.

They picked up their packs and walked along the bank. The soft roar of the waterfall faded as they went. Haley had the strange feeling they weren't alone. She wasn't really afraid, but she kept looking around as they went. She spotted a pair of yellow eyes through the growing darkness. They blinked and turned away. She wondered what sort of creature it was.

They came upon a cleft in a great rock to their left. Through it, they could see a small glade lit up by the moonlight. As they peered in, they held their breath, watching a resplendent creature come out from the evergreen wood.

She had long, brown hair, interwoven with strands of wildflowers, which hung about her in such a way as to hide her bare body. Her face was shining and soft. In her arms, she carried a small brown rabbit and perched on her shoulder was a mourning dove. As she walked into the glade, the twins could see several small deer following her. She reached down to pet one of them gently between the ears. They watched in fascination as she disappeared into the trees on the other side of the glade.

"I can't believe this," Haley whispered. "It's like a dream."

"I know what you mean," Henry whispered back.

They continued along the water's edge, walking as quietly as they could. Up ahead was a break in the trees. They emerged from the wood and looked out at flower covered, rolling hills. The stream narrowed there and wound its way downhill and out of sight. The mountains were vast and the moon lit up the hills in a dazzling display of dark color. Shimmering dewdrops began to appear like shining, little stars.

"I'm hot," Haley said quietly, putting down her pack.

"Me too," Henry agreed.

They took off their winter gear and immediately felt better in the cool of the evening.

"What'll we do with these?" Henry asked. "We can't carry all this, too. The pack is heavy enough."

"We'll have to leave them here," Haley answered. "Let's leave them on the edge of the woods we'll need them when we go home."

They put their snowsuits and shoes in a pile at the edge of the forest and turned to face the hills.

"Let's keep following the stream," Haley said. "Why that way?"

"I don't know, just a feeling."

They followed the stream, which cut its way through miles of hills and lush valleys, winding its way through pretty little spots, which made Haley's heart warm with fulfillment. She felt like she'd been here before. There was something familiar about this place. Maybe it came from a faraway dream.

Night creatures emerged to drink, several times as they came around a bend, they surprised families of deer and great elk. Henry was great at spotting animals. They observed pheasants, turkeys, peacocks, and even a fox trotting along the edge of a walnut grove with some poor animal in its mouth. Haley saw a porcupine and a family of skunks.

The twins were thoroughly enjoying their trek across the countryside. Night sounds made everything seem surreal.

The stream entered a dark wood and they had a difficult time seeing. They kept tripping over unseen roots and rocks, wishing there was a path to follow. Heavy branches hung low and they had to keep ducking as they hiked onward.

Henry had an eerie feeling, as if the wood were alive. They kept hearing noises and would look to see nothing but darkness with an occasional moonbeam shining through the thick canopy.

Every once in a while, a hoot would ring out, causing them to jump.

"It's all right," Haley whispered. "If we just keep moving, we'll be okay."

Henry didn't say anything. He saw to his left, a pair of pale yellow eyes following along with them as they walked. His heart began to beat faster and he quickened his pace, passing Haley.

"Slow down! It's okay. Nothing is going to hurt us here."

The confidence in her voice slowed Henry down and they walked side by side.

"I saw eyes," he whispered.

"So did I," she replied. "Don't worry, nothing is gonna happen. I know."

Henry believed her and relaxed a little. Finally, they reached the edge of the wood. Looking down, they surveyed a wide canyon below. Another stream ran along the bottom, the entire area was thick with trees and bushes.

As her eyes scanned the depths of the canyon to the cliff walls, Haley could just make out steps in the moonlight. Squinting, she could see roads cut into the sides of the cliffs and all along the bottom. Small waterfalls were visible and to their shock and amazement, houses.

"Houses!" Henry exclaimed. "Look!" he said, pointing into the canyon. "And up there!"

Haley looked and saw the soft glow of lights coming from the canyon walls opposite them.

"I wonder who or what lives here."

"Probably people," Henry answered, with excitement in his voice. "Let's go!"

Haley mulled it over in her mind for a moment. "Okay," she agreed. "I think it will be all right, but let's go quietly. I don't want us barging into a strange little village and find out we're not welcome."

"Don't worry," Henry replied. "It'll be fine. I know."

"Are you mocking me?" Haley asked, sarcastically.

Henry looked and saw her smile. He smiled back. "Yeah," he answered.

Giggling, they turned right and followed the edge of the canyon wall. It wasn't long before they came upon a road, heading down into the canyon. It was a narrow grassy dirt road filled with ruts and tree roots, overgrown by tall bushes. Sunflowers and tiger lilies poked their heads out of tall grasses along the way.

"I have never seen flowers grow so tall," Haley remarked as they went.

"This canyon must be at least three hundred feet deep," Henry said, as the road switch-backed ahead of them.

They turned several times, following the road as it went back and forth and lower into the canyon. It got wider as they went, halfway down it turned from dirt to cobblestone and grew to two lanes.

Henry and Haley slowed down and walked as quietly as they could. As they rounded the next bend, a grand house, visible up ahead, was built into the side of the canyon. Old-fashioned iron lamp stands lit up a well-groomed front yard and flower-filled boxes lined the windows. It was two stories and all was dark inside.

They quietly walked past, craning their necks as they went. After another half mile or so, they passed another house, then another. Each one was as lovely as the last. Most were dark, but every so often they saw the soft glow of a lamp inside and several burning candles.

The twins were fascinated by this picturesque little town and drank in its charm. At the bottom, a large cobblestone street ran parallel to the stream, which ran fast, dotted with large rocks and waterfalls. The main street was also lit with iron lamp stands. Shops lined both sides, with quaint little cottages in small neighborhoods behind them.

They walked quietly through town, taking in all the sights. As they rounded a corner, the sound of merriment echoed toward them. Ahead, several horses were hitched to small wagons, outside a pub on the corner.

They walked past the horses and stopped, listening to the commotion coming from inside. A dirty, colored glass window lit the sidewalk in dull red and blue shadows.

The sound of rushing water behind them drew Haley's attention.

She was pleasantly surprised to see, set back in a little hollow around the corner, an old waterwheel turning slowly. To the left, another waterfall roared; on the right was a cottage with a terrace running the length of the building, including several umbrella covered tables. A sign overhead said "Mathilda's."

Haley turned her attention back to the pub. It was an old, run down building. A shutter on one of the windows was hanging by one old rusty nail and the canopy hanging over the sidewalk was badly in need of repair.

"What do you think?" Henry whispered. "Should we go in?"

Haley was nervous.

"Maybe we shouldn't," she answered. "We don't know who or what, is in there."

The roar of laughter inside made her uneasy.

"Come on," Henry whispered. "I'm tired and I need to sit down for a while."

She nodded.

"I don't know if this is a good idea," she mumbled under her breath.

They walked up and tried to peer through the window but couldn't see anything.

"Well, here goes," Henry said, turning the iron knob. He slowly opened the door. Red light flooded his face as he entered. It was an extremely large room, much bigger than it looked outside. It had a long bar on the left side and a half dozen tables lined the right. He was shocked to see a pool table in the center of the pub.

The room became silent. Haley looked at the occupants standing at the bar, staring at them. The pub keeper was a tall, skinny man with long gray hair, pulled into a ponytail. His bushy beard went down to the middle of his stomach and he had deep, chestnut colored eyes. After an awkward silence, the pub keeper cleared his throat.

"Good evening," he said, coming out from behind the bar. "What can I get you?" he asked, gazing down at them.

"Ah, what do you have?" Henry managed to ask, nervously.

"Why don't you two sit down?" he said, ushering them over to a table. "And I'll bring you some nice rainbow dew. How does that sound?"

The twins sat down, putting their packs on the floor while the pub keeper went back behind the bar. They watched him in silence as he took out two large mugs and poured in some smoky looking liquid, walking back to where they sat. He set down the mugs, paused for a moment as if he were about to speak, then changed his mind and went back to the bar.

The rest of the patrons standing at the bar, talked in low tones. Some were huddled together, whispering, while others blatantly stared at them.

Haley immediately picked up her mug and began to sip the cold beverage.

"And who might you two be?" the pub keeper asked, seemingly a little braver now that he was back behind the bar. He leaned over the bar with a curious gaze.

"My name is Henry and this is my sister, Haley."

The pub keeper looked from Henry to Haley and back.

"I don't think I've seen you in here before. Where are you from?" he asked, almost demandingly.

"We're from Bonners Ferry," Henry answered.

The group at the bar stopped their whispering and turned their complete attention to the twins. One man standing by the pool table with a cue in his hand was quite grotesque looking. He wore a torn ratty old brown hat over messy dark gray hair. His beady black eyes stared at them over a long hooked nose. Half of his teeth were missing and his clothes were worn and dirty. He stood hunched over and grinned at Haley. He shuffled toward them. Haley saw that he was shoeless and had long, thick, yellow toenails. She watched him walk toward her, with growing unease.

"You say yous from Bonners Ferry?" he asked. Haley didn't answer. He walked toward their table, and he was shaking like a leaf.

"Eh? You say yous from Bonners Ferry?" his voice croaked.

"That's right," Henry replied.

They sat there, looking up at the old man as he reached their table, while some of the others came up behind him.

"You be kin to Zebulan?" the old man asked, poking Haley in the arm with a long bony finger.

Henry stood up. The crowd backed up a couple steps. "No, we're not related," Henry replied in a slightly stern voice.

Haley looked at her brother, shocked at the authority in his voice. She was impressed. She'd never seen nor heard him act like this and she felt safe. She turned to the man and replied, "No, we aren't related to Zeb, but we have heard of the growing troubles and have come to help."

She spoke in such a calm, soothing voice, the group seemed to relax.

"No harm intended, ma'am," the old man croaked.

Just then, the door in the back opened and in came a towering, virile creature. He had golden hair and pale blue eyes. His face was kind and rugged, he wore no shirt. Haley's breath caught in her chest at the sight of this handsome creature. When he spoke, his wings fanned themselves slowly.

"Good evening, gentlemen," he said.

"Valian," some responded in acknowledgement. "Evening," said the others, as they backed away from the twins' table.

"I hope you have made our young friends feel welcome," Valian said, looking at the pub keeper.

"Oh yes-yes, Sir Valian. I've brought them some nice rainbow dew and got them comfortable at the table here and—"

"Very good," Valian interrupted. Turning to the twins he addressed them. "Henry, Haley, welcome to the outskirts of Roan. I am Valian, guardian of the realm of Roan and brother to Sersha, whom you have already met."

Haley stood, sighing with relief. "Oh! I am very pleased to meet you," she replied, blushing and offered her hand.

Valian gently grasped her fingertips, bowed and kissed her hand. Her heart pounded as he smiled at her.

"It is a pleasure to finally meet you, milady. Sersha has told me of your kindness and desire to assist us." Valian was still holding her hand and she continued to blush.

"Thank you, Sir Valian," she said, in almost a whisper, pulling her hand from his. She quickly sat down. "Would you like to sit down?" she asked.

Her heart was going a hundred miles an hour. She met cute boys before at school and often found herself daydreaming about them, but Valian, he was so handsome, powerful, and commanding. She stole a glance at his muscular stature then quickly looked away. Clearly, she was attracted to him.

Henry looked at his sister then back at Valian and rolled his eyes. He could see where this was going. He always told her, she was boy crazy, but she would always deny it. Haley was completely captivated by Valian's charisma. He pulled up a chair and sat down.

"Ahem," Henry coughed. Valian turned his attention toward Henry and shook his hand.

"Welcome to Roan, Sir Henry. I am glad you have chosen to take on this burden with us. The situation is worsening and we don't have much time. We'll rest tonight and leave for the palace first thing in the morning. I have arranged sleeping quarters for you but first, I'll bet you'd like to clean up and have something to eat. Are you hungry?"

"Starving!" Henry burst out.

"Yes, I would like to clean up," Haley replied shyly.

"Come," he said, getting up. The twins followed Valian toward the rear door, lugging their packs behind them. Haley marveled how Valian's wings magically folded themselves as they went through the door. Glancing back, Henry saw the patrons at the bar watching them as they left then gathered together to gossip about the two strangers that came out of the dark from the *other side.*

They walked past the waterfall and went up a couple of blocks, behind the storefront. The cobblestone streets were well lit by the iron lamp stands, which lined the walkways. The neighborhoods were peppered with great maples and groves of birch. They walked past ponds and water gardens.

The bottom of the canyon had many hidden nooks, crannies, and hollows each with small gardens, flowers, and ornaments. Some homes were built of stone and brick, while others with great logs. Some looked like sod houses with thatched roofs. Chimneys spilled out their burden in plumes of colored smoke as if by some mysterious incantation.

They arrived in front of a small brick cottage. The twins followed, up a stone walkway to a heavy, dark wooden door with a brass gargoyle knocker. Valian grabbed the fang bearing lower jaw of the knocker and wrapped twice. The door opened by itself.

Looking past Valian, Haley saw many lanterns mounted to the walls of the hallway. They walked through and to the right was a large open doorway, leading to the living area.

Entering the room, Haley was impressed with the décor. It was carpeted with thick, soft grass and filled with large, overstuffed chairs and low tables. The wall-mounted lamps around the room gave off a cheery glow. Pillows were piled up in front of a large hearth where a strange blaze crackled and popped.

The kitchen, to the right, had an open ceiling with brass pots and pans hanging from a wooden brace running its length and a huge butcher-block table stood in the center, full of drawers and shelves. Wire baskets hung in front of the stained glass kitchen windows, full of garlic cloves, onions and herbs of all sorts. Strange looking plants adorned the long, deep shelf under the window ledge and Haley thought she could see tall, gray toadstools growing out of a large pot in the corner of the counter.

There were many pictures of landscapes in the front room and she could swear the leaves on the trees were moving.

"Where is she?" Valian wondered out loud.

They followed him back to the hallway, which led past several other rooms, to a stairway. Upstairs two doors stood open, revealing cozy candle lit bedrooms.

"Go ahead and get cleaned up, while I go see if I can find Hilda."

"Hilda?" the twins whispered to each other as Valian went back downstairs.

"Go on," Haley whispered as she entered the first bedroom. Henry took the other.

There was nothing strange about these rooms. They looked like ordinary bedrooms, with a bed, dresser and closet. Looking around, Haley found the bathroom, complete with a shower and tub. She put down her backpack, shut the door, and went to the tub. She turned the handle, but it wouldn't budge. She turned with all her might, but it was stuck fast. She climbed into the tub and turned with both hands.

"Turn on!" She said, frustrated. Suddenly, hot water gushed from the faucet, startling her. She let go of the handle, it hadn't even moved. The hot water was starting to burn her feet. "Cold," she whispered.

The water came out faster. Testing the temperature, it was still too hot.

"Colder," she said. She put her hand back under the water. It cooled enough to be comfortable. "Ahhh . . . " she said, sitting down.

She smiled to herself as the tub filled up.

"Warmer, please." It became warmer, soothing her tired body. "Bubbles please," she said on a whim, quite suddenly, bubbles began to appear.

Soon the tub was filled with foaming bubbles. She was delighted and soaked for a good half hour. After her bath, she rummaged through her backpack for some fresh clothes, got dressed, and walked into the hallway. Wonderful smells drifted up the stairs. She went to Henry's door and knocked. After no response, she opened the door and peeked in, finding the room empty. She quietly went downstairs.

In the kitchen where the butcher block table had been, now stood a large, round table laden with steaming dishes of food. Henry was there and already eating. Valian was at the counter, helping a rather plump black haired woman with several steaming bowls.

She walked into the room.

"Hi Haley," Henry mumbled, between mouthfuls. "Come in and meet Hilda."

The woman turned and looked at Haley. A great big smile came over her face. Wiping her hands on her apron, she bustled over to Haley, grabbed her hand and began shaking it roughly.

"I am so happy to meet you, Haley. I've heard so much about you."

She kept shaking her hand and grinning. Haley felt like a yo-yo. Finally, Hilda let go and put her arm around Haley's shoulder, ushering her over to the table.

"Come now, dear. Let's get something in that stomach of yours."

Valian brought over two steaming bowls of soup, sitting one in front of Henry and one in front of Haley.

"Mmm, that smells good," Haley replied. "What kind of soup is it?"

"It's a special recipe of mine," Hilda answered. "I call it midnight mushroom."

Haley began eating. She hadn't realized how hungry she was until now. Valian came back to the table with bowls of soup for himself and Hilda then sat down opposite Henry.

There was fresh bread, a variety of cheeses and fruits, and several dishes Haley didn't recognize. It didn't matter. Everything tasted wonderful and she finished two helpings.

Sitting back, stuffed, the warmth of the fire made her sleepy. She looked over at Henry and saw him drifting off, jerking his head back as it fell forward. She smiled and before she knew it, she was nodding off herself.

Valian and Hilda looked at the sleeping pair with tenderness and warmth.

"I hope they are the ones we've been waiting for," Hilda said, softly. "They're our last hope, I'm afraid."

"I know," said Valian. "I believe in them, especially Haley. There's something about her. I believe she is destined to make a difference. I feel it."

"I hope so. Come, let's get them up to bed. They have a busy day in store tomorrow."

"Right," answered Valian. He walked over and gently lifted Haley into his arms and carried her up to her room. Looking down onto her sleeping face, he thought to himself, she was exquisite. He felt himself drawn to her beauty. He laid her on the bed as Hilda came into the room.

"Okay, let's get going, Sir Valian, shoo."

He looked once more at Haley and felt his heart go out to her, then walked out of the room, heading downstairs to get Henry.

Hilda waved her hand over Haley's bed, spoke an incantation and magically Haley was in pajamas. She pulled up the blankets and tucked her in. Gazing down at her, she spoke, "Sleep well, sweetness. May celestial spirits be your guide." She waved once more and the candles went out.

Haley slept hard that night and when she woke, it was with a silent scream on her lips. She had another dream about Henry being in terrible danger. She tried in desperation to save him but woke up before she could. The dream faded fast and she couldn't remember what happened; only the feeling of terror remained in her memory. Sitting up, she tried to think of what happened, but it was no use.

She took a deep breath, calming her nerves and pounding heart. The room was full of sunshine. Hilda had come in hours ago and opened the curtains. Haley climbed out of the soft bed and went to the window. Looking outside took her breath away.

The canyon was bright, colorful, and alive with activity. Opening the window, she stuck her head out and breathed in the freshest lungful of air she'd ever felt. She could hear dozens and dozens of birds twittering in the morning light and people were out busying themselves in their gardens and yards.

Real people, she thought. These must be some of the humans Sersha told her about, the ones that came into fairy world and chose to stay. There were several odd looking creatures a couple cottages down from Hilda's, digging in a bare patch of dirt, she wondered what they were.

There was a nice breeze blowing and it invigorated her. She soon forgot about the dream and hurried to get showered and dressed. She told the shower to turn on and smiled when the water began to run.

She bounded down the steps to greet Hilda, who was hurriedly going back and forth from the living room to the kitchen, putting things away and cleaning up.

"Mornin', love," Hilda called to her, with a smile. "Good morning."

"Gotta run, gonna be late if I don't hurry," she said, running into the kitchen again. "There's food in the oven for you," she said, zipping by Haley in a flurry, her cloak flying behind her.

"Where are you going?" Haley called after her. "Gotta get to work. I run a little shop in the outskirts.

Got to be open by nine. See you later, good luck today!" she called out, disappearing down the hall.

Haley looked around the room, slightly flabbergasted. She was alone and had no idea where Henry and Valian were. In the kitchen, she smelled fresh cinnamon and opened the oven. She gazed down hungrily at a dozen sweet rolls that were already frosted. Grabbing a potholder from the counter, she pulled the sweet morsels out and set them on the stovetop. To her surprise, the pan wasn't hot. She touched it quickly and found it cold. Haley picked it up with her bare hands and was amazed. The rolls were steaming. She sat at the table and took a bite of the sweetest, tastiest roll she'd ever eaten.

"Wish I had some milk," she said to herself.

Immediately, a glass of milk popped out of thin air.

"Holy cow!" she exclaimed. "This is totally amazing."

She finished off two rolls and felt completely full.

Looking at the sink she thought for a moment. "Dish, clean yourself."

Haley watched, astounded as the plate she'd been using became clean, flew through the air, and into the cupboard. Shaking her head, she got up and wandered through the house, peeking into the rooms she hadn't seen the night before. Downstairs was another bedroom, a study, bathroom, and a room full of plants. It looked like a small greenhouse with glass walls. Great flowers towered against them, strange looking vines and Venus flytrap type plants were scattered about the room in all sizes of pots. Several gigantic flowers' with huge heads stood behind a glass wall all by themselves, their head's hung as if sleeping.

She continued down the hall to the door at the end, looking out, she discovered a cheerful flower garden outside with a small fountain in the left corner of the yard. It was a large yard bordered by a tall hedge. The next house was quite a distance away and barely visible.

Haley stepped outside and heard voices just past the hedge. She peeked through it and saw Valian looking up in the air. Wondering what he was looking at, she stepped through the opening and looked toward his gaze. She let out a small shriek.

High in the air, Henry was hovering. His shirt was off and wings protruding out of his back, it made her stagger in disbelief. She landed square on her backside. Valian dashed over to her. Taking her by the hand, he helped her to her feet.

"Are you hurt?" he asked, with obvious distress.

"Oh, I'm fine," she answered. "Just a little embarrassed at my clumsiness."

Valian smiled down at her. "What do you think of your brother?"

Haley looked up and watched as Henry flew back and forth, up and down, doing spins and somersaults in the air.

"He's a natural," Valian beamed.

"Haley! You gotta try this!" Henry yelled, swooping down and landing next to her with a huge grin. "Valian gave me an elixir and I grew these!" he said, turning his back toward her, fanning his wings.

"Wow, Henry! I don't know what to say. They're amazing!" She smiled, her eyes wide. "Will I be getting them, too?" she asked, turning to Valian.

His eyes were bright and shining, his smile made her weak in the knees.

"Yes, you'll need them to get to the palace," he said, producing a tiny brass stein. "Drink this," he said. "But before you do, you will need to change out of those clothes."

Walking over to a picnic table, he brought back a shiny peach colored gown. It sparkled like snowflakes in the sun and was soft as rose petals. It looked similar to the one Sersha had worn the day they met. It was backless and had practically no weight.

Haley took the gown and went back into the house. A few minutes later she emerged, stunning. The peachy color brought out the blush in her cheeks. Henry whistled.

"Shut up, Henry!" she said, embarrassed again, but inside, she felt pretty and feminine. She went toward them, barefoot, her long brown hair bouncing in the sun. She was dazzling. Valian handed the stein back to her.

"What will happen?" she asked, a little afraid.

"Piece of cake," Henry grinned, bursting back into the air.

"You'll feel a little lightheaded at first, but that will subside. Your back will get warm, and you'll feel a kind of fluttering sensation," Valian answered.

"Will it hurt?" she asked, with a small frown.

He smiled reassuringly. "Not a bit. Trust me."

Haley looked up in his pale blue eyes and lost all sense of fear. "I do," she answered, softly. Haley looked at the stein and back at Valian, then raised it to her lips. It smelled horrible, but she drank it down quickly anyway.

He took the stein from her hand and stood close beside her.

Almost instantly she became lightheaded and her legs felt like they were made of rubber. She lost her balance and almost sank to the ground, but Valian put his arm around her waist and held her. Haley bent over, feeling out of breath as an intense wave of heat moved from her neck and down her back. Valian held her steady as she breathed deeply. Slowly, she began to feel better and felt a strange sensation in her back. It felt tighter and then humps appeared. She couldn't see what was going on and Henry thought it was a good thing she couldn't. Haley would have freaked out if she actually saw what was happening. Quickly, a glittering wing popped out. First on one side, then the other, opening slowly like a butterflies wings, then spread out in the sun. Haley stood up straight and turned her head to look. She squealed with delight when she saw the glittery protrusions behind her.

"You'll need to keep still while they dry," Valian said softly.

Haley hadn't noticed until now that Valian was holding her. She looked up at him.

"Well, I think you'll be all right now," he said, letting go.

Her wings dried in no time. Valian inspected them for any problems.

"They're perfect," he said, behind her. "Go ahead and try them out."

Valian explained how to use them, along with Henry's help, and together they had her flying like a pro in no time. Haley never felt so light and free, just like a bird. She could go anywhere and see anything.

She could explore the new world like Columbus did centuries ago, only by air. What treasures she would find. What fun. She was so excited, she could have stayed up there all day. Valian had to fly up and coax her down. There was much to do and the morning was waning fast.

Once they were back on the ground, they went into the house and left Hilda a note, thanking her for her hospitality and kindness. Valian decided they would stop at Mathilda's for some rainbow dew before they left.

The three of them flew across the neighborhoods, toward the main street. They landed and went up the cobblestone walkway into the food court and picked out a table.

The twins surveyed the fantastic view around them. They could see for miles. A grungy little creature in a dirty apron and crumpled hat waited on them. It brought over a large goblet and three mugs, setting them down with a grunt, then turned and shuffled back into the cottage.

"What was that?" Haley asked, raising her eyebrows.

"That was a brownie," Valian answered. "They're not much to look at but they are very devoted, if treated well."

"Brownies? I've read about them in books," Haley replied, taking a sip of her rainbow dew. "Mmm . . . this is wonderful," she continued. "It tastes different from the rainbow dew at the pub last night."

"That was an imitation of rainbow dew," Valian explained. "Half of the pubs in the outskirts water it down, so it loses some of its flavor. They sell more that way."

Valian took a small silver box from inside his vest pocket and opened it. Inside were two small objects that looked like frozen water droplets. Taking them out of the box, he handed one to each of them.

"Eat these," he said.

"What are they?" Henry asked.

"They're called dwindle drops," Valian answered. "They make you shrink to a smaller size."

"Shrink?" Henry repeated, excitedly.

"Once you eat one, you will never have to eat another."

"How small will we get?" Henry asked. "Will we stay that way?"

"No," Valian answered. "You won't stay that way. You can shrink to whatever size you need. Just like flying, all you need to do is imagine the size you want and you'll change. Then, just think of being big again and you will be. The mind is an amazing tool, Sir Henry," Valian continued. "You can't even begin to imagine the things you'll be capable of doing once you get the hang of it. When we near the edge of the city, we will need to change to about seven inches. You'll see. Just look at your surroundings and you'll fit right in."

They each took a dwindle drop. Henry ate his without hesitation. Immediately, with a snap of flash and glitter, he disappeared. Haley let out a startled squeal. Valian burst into laughter.

Henry was still in his chair; he was five inches tall. Haley began laughing as Henry jumped up and down with excitement. Suddenly, with another snap of sparkle, he was back to his own size.

"What a rush!" Henry exclaimed. "This is gonna be fun!"

"Let's finish our drinks," said Valian. "We need to get going."

They finished their rainbow dew while Valian went inside to pay the brownie, then took to the air and flew north toward the capital city of Roan.

Chapter Nine

TOURING ROAN

The scenery was spectacular; the trio flew at tree top level. Looking down, the twins saw lush forests and parks. Several fields zoomed past, ready for harvesting. They surveyed crystal clear brooks and streams, ponds and waterfalls were everywhere, strategically placed among the forests and glens.

Haley was breathless, feeling so much joy and wonder at this place. As they flew, the trees grew taller and much larger. She wondered if these were Sequoias or maybe Redwood trees she had seen on television.

"It's time to change!" Valian called out.

With a snap of spark, they changed size, dwarfed by their surroundings in an instant. The twins glanced at each other with broad smiles as they followed Valian's every move.

Up ahead, cottages and tiny houses appeared, nestled in the branches. Down below, they could see streets and roads in many directions. Windows sparkled like diamonds and small plumes of smoke wafted from the chimneys.

Haley was in heaven with all the flowers everywhere, along the roads, in pots on front porches, and great gardens. They followed Valian higher and higher until they were above the canopy, up ahead, a sparkling castle gleamed in the afternoon sun.

The twins could see dozens of fairies coming and going from the castle courtyards, flying in every direction, going about their daily business.

They came to rest on one of the great open cobblestone terraces with large white columns supporting the roof. Tables with umbrellas and benches were set up in rows like a restaurant, filled with chatting fairies.

As they landed, all eyes turned toward them. Everyone was smiling and it made the twins feel important. Valian showed them around, introducing them at various tables. *There are so many of them and they're all so beautiful,* Haley thought to herself.

Every one of them stood as they approached. The males bowed and the females curtsied. Haley wondered how she would ever remember them all.

"Come, it's time," said Valian, leading them through the courtyard to an inner chamber.

They walked down a long corridor and through a cut glass door, in every color of the rainbow. Once inside the room, they were impressed by the glass ceiling, supported by heavy, wooden beams. The walls, also made of glass, were tinted so one could see out, but not in.

It was carpeted in plush, deep crimson, which made Haley think of home at once. Large plants stood in each corner. There was a sunken living area with long, crimson and midnight blue couches shaped in a large square, with a large glass table in the center.

The twins were taken aback at the great bowls sitting on several pedestal tables. They were made of clear glass, and full of gems. Bowls full of emeralds, rubies and diamonds.

The table in the center had a flower arrangement, with small jewel filled bowls around it. Heavy, midnight blue drapes, were pulled back to let in the light. *This is a heavenly room,* Haley thought to herself.

"Make yourselves comfortable," said Valian. "I will be back soon."

He went through a different door, leaving them to look around. Haley went to one of the many windows and gazed out, while Henry went to examine the glass bowls.

"My gosh, Haley!" he exclaimed. "Look at these . . . they're real!"

Haley walked over and scooped up a handful of rubies.

She moved her hand about, making the gems sparkle.

"They're beautiful," she said, dropping them back in the bowl.

Henry looked at her strangely. She wasn't interested in the hoard of wealth before her and she turned back to the window. Her brother watched her and looked back at the bowl. Somehow it didn't seem as exciting as it had a moment ago. Compared to everything else they'd seen and discovered, the gems seemed small and insignificant now. He walked over to the window and stood by her, looking out.

"This is incredible, isn't it?"

She turned to look at him. He was again taken aback by the look on her face. She seemed so peaceful and relaxed. Tenderness and compassion just radiated from her. Henry felt as if he were looking at someone of royalty. She wasn't just his sister anymore. Just then, the door opened, and Valian came in followed by a most striking woman. She wore a crown of deep blue sapphires and gold upon her long, dark, auburn hair. A silk gown of midnight blue, flecked with silver, hung gracefully over her shoulders and flowed behind her. Haley felt small as the woman approached. She stopped in front of them and spoke. Like all the other fairies, her voice was magical, as with melody. Haley felt like she could listen to her speak for hours.

"I am Lilia, queen of Roan. I wish to extend to you, the deepest greetings of welcome to our realm."

"Thank you, your majesty," Haley said, with a curtsey.

Henry bowed, feeling slightly awkward.

"Your majesty," he said, as his face grew red.

"Come, sit down," she said, motioning them toward the couches.

They all sat. Haley was surprised to see the queen had no wings.

"I trust your journey was pleasant?"

"Oh yes!" Haley said. "It was grand. We never dreamed it would be so beautiful and . . . and magical!"

"Yes, I'm quite sure it's been unexpected, not to mention strange to you. I wish the circumstances weren't so grave. As you have been told, Zebulan has been . . . " she paused, searching for the right word. "Overcome by an evil presence which occupies many of the outer realms."

Haley was surprised at this statement.

"I thought the evil one only had control of one realm," Haley responded.

"I wish it were so," said the queen. "The evil one dwells in one realm in particular, however its influence has infected several other realms as of late, and it seems it is getting stronger as time passes. Soon Zebulan will complete the change, and we fear what affect it will have on him and other realms, and not to put it lightly, fairy world as a whole."

The twins sat, pondering this latest information. Haley was obviously troubled by this news and wondered if they would be able to help, and if they were in time.

The queen watched Haley's expression with great interest. No one said a word for quite some time. A young brownie entered the room with a tray, and walked up to Lilia, bowing slightly.

"A crumpet or cake, your majesty?" he asked, with reverence.

"No, thank you, Reed."

The brownie went around the table and bowed to each of them, offering the tray. He stole several glances at Haley as he served them.

"That will be all, Reed. Thank you," said Lilia.

Reed put the tray on the glass table and left the room. Everyone but the queen helped themselves to cakes and rainbow dew, eating in silence.

Haley put down her mug and went over to the window, looking out, an idea began to form in her mind. Was it possible? If so, would it actually work?

Lilia broke the silence. "What is it?" she asked, studying Haley.

"Sersha mentioned something to me the night of the festival, about time being different in fairy world."

"Yes," answered the queen, with curiosity. "Time is very different here than on the other side, among other things."

Haley turned to look at her. "Have you ever heard of time travel?"

Valian and Lilia looked at each other with growing realization at the implication of Haley's question.

"Yes, I've heard of it," she answered. "What are you suggest—"

Haley interrupted. "I beg your pardon, your majesty. Is it possible?"

After some hesitation, Lilia nodded her head, looking down with apprehension.

"Yes it is possible, but it hasn't been done in centuries.

It is complex and rather involved."

"What are you thinking, milady?" Valian asked, with unease.

"I don't know what help we can be at this moment in time, now that the situation has already spiraled out of control, but if we could go back, maybe we could change the course of events."

"Hmm," said the queen, standing up and pacing the floor. "It would be dangerous, but I don't think it will interfere with our future events. Zebulan hasn't been here that long and since you would be going back on this side, you won't be doing anything to change events in your world. It is possible. What's your plan?"

"Well, if we could be there when Sarah and the girls are pulled through the portal, we may be able to stop them from being captured. We'll be there waiting and rescue them, take them somewhere where they will be safe until Zeb comes through. What do you think?" Haley asked, rather excited about her idea.

"Brilliant!" Valian exclaimed. "Why didn't *we* think of that? We'll just hide out at the swamp and grab them as soon as the hag pulls them through. Simple!" Valian said, getting excited, himself.

"All right then," said Henry, slapping his knee, startling everyone. "Let's do it!"

"Not so fast," Lilia interrupted. "There are preparations to be made."

Just then, the door opened and Sersha walked in.

"Sersha!" Haley cried.

Haley ran over to the princess and they embraced. Henry and Valian stood as Lilia went over and hugged her daughter. You could tell they were mother and daughter as they both had striking auburn hair and the same facial features. One thing that struck Haley was the fact that Lilia looked just as young as Sersha.

After the greetings were over, Lilia related Haley's plan to Sersha.

"Excellent plan," said Sersha. "Now, why didn't we think of that?"

Everyone smiled.

"Valian, I'll need your assistance preparing the sphere. In the meantime, you two see some of the sights, have something to eat and get some rest. We'll send the four of you back tomorrow."

Lilia dismissed herself and Valian escorted her out of the room.

"Why doesn't the queen have wings?" Henry asked Sersha.

"She does," Sersha replied. Seeing their bewildered looks she explained. "My mother is a descendant of the primeval Manwan's. The true lineage passed down from generation to generation. They were the only ones who have the ability to hide or shroud their wings. Valian and I are also descendants." She turned and to the twin's astonishment, her wings were gone. "I don't usually shroud them. We have no need to, except when we're in your world. Come, let's fly to the square an shop around awhile."

The three walked out onto the private veranda and took to the air.

Sersha dazzled the twins with a tour over the sparkling city, pointing out various sights.

Gems were everywhere. They were used to make so many things, beautiful goblets, chandeliers, dishes, and lampposts. It was hard to get used to the fact that they had no monetary value, mostly due to the fact they were everywhere and so easy to find. Haley compared it to the same worth sand would have.

They flew from tree to tree, looking through storefront windows, nestled snugly in the massive crooks and branches. It was like looking at whimsical tree houses, perched high and low. Quaint little shops and boutiques lined each storefront. The twins did a lot of window shopping. There were several places, which caught Haley's attention. She ventured into Bella's Blossom Shop by herself, while Sersha and Henry went into the store next door. Bella's had every flower under the sun. There were rows and rows of seeds, bulbs, and seedlings. A great nursery stood out back, chock-full of plants, great and small. Haley discovered the most unusual and uncommon things back there. There were plants that bled if you touched them the wrong way, plants that could hold a conversation, and plants that sang when they were fed.

Back in a corner of the room, behind a tall iron grate, were the most captivating flowers. A wide, black line was painted on the floor fifteen feet in front of the grate and the sign standing by the display read: *STAND BACK! DO NOT APPROACH! DANGER!*

Some of these flowers stood twenty feet tall, with purple and orange heads the size of bathtubs, surrounded by smaller varieties. As Haley approached, she saw the branches of these great flowers were moving. They shivered and shuddered as if a strong wind was blowing behind the grate. Haley watched them, fascinated, wondering why they were protected. She glanced around the room trying to spot a clerk. The shop was teaming with browsers. Fairies, pixies, and sprites milled around examining various plants and making purchases. A petite young fairy wearing an apron came over to where Haley stood.

"Interested in a bulwark?"

"What?" Haley asked.

"A bulwark," she said, pointing toward the grate. "You know, for protection. We get a lot of orders for these. Pesky things they are, but they do the job."

"I'm new here," Haley replied. "And I've never seen a bullark."

"Bulwark," the fairy corrected her.

"Bulwark," Haley repeated. "I've never seen a bulwark before. What do they do?" she asked.

"They're guard flowers."

"Guard flowers?" Haley repeated, fascinated.

"Yes. You plant them close to your front door or wherever you want protection. They eat anything. Bugs, weeds, unwanted critters and beasts. They especially like wood elves and goblins. And sometimes they'll grab a brownie if they're especially hungry. Occasionally, they may even grab a fairy when they're feeling ornery or spiteful. They may bite off an arm or head, but they spit it out right away. Guess we're not that tasty. We even carry the walking variety, but we're out. Had an ogre come in and clean us out yesterday. They work especially well for large grounds. We can rush the order if you need them right away."

"Oh," Haley replied, a bit lost for words. "Thank you for telling me about the bulwarks."

"Would you like to try one out?" the clerk asked, hastily. "I'd recommend a small one unless you're planning on guarding your grounds or a castle.

The larger ones work much better for that and you don't have to plant them close to the entrance."

"Well-l-let me think about it," Haley replied and turned to go. The fairy started after her.

"They're on sale! I can knock off ten percent!" she called, as Haley hurried past a display of various mushrooms and toadstools, exiting the shop.

She walked down the boardwalk, peeking into each shop, looking to see where Henry and Sersha went. A candle shop caught her eye and she entered it. There were tons of candles in every shape, size, and color. They lit up the room in a warm, flickering glow, giving off a soft feeling and she left with the impression they were charmed. She walked past several more boutiques, a bakery, and an enchanted workshop where the tools worked by themselves, hammering and sawing, building miniature houses and castles. Tiny brushes delicately painted each piece with precision. Each dwelling was open to view the intricate designs inside. The tiny chandeliers and lamps all worked as did the fireplaces. She was delighted and wished she could have had a house like one of these to play with when she was little.

Next door was a doll shop, with dolls large and small. Many walked and talked. Some could dress themselves and comb their hair. There were a few families inside with small fairy children. This was the first time Haley had seen a fairy child. They were truly sweet and lovable, pure, full of wonder, and well behaved. They graciously followed their parents down the aisles, admiring the various dolls. Haley was truly impressed by their respectful dispositions.

As she continued walking, she wondered about all these shops and emporiums. What did fairies use for money? She hadn't seen any and no one asked her for any when they were at the pub or at Mathilda's. She remembered Valian dismissing himself to go pay the brownie and wondered what their money looked like.

She approached an old stone building. It was small and stood three stories. An illuminated sign hung in one of the windows, which read, *Tea House.* Feeling a bit parched, she walked in. There were candles and lamps burning all around the room, but it seemed quite dark, like a cozy, secluded bistro. There were quite a few tables, mostly empty, but a few fairies and other creatures were seated at some of the booths that lined the room. Straight ahead was a wide staircase, leading up to the second story. She went up the steps and pulled back a heavy drape that hung in the doorway. Bright light lit the room, which blinded her for a moment. When her eyes became accustomed to the light, she spotted Henry and Sersha seated in a booth in front of one of the large windows. Seeing Haley, Henry waved her over.

"We were just about to send a courier to find you," Sersha announced. "We were getting hungry and thought we'd stop for a bite. Come sit down."

Henry got up and let Haley scoot in by the window. Almost immediately, he began jabbering about all the shops he'd visited.

They checked out a broom and cloak shop.

"Did you know they have real witches here, Haley?"

"Witches?"

"Yes. Then we went into a store that sells digging tools to gnomes. And did you know there are fairies that glow in the dark like lightning bugs and are as small as a ladybug?"

Haley listened to his discoveries with growing interest. She had no idea fairy world was so diverse. A fat fairy waddled over to take her order. Haley wasn't very hungry and ordered a mug of rainbow dew. They chatted about the shops and the city for a half hour or so then decided to get back to the palace. As they walked toward the door, Sersha said she'd be right back and went through an open side door. Looking around her, Haley thought she saw a cash register and again wondered what they used for money. As they descended the stairs, Haley asked her about it.

"Money, what's money?"

"You know, it's what you pay for services. If you want something from a store, you give the storekeeper money as payment."

"Oh," Sersha replied, "that's what you do on the other side. I forgot about that. We don't have money here. We exchange services. I think the technical term for it is bartering. Trading, swapping, we offer one service for another. You see, everyone here has a talent or a trade to offer. Take me for instance, I weave."

"Weave?"

"Yes. I am a weaver of silk. I make and design many of the gowns you see everyone wearing. Everyone is taught from the earliest age, some kind of craft. Something that fits their personality."

Haley found this interesting and urged Sersha to explain more.

"When a fairy is born, they are brought before my mother and one of the high councils. Then they go to the sacred chamber, where their talent is revealed through the sphere and they are announced to their parents. From the time they begin to walk, they are taken to the proper tutor and they learn that craft."

She paused for a moment.

"Go on," Haley urged. "Tell me more."

"Well, there's not much more to tell. The baby fairy is trained by their tutor, for as long as it takes to master their art, then they are free to trade just like the adults. There are callings of every kind. There are bakers, farmers, builders, singers and entertainers, also gardeners, florists, and innumerable craftsmen of all sorts. When we want something from a shop or boutique, we bargain our services. To pay for our drinks at the *Tea House*, I arranged to make a set of curtains for the waiter that served us. It's all very simple."

"Wow, that's really neat!" Haley exclaimed. "It's too bad we can't do that in our world."

"Tell us more about this sphere," said Henry.

"The sphere is the most sacred thing in our entire universe. It is the pinnacle of our very existence."

"What does it do? Where did it come from?" Henry asked.

"No one knows from whence it came. It has always been here. The kings and queens from the beginning were the only ones to have access to it and those most committed and trusted by them. Not only is it sacred, but it also could be an extremely dangerous tool, if it's ever in the wrong hands. That is why it is kept in a hidden chamber and protected by sentries, not to mention spellbound by enchantments."

"What does it do?" Haley repeated Henry's question.

"Well . . . it can see. It can see many things. It can see the past as it was written, it can see the present. And, as you already know, it can see the hidden talents of the fairies and many other species as well. It is also a timekeeper. It has converse time-lapse capabilities."

"What does that mean?" Henry asked, confused.

"It means the sphere is able to reverse time, to reverse the order. Time can be manipulated to slow down and reverse the process. So, you can understand why it is concealed and protected."

The twins stood there unable to say anything. They were quite speechless. Finally, after watching them for a moment, Sersha asked, "Are you two well?"

"Yes," Haley answered. "We're just at a loss for words. This place is so incredible. All we have seen and learned about your world affects us. Our reality gets confused. Sometimes we wonder what is real and what isn't, do you know what I mean?"

Henry nodded his head, in agreement. "You hit the nail right on the head," he replied.

"I understand," said Sersha, with tenderness in her smile. "It must be a bit overwhelming for you. Don't worry, it'll get easier. You'll get used to your surroundings and the way things work here. Before you know it, it'll seem totally natural. You may even find it difficult to remember the way things work in your world. Come, it's getting late. We need to get back to the palace soon, before they begin the feast without us."

"Feast, what feast?" Henry asked, with anticipation.

"Henry, honestly," said Haley. "Is that all you think about anymore?"

He looked at her, a little hurt.

"I can't help it. I constantly feel hungry. I don't know why."

"It's the air," Sersha replied, as they took flight. "The air here make's many of the human males feel famished much of the time. I think they use up much more energy than back on the other side. The air is pure here! No pollution whatsoever!" she yelled, over her shoulder.

They flew between great trees, dodging branches, scaring up a nesting flock of birds. As they arrived back at the palace, the twins were shown to their rooms to clean up before the feast. Haley had a new gown to wear made especially by Sersha. She was stunning as usual, in the pale orange and yellow gown, with just enough sparkle. Henry was also quite handsome in dark blue, with a bronze colored vest. A knock came at Haley's door.

"Who is it?" she called out.

"It's the steward, milady. I've come to escort you to the great hall."

"I'll be right out."

With a last look in the mirror, she went to the door and followed the steward toward the great hall.

"Where is Henry?" she asked.

"Another steward is escorting him, milady."

She followed him down several long hallways and into a small room.

"Wait here, milady," he said, leaving the room.

There were a couple of small sofas in the lamp lit room and she sat for a moment. There were no windows, so she couldn't tell where she was for sure. After a couple of minutes, another steward came in, with Henry close behind.

He was instructed to wait as well and the two of them sat together, wondering what was going on. They didn't have to wait long. Sersha, Valian, and Lilia came in. After a few pleasantries, the stewards escorted the group to the great hall.

It was an exquisite room. Great, sparkling chandeliers hung throughout the columns. Beautiful tapestries lined the room, along with colossal paintings of landscapes and many portraits. Again, Haley could swear the leaves in the pictures were moving.

The tables were covered in linens and fine lace, already set. They marveled at the plates and platters, all made from colorful gemstones. The table was also laden with large vases, filled with a wide variety of flowers, and of course, there were glass bowls filled with colorful gems.

The great hall was already crowded with many fairies, aside from a few latecomers that quickly entered to take their seats. There were small groups hovering here and there, in light conversation while others were standing by their seats, waiting.

As the five-some entered the room, a sound rang out, like hundreds of wind chimes being shaken at once. All eyes turned toward them. A hush came over the room. The hovering fairies landed and everyone bowed and curtsied.

"Welcome to all," Lilia said, with authority. "Lords and ladies of the council, may I introduce our two very special visitors from the other side. May I present Haley and Henry Miles," she said, motioning toward the twins.

Immediate applause echoed through the room, along with many more bows and curtsies. The twins, who had been standing behind Sersha and Valian, were coaxed forward to be recognized. They were both embarrassed and grinned shyly.

When the applause subsided, the queen continued, "They have graciously offered to help us, in this time of adversity. We shall honor them in celebration with a feast, after which, everyone will adjourn to the council chambers."

The chimes rang out again and everyone took their seats. The queen sat at the head of one of the tables. Sersha and Henry sat on one side, while Haley and Valian sat on the other.

A moment later, a door opened at the far end of the room where a long line of brownies stood waiting. They entered, bearing large platters of food and drink. There were roasted turkeys, smoked hams, and plates of sausages. Every vegetable under the sun was cooked to perfection and dishes were brimming with strange casseroles and salads. There were desserts galore, some of which the twins had never seen before, and large goblets of rainbow dew.

"I can't believe you eat the same kind of foods we do," Hailey exclaimed.

"We're not completely different from you," Sersha replied, helping herself to a scoop of mashed potatoes. "You have to remember; our worlds were one. We live and eat in much the same way. Some things haven't changed that much since the split. Some have. For instance, we don't eat animal flesh. What you see here, is charmed into existence."

"I have a question," Henry said, looking at the others. "If our worlds were one, does that mean there were fairies and other creatures living on our side?"

"Yes," Lilia replied. "There were many at the beginning, but those that didn't come to *our side,* died out soon after the division took place. Many fairies were lured by the promise of power and control, but something happened during the tear. No one is exactly certain what it was. Maybe it was evil that slowly killed them one by one. Maybe it was the air. Nobody knows. Only the humans were able to survive. As near as we have been able to figure out, human beings have something we lack. They have a resistance, strength, and resilience toward calamity and evil. Most are born with the ability to fight it and that ability is nurtured as they grow. That is why we wanted a human to aid us," Lilia finished, with a sigh of hope.

The twins finally understood their role and the challenge ahead. The sound of music filled the great hall. The twins craned their necks to see, back in one of the corners, a dozen or so fairies gathered together with instruments. The sound was beautiful. Horns, harps, and violins, along with flutes and strange looking instruments they had never seen before.

They finished dinner completely satisfied, physically and mentally. When the chimes sounded the end of the feast, they left the great hall feeling like they could take on the world.

Everyone assembled in one of the larger council chambers. The meeting was called to order, Lilia explained Haley's idea on time travel and the plan to intercept Sarah and the girls. She asked for comments and any other ideas to aid them in their quest. Everyone agreed this was an excellent plan and were excited about it. Manwan fairies were not conniving and sneaky, they were thrilled about the plan. They adjourned, unanimously agreeing to expedite the plan right away in the morning.

The twins had a tough time sleeping that night and were both up with the sun. It was another gorgeous day. They were both showered and dressed within thirty minutes, meeting each other in the corridor.

Not sure where to go, they walked in the direction of the great hall. They ran into Valian coming in from the terrace.

"Well, good morning, Sir Henry, milady," he said, walking toward them. "You two are up early. Come out to the terrace. Breakfast is just being served."

They followed him outside and took a seat next to the ledge, where they could view the city and forest below. Sersha joined them a few minutes later and they went over the plan one more time.

"Mother has the sphere almost ready," she said, excitedly. "How are you two feeling? Are you ready?"

"We're ready," Henry said, a little nervously.

"Don't worry," said Sersha. "Everything will be fine. We'll be right alongside you."

That statement made them both feel a little better and they enjoyed a delicious breakfast of bacon, eggs, and toast, along with a refreshing mug of rainbow dew.

Finally, Sersha announced it was time to go and they felt the nervous feeling creeping back in. They followed her through a maze of well-guarded rooms and corridors for what seemed like an eternity, until they were thoroughly lost. With a wave of Sersha's' hand, they went through a tall, skinny door. It looked like every other door they passed and they knew they would probably never be able to find it themselves if they had to.

Inside was a dimly lit room. There were four cushy, high backed chairs and several heavily draped windows, but the most dazzling and interesting thing about this room was a six foot wide, round glass ball full of light pastel colors moving across the inside surface. Lilia was seated in one of the chairs placed in front of the sphere. She turned to them as they entered.

"It's ready," she said, sounding fairly excited. "Where's Valian?"

"He'll be here momentarily," Sersha answered.

Valian entered a minute later, equipped with a bow and a quiver of arrows. Sheathed, at his side, was a long silver sword with a jewel-encrusted handle. He walked over to a long chest and pulled out another bow, quiver, and sword, handing them to Sersha.

"What are those for?" Henry asked, alarmed.

"Protection," Valian answered.

"You will recall," Sersha spoke up quickly. "When Sarah and the girls were pulled through the portal, the swamp hag told Zeb they had been captured by moss trolls. Now, I don't know how much time it took from when the Bonners entered, until they were captured. I am assuming it was rather quickly, because of the fact that the swamp hag didn't get a chance to devour them. She is a swimming stomach and most testy. I'm banking on the moss trolls being there almost immediately. Also remember, the little girls couldn't swim, so we must act quickly when they first appear."

The twins nodded their heads.

"As soon as Sarah is pulled through, Henry and Haley, you grab the girls. Valian and I will keep the swamp hag occupied until you can get them away from the water. We'll then bring them through the sphere and back to our present time."

"Why are we bringing them back through the sphere?" Henry asked. "Why don't we just wait for Zeb to come through?"

"Zeb doesn't come through right then," Sersha answered. "We didn't go get Zeb for weeks. In the meantime, we have to get Sarah and the girls to safety. They will be vulnerable and need protection. Besides, we only have so much time to get back. The sphere is a complicated instrument and can only do things in the proper order. It will give us probably a thirty minute window to do what we need to do and get back," she finished.

This news put more pressure on the twins and they were more than nervous now.

"Don't worry," said Lilia, with a gentle smile. "You're in good hands. Sersha and Valian are the best guardians in Roan. You'll be fine."

The twins glanced at each other with hope, but they were still feeling quite uneasy.

"Oh, Haley, you'll want to leave your necklace here for safekeeping," said the queen.

Haley put her hand to her heart to remove the necklace and realized she wasn't wearing it.

"I must have left it in my room," she said, wondering where she had laid it.

"Okay," Lilia said. "The sphere is ready. Go quickly. Fare-thee-well. Go one at a time. Now!"

Chapter Ten

A DARING RESCUE

Immediately, Valian jumped into the sphere. The twins were shocked. It looked like a solid glass ball.

"Go!" Lilia shouted, with her hand on Haley's back.

Haley jumped through, followed by Henry, then Sersha. The twins felt like they jumped into the middle of a tornado. Then it was over. Just a fraction of a second passed and they were standing in the middle of a wide bog.

"This way," said Valian, leading them through wet ground and tall grasses.

It looked like they were following some kind of trail. Valian's sword was out, as was Sersha's. The foursome stopped, just outside the border of the swamp. Sersha and Valian were in front and peered through the tall weeds, searching for the hag. There wasn't a sound or movement in the water. Valian motioned them to follow him around the edge of the bog, toward the opposite bank of the swamp. There they stayed, crouched in the weeds, waiting.

The twins' hearts were pounding a mile a minute. Haley was sure it could be heard for miles. Valian and Sersha were composed and made no sign of nervousness or fear, which comforted her greatly. Suddenly, a coughing scream rang out from further down the bank. Alarmed, the twins both jumped. Valian quickly put his arm out, to keep them from moving.

They watched as the swamp hag gripped a thrashing child. It was a little girl, screaming and coughing, trying to wrench herself free. The hag had a strong hold on her and stood a few feet from the bank. Putting her slimy arm under the water, she waited. A moment later, another screaming child appeared. The swamp hag had a hideous grin on her face and licked her lips hungrily.

Just as she was about to sink her needle sharp teeth into the neck of one of the girls, she stopped. Looking down into the water, she stood still, listening.

Without warning, she threw both children onto the bank and dove under the water. That was exactly what Valian had been waiting for. With a shout to the others, all four dashed out from behind the weeds and ran down the bank. It all happened in a split second. Haley grabbed one child, Henry the other.

"Get back into the weeds! Quick!" Valian shouted.

The twins ran, half dragging the girls behind them. They quickly took cover, whispering to the terrified children that they'd be all right and to be as silent as they could. They covered the girl's mouths, as they were shaking and crying. Valian and Sersha crouched on the bank, waiting.

It took several minutes before the swamp hag emerged with a hysteric, terrified, yet fighting woman. As soon as their heads broke the surface, the twins could see the woman scratching, kicking, and swinging her fists at the hag, who wasn't prepared for such a fight and lost her grip on the woman. At that moment, Valian and Sersha jumped into the water, swinging their swords. Sersha grabbed the woman and made for the bank, while Valian rushed the hag. Just as the hag dove under the water, fleeing from the mighty fairy, a scream pierced the air. Valian turned and saw six or seven moss trolls, dragging the twins and the children toward the forest. Valian immediately took flight as did Sersha, they flew like lightning toward the terrifying scene. The trolls dropped their prisoners and raised their clubs.

The battle didn't last long. Valian and Sersha were much too quick and powerful. Swords met clubs, cleaving them in two, leaving the trolls defenseless and running through the weeds, into the forest with their tails between their legs.

"Quickly!" Valian yelled. "We must get back to the sphere portal, before it closes!"

The seven people ran. The little girls couldn't keep up. Valian and Sersha each grabbed a child and took flight. Together, Henry and Haley each took an arm of the distressed woman and followed. A moment later, they entered the portal. Sersha went through with her girl first, Valian and the other weeping child followed, and finally the twins with their charge. A moment later, the portal closed and they were all standing in the sacred chamber panting, shaking, and dripping wet. The queen was waiting to comfort the newcomers, with towels and hot drinks. The woman quickly moved toward her children, wrapping her arms around them, talking gently. Sarah looked around at the spectacle before her, alarm on her face. Finally, she was able to speak.

"Who are you people? Where are we?"

The queen ushered the three frightened individuals over to the soft, high back chairs.

"You're safe, Sarah," the queen said, softly. Her eyes shone with gentleness and her smile put Sarah at ease, just a little.

"How do you know my name?" Sarah asked, in a small voice.

The twins, Valian, Sersha, and the queen exchanged glances. Sersha suggested they all retire to a more comfortable place to talk. The queen agreed and they left the sacred chamber. Lilia led them all to a room where they could change into dry clothes. When everyone was ready, they went to the beautiful room with the deep crimson carpets and sunken living area. Reed came in with refreshments and then left quickly. Sersha and Valian each took a mug, added a pinch of a powdery looking substance and poured in some rainbow dew. After mixing, they handed the mugs to the two little girls, who took them apprehensively. Several minutes later, the children fell asleep, much to the dismay of their mother.

"I am sorry, but we had to sedate your girls," the queen said to Sarah.

A look of alarm came over Sarah's face, but the queen quickly reassured her they were quite all right.

"We need to tell you what has transpired and didn't wish the children to hear."

Sarah looked around at the others, who were now seated on the other sofas. Finally, with a sigh, Lilia began to explain the long course of events, which led up to the Bonner children and Sarah's arrival to Roan.

When she was finished, Sarah looked as though she'd been slapped in the face. She couldn't believe her ears or her eyes. Her emotions were rising and falling; fear, relief, and joy jumbled together. She looked at Haley and did a double take. Up until now, she hadn't had a good look at her and now seemed dumbstruck. She slowly stood up and walked over to Haley, who was unsure what was happening.

Haley studied Sarah's face. The two gazed at one another, without saying a word. Finally, Henry broke the silence.

"You see? I told you, you were dead ringers."

Haley reached up and took Sarah's hand, motioning her to sit down beside her. With a smile, Haley spoke. "I never dreamed it was possible," she said. "My living in the exact same place as you, you and I looking exactly alike . . . this is the strangest thing I have ever felt."

"I feel the same," Sarah said, shyly. "This whole story is unbelievable. It's tragic, yet I am so happy things have turned out differently than what you've told me happened in the past. I am glad to be alive and in this place, but tell me, where exactly are we? You said that this . . . Roan was a tiny little city in the trees, in a fairy world unknown to humans. Where are we now?"

"You *are* in Roan, Sarah," the queen said. "Come take a look."

Lilia guided Sarah to one of the windows. Sarah gasped at the shining city spread out all around her. She could see fairies flying around, coming and going.

"It's beautiful, but you said everything was supposed to be tiny. It doesn't look tiny. I'm not tiny nor my children. I am a bit confused."

Lilia looked at Sarah. "I understand your confusion. You are tiny and so are your beautiful daughters. We all are. When you were brought through time and space, you were changed with the rest of the party. When transporting from one time and place to another, your body automatically adjusts to suit your destination during the journey. This change is only temporary, which reminds me, Valian, we will need the dwindle drops to keep them from popping back to their original size."

Valian left the room at once and was back moments later with three small pills.

"Here, eat this," he instructed Sarah.

"What about my girls?" she asked.

"Wake them," said the queen.

Sarah and Haley went to the sleeping girls and gently shook them. They awoke, both looking into the face of their mother. As soon as they realized there were two Sarahs, they became alarmed.

"It's okay," Sarah said, softly. "It's Mama. This is Haley. Haley is a friend. She is like my twin."

The girls looked from Haley to Sarah, and back to Haley again.

"Is she your sister?" little Rose asked, in a small voice.

"No," Sarah said, laughing. "Haley is just someone who looks a lot like me, that's all."

Susan looked up and smiled at Haley and gave her a hug.

"We have two mothers."

Everyone laughed.

"Here, eat this," Sarah said, handing a pill to each of the girls.

"Why?" said Susan.

"It's medicine," Sarah said, feeling guilty for having to lie.

"Are we sick?" Rose asked.

"Well, not physically sick," Sarah answered "But you have been through quite a lot today and mama wants to make sure you don't get sick. Now, eat it up, both of you."

The two little girls did as they were instructed.

"Good girls," their mother told them.

"Now, let's get the three of you to your assigned room," Lilia suggested.

Just then, there was a knock at the door. Valian answered it and spoke quietly with a large, muscular male fairy for a moment. The fairy left and Valian went over to Lilia and whispered in her ear.

"You must excuse me," said the queen. "I have some matters to attend to. Valian, Sersha, please see to our guests," she stated, leaving the room.

The Bonner family was taken to a large room across the hall from Henry and Haley's and went inside to rest.

"We will call for you when it is time to dine," said Valian.

"Make yourselves comfortable," Sersha added, then left the family to be alone.

Valian turned to Henry and Haley. "We have trouble."

The twins followed Valian and Sersha down the corridor that led back to the sacred chamber. Once inside, they saw Lilia with several other fairies, looking at the sphere.

"What is it?" Sersha asked, walking over.

"The sphere, it's malfunctioned," Lilia answered.

"Malfunctioned?" Valian and Sersha said, together. "How is that possible?"

"Something has happened to it. I don't know what."

"Maybe it's overloaded," Henry interjected. Everyone looked at him with surprise.

"Yes," said one of the other fairies. "The sphere isn't designed to take more than one person at a time. When you returned from the past, you entered two at a time and the last to come through was three! It must not have been able to handle the pressure of so many people and short circuited or something. After all, it hasn't been used like this for centuries."

"Can it be repaired?" Lilia asked, greatly concerned.

"I think so," the fairy answered. "This happened once before that I know of, about a thousand years ago. I believe it's recorded in the archives along with the repair, however, it will take some time to fix."

"How long?" asked Sersha.

"Several months," the fairy answered, looking at Lilia.

Everyone's heart sank.

"How are we going to go back and get Zeb in time?" Henry asked in dismay.

"We won't be able to," Lilia answered, sinking into a chair.

"We won't need to," said Haley.

Everyone turned to Haley with puzzled looks. "Listen," said Haley. "We don't need to go back, Zeb is already here."

"But—" Valian began.

"Wait," Haley interrupted. "Look, we can go get him."

The room erupted in protest. Haley held up her hand, indicating silence. When everyone quieted down, she continued.

"You said it yourself," she said, looking at the others. "My finding the necklace, living in the same house as Sarah, looking exactly like her, it means something. There was a reason for it. I was meant to be here. Just like you said. I was destined to be the instrument to change these events. There is no other way. We can't wait weeks. Zeb will complete the change and we may never be able to save him. We have to do it now."

The others stood in silence. They knew she was right but didn't want to think about the task ahead. Haley cleared her throat.

"I have a plan."

For the next hour, the five sat at a table on one of the private verandas and Haley explained her idea to save Zeb.

"I hope your plan will work," Valian said, as they stood up.

"I think we have a very good chance," said the queen. "We have to try."

"I agree," Sersha added.

"Well, I'm famished," Henry spoke up, looking around at the others.

The others smiled. Henry and Haley went to their rooms to freshen up before lunch.

In her room, Haley thought about all that happened. The trip through the sphere, the swamp hag and moss trolls, then the rescue of the Bonner women. She felt good things had gone off without too much of a hitch. On the other hand, things could have been much more difficult, she was relieved. As she was changing into a fresh gown, she remembered the necklace and decided to give it back to Sarah at dinner. She would be so pleased to have it back, after all, it did rightfully belong to her. She looked on the night table next to the bed, but it wasn't there. She checked the bathroom sink. Disturbed, she searched the entire room, looking under the bed, the window ledge, and in the bathtub, but couldn't find it. She thought about where she could have left it and wondered if when the room was cleaned, maybe someone found it and put it somewhere for safe keeping. She'd ask Sersha at lunch.

A short time later, the same steward came to escort her to lunch. In the corridor, Sarah and the girls were being escorted as well. Henry, as usual, was already gone from his room and they met up with him in a different dining room. This one was much smaller and more private. Everyone was seated and the familiar chiming announced the arrival of the queen.

Lilia looked as beautiful as ever, this time in a rainbow colored gown. Her crown was one of gold, diamonds, and emeralds.

The short line of brownies bearing platters of food entered and everyone enjoyed a delicious, quiet meal together. The children were busy chatting with each other, while a small orchestra played soft music in the background.

They were delighted by the wings of the fairies and chose to sit with Haley in between them, so they could admire hers. Every so often, Haley would feel little fingers touching her and would look down to see the bright face of one of the curious children, examining her wings. Haley was also delighted.

After lunch, several female fairy guardians took Susan and Rose to a pretty outdoor flower garden on the palace grounds, complete with playground equipment. The rest of the dinner companions went to a long terrace and watched the children playing below.

Lilia explained to Sarah the latest developments involving the sphere, and Haley's plan to intercept Zeb in the present. Sarah was obviously worried about her dear husband, distressed by the fact he wasn't the same man she married. He became something she could hardly fathom. Sarah thought she probably wouldn't recognize him if she saw him. Lilia explained to Sarah, it would be best she and the girls stayed safe in Roan. Sarah immediately disagreed. She was insistent that she join the others in helping to save Zeb. Valian and Sersha strongly objected.

"That wouldn't be a good idea," Valian said to her. "I beseech you to reconsider this. You need to be here and safe, especially for your daughters."

"No." Sarah was persistent.

Haley watched her, admiring her spirit. She was headstrong and stubborn. Haley had a growing adoration and respect for her double.

"I am inclined to agree," Haley said suddenly.

Everyone looked at her.

"Let me explain," she said, suddenly getting excited. "Take a close look at us. We look alike, we talk alike. We could use her. With the two of us working together, we may have a much better chance to succeed!"

The rest of the group looked at Haley, unable to understand what she was getting at.

"With us working together, Zeb will be totally confused. He won't know which one of us is the real Sarah. We can use that to our advantage. Together we will lure him. Trick him."

"What a conspiracy!" Sersha exclaimed. "It's the most devious scheme I have ever heard of!"

Valian looked at Sersha as if she'd lost her mind. Sersha looked back at him with a beaming smile.

"I understand," she said, answering his bewildered look. "Brilliant!" she continued. "It is a most splendid notion! How did you ever think of it?" Sersha asked Haley, excitedly.

"I saw it in an old movie on TV," Haley answered, smiling.

"What's an old movie on TV?" Sarah asked, a bit perplexed.

"It's a—I'll explain later," Haley answered, wondering how to explain something as complicated as TV to a woman who lived almost two centuries ago.

"It'll still be dangerous," said Lilia. "Are you sure you really want to do this?"

"I am positive," Sarah answered. "He is my husband. It was my doing that got us into this mess. I want to do all I can to save him."

"Then it's settled," said Haley. "Here's what we'll do. We'll sneak into the realm and find out where he is. We'll let him see me. That should get him moving. Sarah will be hiding a short distance away and she'll come out, while I disappear behind a tree. We will both continue to appear and disappear just ahead of him, using the trees for cover. We'll then lead him out of the realm, where we'll have a much better chance. The further away from the evil realm the better. Valian and Sersha will be standing by, hiding somewhere, and the four of us will overpower him and fly him somewhere where it's safe. Then I don't know what we'll do. I don't know if seeing Sarah will do the trick or not. I guess, we'll just have to wait and see what happens."

The others sat and thought about it. Nobody really knew what to say at this point. They were all feeling the same way. Who knew what would happen to Zeb if they got him away from Molock's realm, or what it would take to snap Zeb out of his lethargy, if seeing Sarah would make any difference or not.

Valian spoke up, "I'll bring fairy dust and put him into a deep sleep."

Seeing the looks on the twins faces, he added, "Yes, there is such a thing as fairy dust," he said, with a smile. "I used it when we first brought Zeb to our side. It worked very well."

"Well," said Lilia. "It's the best plan on short notice. You shall go first thing in the morning. Valian, Sersha, you know where the realm is. It won't take you long to get there. With any luck, you will get Zeb away quickly and maybe by nightfall all will be well," Lilia finished, with a hopeful look.

"All right let's prepare for the journey—" Sersha began. "Oh," she said, looking at Sarah. Valian followed her gaze and realized what she was thinking. So did the twins.

Sarah looked around at each of them, wondering what was happening.

"What?" she asked, feeling a little uneasy. "You haven't changed your minds have you?"

The gentle smile Sersha gave her relief at once.

"No—it's just—you will need wings if you're going to keep up."

Sarah stood before them, excitement in her voice. "Fly? I'm going to fly? Oh, I can't wait! I have dreamed of flying ever since I was a little girl! Just like a bird. High in the sky, flying through the trees in deep valleys and forests! Oh, when do I get my wings?"

"Right now," Lilia answered, taking Sarah by the hand.

The two left the terrace with Valian close behind. Henry left the room, saying he was going to take a nap, while Haley and Sersha stayed behind.

They sat, watching the children play. They seemed so happy. Sersha remarked at how quickly they seemingly recovered from their ordeal.

"It's almost as if they've blocked it out," Haley responded.

They sat quietly for a while and then Sersha cleared her throat. Haley looked over at her. It was several moments before she spoke.

"You know, I envy you. You are the most honest and devoted human I have ever met. To come from such an unpredictable and often frightening world, yet, retain such a strong spirit with such values. You are truly an honorable example of the human race and what they could be."

Haley blushed. "Oh, I've had my moments," she said. "I'm not perfect by any means."

"I don't mean that," Sersha replied. "What I mean is, you have strength. You are able to take a bad situation and figure out a way to turn it around. You have a spirit that can lift you out of misery and despair, willpower. We on the other hand, aren't capable of those things because most of the last few thousand years in our world have been peaceful. Sure, there are outer realm's that are influenced by the evil one, but mostly they have always been contained and not part of our lives. Up until recently, we didn't know such fear and pain had no voice. Now we feel powerless, incapable of defending ourselves against something we can't see. Then you put on the necklace. It was then we felt a pull through the rift. We felt emotion so strong, it was startling. Much of it was scary, like we'd never felt before. It seemed to change us in a way. I think it brought feelings that have always been there, only lying dormant. Many may argue my opinion, but I have a strong suspicion we are more alike than we realize or will admit."

Haley sat, listening. "Do you really think so?" she asked.

Sersha nodded as she looked down at the girls playing hide and seek with the guardians.

"Wow," Haley said, softly. "Maybe there's hope for our two worlds after all."

Lilia came out onto the terrace. "How are you two doing?" she asked, standing behind Sersha.

"Oh, we're fine. Enjoying the quiet afternoon," Sersha replied.

"How's Sarah coming along?" Haley asked.

"She's adjusting," the queen answered, with a chuckle. "You should have seen her. She went through the process really well, but her flying skills will need improvement before you leave in the morning."

"Is she that bad?" Sersha asked.

"It's not that she's bad, she just hasn't quite got the knack of it yet. She wobbles so much, that she's finding it difficult to steer herself correctly. It'll come, hopefully sooner rather than later, for everyone's sake."

Moments later, a dark cloud passed overhead. The three looked up and saw Sarah wobble overhead, then land in the flower garden below. The little girl's squealed in delight, thinking Haley came to play.

"It's me, girls! It's mama! Look at my new wings!" she laughed.

Susan and Rose were shocked and weren't sure it was really Sarah.

"Look! Up there!" Sarah said, pointing to Lilia, Sersha, and Haley.

"There's Haley! Up there!" Rose shouted.

Haley waved at the girls, giggling to herself.

"They can't tell us apart," she said. "What we need, is a way they can distinguish between us."

Suddenly, she remembered the necklace and turned to ask Sersha about it.

"I don't know what could have happened to it," Sersha said, puzzled. "The cleaning staff never touches any personal items in any of the rooms. I can ask if any of them have seen it."

"Thanks," Haley said, with an uneasy feeling. "I can't figure out where it could have gone," she continued. "I can't even remember when I saw it last."

Sersha shrugged her shoulders and repeated that she would ask the cleaning staff about it.

Lilia, listening to Haley's inquiry, felt a bit unsettled by this, but didn't say anything.

The afternoon shadows grew long. Songbirds began to give way to crickets and frogs singing out their chorus at the approaching evening, far below the canopy.

Lights began to twinkle on the roads and paths below them, lamps and candles were lit in the homes wedged in the crooks of the huge trees. The guardians took the children to meet Sarah in their room, to clean up before dinner. Lilia, Sersha, and Haley stayed on the terrace, watching the sun slowly sink before them.

"Let's go for a sail!" Sersha suddenly burst out, making them jump.

"A sail?" Haley echoed.

"Well, not on a boat," Sersha answered, giggling. "We'll sail on the wind currents. It's beautiful flying in the evening, when all the homes are lit up and the night creatures come out. There are many creatures you have never seen," Sersha continued. "Lightning fairies, fire fairies, earth mother fairies, and night flower fairies. Pixies love the dark just as much as some elf and dwarf species. The mermaids are spectacular at night! You want to go?" Sersha asked, already knowing what Haley would say.

"Yes! I'd love to!" Haley exclaimed with excitement.

"You're just like me!" Sersha replied, laughing. "You love to explore just as much as I do."

"I'll sit this one out," Lilia chimed in. "Don't you two be too late! Dinner will be served in an hour or so, don't forget we have other guests to attend to!" she finished, with a knowing smile.

Lilia turned to go inside. Sersha and Haley rose in the air and took off with lightning speed. Sersha flew extremely fast, knowing all the routes, paths, and air trails by heart. Haley had a somewhat difficult time keeping up behind her.

"Slow down a bit!" she hollered.

"Sorry, I forgot. You're new here!" Sersha called out, slowing to an easier pace.

They dodged in between trees, went through gaps in the branches, and skimmed the surface of still ponds. They even flew level with a pair of owls for a short distance before they were discovered and flew off hooting through the dark. Haley was exhilarated by the scenery. The sun was almost down and she could see the stars beginning to pop out in the sky. Sersha took her to the most wonderful spots. They visited waterfalls that shimmered and sparkled in a florescent flowing display and watched the animals come to the water's edge. Small timid deer came to drink and a mama raccoon with four little babies came to fish. They left the waterfall and flew to a hollow that contained many large flower covered mounds. Perching at the top of a willow tree, they waited. Haley began to ask what they were waiting for, but Sersha whispered.

"Shh, just wait."

Haley watched patiently, wondering what would happen. The moon came out from behind a patch of clouds overhead. At that moment, hundreds of tiny bright bugs, or so Haley thought, came flying out in a glowing, flashing stream into the air. They scattered and the sky was filled with a thousand blinking lights. Haley held her breath. The sight was wondrous.

"Fireflies?" she whispered, excitedly.

"No, they're not fireflies," Sersha explained softly. "Those are the lightning fairies I told you about. They don't make lightning; we just call them that because they flash like lightning."

It was a glorious display. A couple of the tiny fairies flew close enough for Haley to get a good look. She and Sersha were well hidden, one flew almost right up to her. She could have reached out and grabbed it if she wanted to. It was spectacular. It had coal black hair, pointed ears and nose, and was clothed in a creamy white short skirt. On its feet were green pointed little boots. As it hovered there for a moment, its entire body flashed a bright florescent green color. Its tiny wings were only illuminated at the edges, so it looked like the entire inside of the wing was invisible. The fairy zipped off through the trees.

"Oh my God," Haley whispered.

"Aren't they something?" Sersha whispered back.

"Marvelous. What do they do?" she asked.

"Watch," said Sersha.

Moments later, dust began to softly shower down little glittering particles. They fell through the air like snowflakes picked up by soft air currents then floated to the ground in every direction.

"What is it?" Haley whispered.

"They're seeds. These fairies pollinate the forests and meadows with all types of plants and flowers. They only come out once a month. What happens is, the fire fairies go through and remove all the brush and undergrowth with fire. They burn it off before the lightning fairies come out, so the seeds will grow."

"I wish I could have seen the fire fairies," Haley whispered.

"They came about a week ago and cleaned out this area. The lightning fairies will cover this entire realm within a week or so and then go back into their mounds to prepare seed for next month."

"Wow . . ." was all Haley could say.

"By tomorrow morning, the seedlings will have already come up and there will be a fresh carpet of flowers and grasses within a couple days," Sersha finished.

Looking up at the moon, Sersha suddenly whispered, "Oh my goodness, look at the time. We're going to be late for dinner!"

They quickly jumped out of the willow, dived toward the ground, and swooped up into the sky, flying back to the palace. When they arrived, they found Queen Lilia, Henry, Prince Valian, and the Bonners already sitting down to eat. Lilia gave Sersha a scolding look but didn't say anything. Sersha apologized for their being late and they quickly took their seats. Haley sat in the only other open seat, next to Valian. He looked at her with his pale blue eyes and winked. She turned her head to her plate, blushing. Dinner that evening was especially quiet. Everyone's thoughts were on the next day's events. The chimes rang out signaling the close of mealtime. Sarah cleared her throat, then announced to her daughters that they would be going shopping with the guardians in the morning. This excited Susan and Rose. They had never been shopping before.

"Will we really get to go inside a store?" Rose asked.

"Yes," Sarah answered. "The queen has graciously offered to let each of you pick out one thing to buy, so take a good look at everything and choose carefully, okay?"

What was really going through her mind was, if they were going to ask her if she was going, too. No sooner had she thought it, Rose asked it.

"You're coming too, right?" she asked.

"No, Sersha, Valian, Henry, and Haley are going to take me on a little shopping trip of my own," she answered.

She was telling the truth, she would kind of be shopping for her husband. She was, however, stretching the truth and it disturbed her. Everyone around her could feel her grief at having to fib, but it couldn't be helped. They couldn't possibly tell the children anything about Zeb. They wouldn't understand any of what happened, it would worry them unnecessarily.

"Come on, it's time for bed," Sarah said, picking up Susan, giving her a hug. Rose took hold of Sarah's wing.

"When will we get wings?" she asked.

Everyone smiled.

"One of these days, if you're very good, maybe you'll get wings," Sarah answered, chuckling.

Several guardians entered the room and escorted the Bonners out. The rest of the group adjourned to a comfortable little nook that overlooked the city. A nice fire was going in the fireplace.

Reed came in with four steaming mugs.

"This is an Ember potion," said Lilia. Before the twins could ask, she continued, "It is filled with the essence of the ruby. As you have noticed by now, the gemstones in our world are pure. The property of the ruby is one of strength and courage. It is cleansing and radiates a warm spirit. It is not a magic stone; it merely enhances the qualities which are already there. Think of it as the heart of the universe working in unison with part of itself. You." The twins looked at each other and back at the queen. Lilia continued, "You are part of the universe. Everything here is related in one form or another. Each serves its purpose. Working together with the other parts, there is harmony, oneness for all who dwell here, including you."

Henry and Haley nodded their heads in understanding.

"I can feel it," said Haley.

Henry nodded again in agreement.

"The potion will help you. It will enhance your strength and endurance. It will help you to draw on the qualities within you, helping your actions become more effective."

"Cool!" Henry said, sipping his drink.

"What about some for Sarah?" Haley wondered, aloud.

"Her mug has been delivered to her room," answered the queen.

Haley let out a sigh. They sat and sipped for a while. The hot potion had a warming effect. The twins were feeling a bit strange. It was as if someone threw an electric blanket over them. It felt good.

Haley felt as if she were wide awake and wanted to fly off into the night, exploring with Sersha again.

"Do you want to go sailing again?" she asked Sersha.

Sersha looked over at her and smiled.

"You won't want to in a few minutes," she replied. "Your energy is just the first reaction to the potion. It will go away shortly and you will want to sleep."

Sure enough, a couple minutes later, Haley was yawning along with the rest of them. Several guardians came in to help them to their rooms. Soon, the four of them were off in slumber land, dreaming of flying and the wonders of the universe.

Chapter 11

THE HUNT FOR ZEB

The next morning came too soon. Nobody wanted to get out of bed, except of course, the queen and the children. The ember potion put everyone into a deep, restful sleep. The stewards came to the door to wake up the twins, Valian, Sersha, and Sarah. Everyone met in the great hall for breakfast.

The children were bright eyed and excited about their shopping trip. They were antsy and had a hard time sitting still during the meal. Chimes rang out then Sarah kissed her girls goodbye, watching as two beautiful fairies adorned in silver gowns ushered them out onto the terrace. A light rain was falling and the guardians fastened large, light-weight umbrellas to their sashes. Lifting the children into their arms, they flew off, disappearing behind the palace.

Lilia looked at the five people in the party. She went up to each one and kissed them on the forehead and repeated, "Go with speed and take care. May the celestial spirits be on your wings."

She stood in the doorway as the band of would be rescuers took to the air, bidding them all farewell. She watched them anxiously until they became specks in the gray sky.

The five maintained a good pace. Everyone was soaked the minute they took off. Fortunately, the rain was warm.

They passed over large fields and meadows. Many ponds and coves appeared below them as they crossed vast forests and woods. After four hours of non-stop flight, the group landed by a stream in a densely covered hollow. It was small but fairly dry and thick with trees. The branches hung low and well away from their trunks, creating a nice dry spot. The ground was covered in soft pine needles.

Everyone sat down to rest. Valian opened a small pack he had secured to his belt, pulling out a container of rainbow dew and some strange looking fruit. It was grayish brown and shaped like a small octopus with tentacles sticking out all over. He handed it out to all members of the party.

"Only eat the arms," he said, biting off one with a crunch.

Everyone followed suit. It tasted sweet and was quite juicy.

"What is this?" Henry asked, finishing his.

"It's called Vimsom. It replenishes the body with natural minerals and water."

"It's very refreshing," said Haley. She wasn't overly hungry, eating only one of the arms and putting the rest into her little pack for later.

"I feel like I've eaten a full meal," said Henry, patting his stomach.

"It's not really a fruit but a vegetable," Sersha said, nibbling on an arm.

Sarah sat in silence, not really eating much. Her thoughts and her heart were divided between her children and husband.

Haley sat enjoying the soft patter of the rain and the soothing sound of the stream.

After thirty minutes of rest, Valian stood up and rearranged his bow and arrow. "Let's get moving," he said, facing the north.

They took to the air. Sarah was doing much better with her flying and was able to take off without wobbling now.

"Where are we?" Henry called out.

"We just left the Woodland realm and are now in Spicewood realm," Valian yelled. "Another hour or so, we'll be at the border of Spicewood and the Cimmerian realm where Molock dwells."

They flew on quietly. The skies grew darker and the forests became dim. The closer they got to the evil realm, the more dreary and forlorn their surroundings became. Everyone could feel the chill sinking into their bones and any cheer or joy they felt grew fainter with each passing mile. The party landed before the border separating the two realms.

"We must use extreme caution," Valian warned, in a low voice. "If you let it, this realm will rob you of all that is good. Keep happy thoughts forward in your minds. This will protect you and may be the only thing that keeps us hanging on. Stay focused."

Everyone nodded, but feelings of sorrow and despair were already edging their way in, trying to invade their minds.

"We can do this," Valian added. "We are strong. We will be victorious."

He didn't know it, but those few words perked up their spirits, they put their hands together.

"We're ready," Henry said, with an air of determination.

They quietly crossed the border, flying slowly and in single file. The surroundings were dark, desolate. It was like dusk. Large blankets of fog hung in what were once trees, which now stood stark and leafless. It was as if a fire came through and stripped them of every bit of life.

After about an hour, the group landed and began to navigate on foot. The forest was too dense to fly through, they couldn't chance going over the tree line in case they were spotted.

They slowly climbed their way over fallen trees and branches. With each step, fear and despair piqued at their minds. It took everyone's strength to continue on. Every once in a while they would join hands, which cheered them up somewhat. It took much longer than they expected to get through the unearthly place.

Many times, they felt they were being watched. Valian finally spotted a break in the forest up ahead, which made everyone pick up the pace. As they were coming out, Sarah let out a cry. Everyone turned and saw her wing was caught in a dead shrub, covered in thorns. Valian and Sersha hurried back and carefully plucked away each thorn. Her wing was slightly torn.

"Oh dear," she whimpered. "It's okay," Valian said quickly.

"Will I be able to fly?" she asked.

"You'll be able to fly, but I don't know how straight," he answered. "Don't worry, I'll be close by. I won't let anything happen to you," he said, with a troubled smile. "Come on, I feel we're getting close. Haley, you and Sarah will have to go on ahead without us. We will be right behind you, but out of sight."

Valian and Sersha's swords were out and ready. Haley and Sarah split up but kept each other in sight. They used the trunks of the decaying trees as cover. First, one would go forward to the next tree and hide, then the other would do the same. For several miles, the two carefully made their way forward, holding their breath, searching the area ahead for any sign of trouble.

They crossed a muddy swamp, surrounded by thick patches of tall weeds. Their long blades cut at their arms. Flies and bugs were everywhere, buzzing around their faces and biting their exposed flesh. They emerged from the swamp as quickly as they could. Up ahead, a bad smell burned the insides of their noses. A bog came into view, covered in bubbling pools of muck. Great plumes of fire burst through the massive black ooze. It was putrid and stagnant smelling like rotting, decomposing flesh and foliage.

It gave Haley and Sarah a horrid feeling. They kept looking back to find each other, making sure the rest of the party was still behind them.

Every so often they came across a jagged, black stone sticking out of the ground. Some were extremely large, blocking their way, so they had to go around. Others were small and barely visible.

Waves of panic and fear began to permeate Haley's thoughts. She kept looking back to make sure the rest of the group was still there. *Valian must be able to read people's minds,* she thought. Every time she started feeling bad or scared and glanced behind to see if they were back there, Valian's head would poke out, making her feel better. She wondered if Sarah was going through the same thing.

Up ahead, she spotted Sarah waiting for her to pass. Haley moved on. When she caught up with Sarah, she stopped beside her.

"Are you all right?" she whispered.

Sarah stood trembling behind a massive fallen tree.

"I'm okay, but I don't know how much more of this I can stand," she whispered. Tears began to roll down her cheeks. "I feel so much despair and fear. I just want to weep and weep."

Haley put her arms around Sarah, they hugged each other for a moment. She looked into Sarah's eyes. A tiny spark of hope began to grow in them. Both women were amazed at the strength they got from each other. They were beginning to feel a power was building between them and smiled at each other. Sarah wiped her eyes.

"That was amazing," she whispered.

"You said it sister," Haley whispered back.

"Sister," repeated Sarah, with a huge smile.

"Okay?" Haley asked.

Sarah nodded.

"I'm going on ahead," Haley said, patting Sarah on the shoulder. "Look back for the others when it starts getting to you. That helps."

Sarah looked back and watched as Valian poked his head out from behind a tree. Reassured, she turned back, watching Haley disappear behind a group of tall thistle bushes.

Haley spotted a worn path, winding its way around a huge black boulder the size of four or five rooms put together. It stood at least twenty feet tall and came to a sharp, jagged point at the top. Her heart began to beat faster. She could almost feel an evil power emitting from it.

I should feel afraid, she thought to herself, *but I don't.* It felt like she was walking with a protective field around her. She made her way around the boulder and stopped on the other side. Haley was standing at the base of a huge dead mountain. She was taken aback at the sight. She couldn't believe she didn't see it before. A cave stood before her with its large gaping mouth like a giant ancient beast. Haley stood holding her breath, wondering if she would have to go inside. She waited for several minutes. When nothing happened, she took a deep breath and started for the entrance. She thought about waiting for Sarah to show up, but she felt she was running out of time. Slowly, she crept into the cave. It was dark inside, but a soft red glow illuminated doorways to several passages. She wondered which one to take or if this was really a good idea to in go alone. Haley remembered thinking it was her destiny and chose the center door. The passage was long and winding, she felt like she was descending. The passage was a little brighter here, lit up by a dark red substance on the lower half of the walls. The passage got wider the further down she went. Putrid smells burned her nostrils and she found it more difficult to breathe. It was also getting warmer, like a humid day.

Haley emerged from the passage into a large cavern, filled with enormous stalagmites and stalactites, giving off a florescent white and green glow. In the center, was another bubbling pool of black sludge-like muck. The room was eerily absent of life. She stood listening, only able to hear the *glug! glug!* noise of the pool and a faint clinking sound. Haley spotted another doorway and proceeded to the entrance. Again, she stopped to listen. The clinking sound was coming from the right. She didn't walk far before the passage ended in a small alcove with another opening to the right. Haley stopped dead in her tracks. The floor was covered in bones, bleached white and lying in piles around the room, filling her with fear and dread. She tried to pull herself together, thinking about Henry, Sersha, and Sarah. She imagined her parents, the queen, and the beautiful joyous city in the trees.

Visions of Valian's kind and rugged face smiling at her gave her courage. She tiptoed through the bones, to the archway on the right. Summoning all her strength, with her back to the wall, she edged toward the sound. It grew louder and louder as she inched her way forward. She peeked through the opening and stifled a scream. There, chained to the walls, were at least twenty fairies.

They looked horrendous. They barely resembled fairies anymore. They were scarcely alive, their heads drooped forward in silence. Most of them were skeletons covered in taut, pulled back skin. Every few seconds, a fairy would quiver, making the chains binding it clink against the stone wall. Haley was sickened and appalled, even more, she was outraged.

"Who in God's creation could do something like this?

Even think of something like this?!" she said aloud.

Haley stormed into the room and spotted a key hanging on a hook, just out of the fairies' reach, like some torturous reminder of their captivity. She began unlocking the chains that bound them. Haley worked quickly to help each fairy to the floor. They were so weak. She felt such compassion and tenderness for them. Freeing each one, her heart broke; looking at the raw stumps on their backs where their beautiful wings once grew. She became angrier with each passing minute. After they were all free, Haley looked at them slumped on the floor. Her mind raced, thinking about what to do next. Then she remembered the vimsom in her pack. She pulled it out with trembling hands, broke off pieces, and began to feed each of them. The fairies had great difficulty holding up their heads, let alone chewing. However, the effects were apparent almost immediately. Slowly, they began to look up. The light in their eyes began to appear, hope was flooding the room. Some were trying to get up, but they were still too weak. One of the fairies opened her mouth to speak, but Haley quickly quieted her and whispered, "Don't speak. Sit quietly and gather your strength." *I'll get you out of here somehow,* she thought to herself.

Suddenly, several of the fairies bent over, as if in pain. They were having difficulty breathing and Haley began to panic. Running over to one of the fairies, she saw what was happening. Wings began to pop out, like blooming flowers. Surprised, she went to check the others. In all, ten of the fairies got their wings back. Haley began to get excited, and joy started flooding back into her heart. Those who hadn't gotten their wings back began to stand up, gaining strength.

After everyone was on their feet, Haley whispered, "We have to get you out of here now. Is everyone ready to move?"

They all nodded and she motioned them to the door. She was still angry and felt prepared for anything. Quickly, she peeked out of the opening. The coast was clear and they followed her down the passage, through the bone room and up into the large cavern. All was quiet—too quiet. Haley thought she was unusually lucky so far. It made her suspicious and she hurried them along even faster. The fairies were now much stronger, however, they seemed confused. Haley knew from the stories she'd heard, how the evil Molock tortured the minds of its victims, confusing them while sucking all their hope and joy from them. She wondered if the fairies would be able to function because of the vimsom she gave them. Well, they were functioning and she put her questions aside for now. The group quickly moved up the long corridor, toward the cave entrance. She moved them along faster now and actually took flight. The others followed her example, helping the wingless fairies along. Finally, the mouth of the cave loomed into view. The dark sky outside was too bright for the fairies. They gathered inside the entrance, shielding their eyes until they became accustomed to the light.

Haley looked all around but didn't see anyone. Sarah wasn't there. None of the rest of the party was there either. It was silent, which made her uneasy.

As the fairies began to take their hands away from their eyes, a long loud scream pierced the air. Off in the distance, they heard the faint sounds of swords clashing and many voices in battle. Haley began to run. Down the path, around the black boulder, and through the tall brush she raced with her heart pounding in her chest. Fear crept back in, she was terrified of what was happening up ahead. Several fairies flew over her head in that direction then she suddenly remembered she had wings too. They flew like the wind over the bubbling pools and the swamp. Over the dead forest, Haley came to a halt in mid-air.

Looking on in horror, she spied below, an army of ferocious looking creatures. Valian, Sersha, and Henry were desperately fighting to keep from being overtaken. The creatures surrounded them, carrying big heavy spiked clubs. The sound of clashing metal rang out through the dried up glen. Limbs were flying and the sound of hoarse screams filled the air. Haley and the rest of the fairies that could fly dove down toward the battle. One of the horrible creatures looked up and cried, "Incoming!"

Most of the band scattered in every direction. The three fighting one on one with Valian, Sersha, and Henry turned to flee and were cut down by Valian and Sersha's shining swords. Henry, using the bow and arrow, shot the last creature standing. Everyone stood there breathing hard and fast, bent over trying to catch their breath.

Haley looked down upon the corpses strewn about. They were the most horrible, scariest looking creatures she had ever seen. They had the heads of large pigs with long slimy snouts, huge tusks two inches thick curling up into sharp points, and small beady eyes. All the creatures were clad in various types of armor and their large clubs were spiked. Merely glancing at them gave her the creeps. She ran over to Henry and hugged him hard. Visions of her dream passed through her mind. He let out a cry of pain.

"What is it?" she asked, frantically.

"My arm, it hurts," he moaned.

Valian and Sersha ran to the rescued fairies with open arms, hugging and patting them on the back. It was a joyous reunion, but a short lived one.

"Valian!" Haley called.

Valian came over and Haley showed him Henry's arm. "It looks like it may be broken," he said. "Don't worry, it will heal up in a few minutes." Valian called out to the others. "We need to get out of this realm quickly before they regroup and bring back reinforcements!"

"Where's Sarah?" Haley called out, looking around.

Everyone stopped and turned their heads, looking for her. Sarah was nowhere in sight.

"She was with us when we were first ambushed!" Sersha yelled.

Everyone fanned out to search when a long loud scream pierced the air. It came from just inside the dead forest. Everyone flew to the edge of the forest, searching. They took different directions but had to walk slowly because of the denseness of the woods. They trampled through the trees, calling out Sarah's name.

Henry and Haley paired up. At the top of a steep gully, with dread, they spotted Sarah lying at the bottom with a man lying across her. She appeared unconscious, as did the man.

Haley quickly called out to the others and descended to the bottom. Henry rolled the man off of Sarah with his good arm. She didn't look injured, but the man was cut up.

He had black, long shaggy hair and a long, matted beard. His eyes were closed, but he was twitching. Every once in a while he would convulse then lie still. The others arrived one by one, gathering around them. "It's Zeb," Sersha whispered, softly.

Zeb twitched again.

"He's going through the change," Valian added.

"Look! Look what he's got around his neck!" said Sarah, in horror.

She pulled open Zeb's tattered shirt, pulling out a silver chain. On the end hung a black stone about the size of a large grape. In disgust, Valian yanked it from Zeb's neck, then threw it on the ground and smote it with his sword.

"It's obsidian," he said, in disgust.

At that moment, a long terrifying screech echoed through the forest. A continuous howling followed right after, like a dog had been injured and ran yelping with its tail between its legs. Everyone looked at each other.

"Come," Valian said again. "We need to get out of this realm NOW!"

Valian and Sersha picked up Zeb and carried him to the edge of the dead forest. Haley and one of the other fairies took Sarah, while the others helped the wingless ones out. At the border, they took flight in the nick of time. Not more than a few hundred yards away, another band of boar soldiers gathered, ready to do battle again. As the fortunately triumphant group flew over the band, they were screamed and jeered at as clubs were thrown into the air in unsuccessful attempts to pick them off. Soon the fairies were miles away and flying toward safer realms.

Chapter Twelve
THE RETURN JOURNEY

Haley was amazed. *We pulled it off,* she thought, as they flew over a deep gorge. Everyone was all right, except for Henry, of course. She was especially thrilled they were able to find the captives and save them from certain death. Haley, Sersha, and Valian flew in the front, while Henry fell back with the others. It was a little slower going for the rescued fairies, as they were still weak from their ordeal. The group flew about forty miles or so, before Henry called out for a pit stop. They landed and he quickly examined his arm. He moved it up and down, around and around.

"It's healed!" he exclaimed, pleased.

They were safe inside the Woodland realm and landed in a large poppy field. The colors were brilliant and dripping with rain. A small group of peacocks took refuge under a few chestnut trees there.

Everyone found a fairly dry spot to sit, the weak and injured were tended to. Valian pulled out the rest of the vimsom he had and passed it around. Henry surprised everyone when he pulled cookies, small cakes, and several sandwiches out of his pack.

Haley smiled and rolled her eyes. *Always thinking with his stomach,* she thought as he handed the goodies to Sersha to pass out.

She looked down at her brother, like a parent tending to a sick child.

"You scared me back there," she said, in a motherly tone.

"I scared myself," he replied, his word's muffled by a mouthful of cookie.

She shook her head and squatted down beside him, examining his arm.

Valian came over and sat next to Henry. He looked over at Haley in amazement.

"How did you ever get them out of there?"

Haley relived the scene. Valian shook his head in disbelief. Sersha joined them and couldn't believe her ears. When Haley finished, she looked around at the others.

"What happened to you guys? I looked behind me right before I went into the cave and didn't see anyone."

All three of them began talking at once. Haley held up her hand. "One at a time, please."

Valian began to tell the story, when Sarah, who was sitting under a tree by herself, called out. Valian, Sersha, and Haley walked over, while the others looked on. Zeb was convulsing again, this time for a much longer period.

"What's happening to him?" she asked, looking up at Valian with fear, feeling helpless.

"He is going through the change," Valian answered, looking down at the unconscious Zeb. "I hope we aren't too late."

"What change?" she asked.

Valian explained what human's go through, after being in the fairy world for so long. How they leave their mortality behind and become immortal.

Sarah looked down at her husband and wondered what would happen when he woke up. Would he be his old self again, or would he remain the evil thing he had become? What would happen to her and the girls if he were immortal and they were not? Would she grow old before his eyes and depart from this life, leaving him behind and alone for all eternity? A thousand questions ran through her mind.

Valian could see what she was going through.

"It'll be all right," he said, reassuringly. "All your questions will be answered soon. Zeb has a good heart. I'm sure he'll pull through and be the same Zeb you knew a few days ago."

"Desperation and despair are powerful tools when under an evil influence. Molock knew this when he ensnared Zeb. He took advantage of your husband's situation and upon their meeting, used the obsidian stone to control him."

Sarah didn't understand. Tears rolled down her cheeks. "I love him so," she said, weeping softly.

"I know you do," Valian replied. "Your love is what will pull him through. You need to stay strong for his sake, as well as your own and that of your children."

She looked up and nodded. "I will," she said, with determination. She put on a happy face, but inside she was scared.

The group sat for another half hour or so, resting and eating. The wingless fairies were getting stronger, but still looked like skeletons.

Valian, Sersha, and Haley moved away from the others for a moment.

"It will take much time and council to help them," Valian said, nodding toward the fairies. "I don't know how they survived for this long."

"Well, there's power in numbers," said Sersha, looking over at the pitiful group. Suddenly, a realization dawned on her face. "Valian," she said, taking him by the arm. "Look at them. Look at them closely."

He looked at each one, studying them. Moments later he began to smile.

"What?" Haley asked, looking at the both of them.

"Look at them," Valian answered.

Haley looked at each fairy but couldn't see what they were seeing.

"Each fairy is still wearing their given gems!" Valian exclaimed.

"Given gems?" Haley repeated.

"Yes!" Sersha answered. "When we are born, each fairy is given a jewel, after being taken before the queen. Each gem represents certain qualities. All these fairies are still wearing them. Molock obviously didn't see them as a threat. The only stone he is interested in is obsidian."

"Look," Valian interrupted. "Half of these fairies are bearing diamonds. Diamonds symbolize the lifeblood of the earth. They are made from the tears of the night, weeping for the lack of light. And look, several are wearing rubies, which represent courage and the fiery spirit. They are the heart of the world. And the rest of them, they all have bands of gold around their necks. Gold is light. It enhances intelligence and understanding. It is created when sunbeams hit the obsidian rock.

Obsidian can't absorb the sun because of its corruptive nature. This is very curious," Valian said, puzzled.

"What is?" Sersha asked, wondering what Valian was getting at.

"If Molock doesn't perceive the properties of the gemstones that could lead to its undoing."

"How?" she asked.

"I'll explain later," he answered. "It's time we got underway."

Sersha nodded, and the three gathered everyone together.

They traveled most of the day, stopping every once in a while, whenever Zeb began convulsing again. By the time they reached the outskirts, most of the party was exhausted. Valian and Sersha decided they would need to stop for the night and set off in the direction of Hilda's place.

They arrived just before nightfall. Hilda greeted them at the door, as if she were expecting them.

"Broom Hilda!" the twins called out to her.

Hilda gave them a huge grin and rolled her eyes. After many hugs, Hilda directed the fairies and the members of the rescue party to their bedrooms for a long overdue bath then left to busy herself in the kitchen. Henry and Haley did a double-take when they entered the cottage. When they last visited, there were only three or four bedrooms. Now there were enough rooms for everyone. When they entered the living area twenty minutes later, they were stunned to see a huge room with enough pillows and sofas to go around. The kitchen was massive as well.

Hilda, seeing the puzzled looks on their faces, explained she felt like doing a little redecorating.

"You mean, you can just change the size of your home at will? Henry asked.

"Of course," Hilda answered. "Did you forget where you are? she asked.

Everyone within earshot laughed. The recuperating fairies settled down onto the comfortable sofas, chairs, and pillows after cleaning up, relaxing before dinner. Haley went up to check on Sarah and Zeb.

Zeb was still unconscious and convulsing at regular intervals.

Sersha came in a few minutes later. "It won't be long now," she said. "The change is becoming more rapid."

Just then they heard a soft gong-like sound.

"That's the doorbell," said Sersha, and left the room. Moments later, she reappeared with three guardian scouts. After introductions, Sersha announced that two of them would remain by Zeb's side until the change was complete. The third would be leaving shortly to fly to the palace and inform the queen of their safe return.

After the guardian scouts were seated and comfortable, Haley took Sarah by the arm.

"Why don't you come downstairs and have something to eat. Hilda is cooking up a feast."

Sarah looked down at her husband with apprehension. "It'll be all right," Haley said. "He's in good hands. There's nothing you can do now except wait it out."

Sarah reluctantly agreed, following Haley down the stairs. Sarah walked around the rooms in awe. She wasn't used to this kind of furniture and décor. She was fascinated, loving each thing she looked at. She felt rather shy and out of place around these strange and wondrous creatures. However, she took to Hilda like a daughter to a mother. She busied herself in the kitchen, helping where she could. Hilda took Sarah under her wing, making her feel at home. Sarah watched in awe as Hilda told the table to set itself and marveled when the dishes came out of their cupboards upon her command.

A half an hour later, as they were just sitting down to eat, another gong sounded at the door.

"I'll get that," Valian said, leaving the room.

Large platters and bowls were passed around, heaping spoonfuls of steaming food were piled high onto the plates. Henry had an extra-large plate set before him. He was in hog heaven.

Valian came in, followed by a long line of guardians, who walked into the large kitchen one by one, standing behind each fairy in the party, silently at attention. The fairies acted like they weren't there, as they were engrossed in the feast which lay before them.

Hilda cleared her voice and got everyone's attention. She looked at each of her guests and finally spoke, her eyes brimming with tears.

"We can be truly thankful for the safe return of those in peril. Let us rejoice and be glad, especially for Henry and Haley. Without their help, this celebration would not have been possible. A toast," she said, lifting her goblet.

Everyone raised their goblets and toasted the victory.

"Let's eat," Henry said, after the clink of everyone's drink.

The whole group dug in. Sersha came down and joined them, they had a wonderful dinner. The rescue party did most of the talking, reliving the day's events while the fairies were silent and occupied with eating.

When the meal was finished, the guardians escorted their charges up to the bedrooms and stood watch outside their doors. Sarah went up to join Zeb.

The twins, Sersha, Valian, and Hilda retired to the living area and started a fire. They discussed in greater detail what happened. Hilda sat there with her mouth open half the time, nodding in all the right places. When they were finished, she shook her head in amazement.

"Jumping jellybeans!" she exclaimed. "That is the most horrifying and exciting story I have heard in a thousand years! You are heroes! The four of you! I wouldn't be surprised if they make up songs about you. Your feats will be written in the archives."

The four smiled.

"Well, I'm beat," Henry said, yawning.

"Me too," Haley agreed.

They decided to call it a night and everyone went to bed. Hilda told the dishes to wash themselves and went to her own room downstairs.

The next morning Haley woke up to the familiar sound of hundreds of birds. She smiled to herself, remembering yesterday. She showered, dressed, and went downstairs.

Hilda closed her shop for the day so she could stay home and bake. When Haley entered the kitchen, Hilda informed her of a celebration being planned for that evening.

"The whole of Roan will be there! It will be declared a holiday. There will be dancing, singing, and feasting!"

Hilda seemed truly excited about it.

Haley was pleased, but she felt she and Henry were being given too much honor and esteem. She didn't do anything more than anybody else would have done in the same situation. *I guess I'm just not used to being in the spotlight,* she thought to herself.

Haley didn't fully realize what she accomplished. Due to her humanity, she grew up being able to rationalize and learn the abilities of deductive reasoning, as well as problem solving. She hadn't grasped the fact that fairies didn't have those skills. This was the reason they hadn't been able to find their own solutions. She thought about it while she helped Hilda mix up a batch of cookies.

"Vanilla, please," Hilda spoke to the vanilla bottle. "One teaspoon."

Haley thought about yesterday's events, something Valian said came to mind. When he found the fairies were wearing their given gems, he said the gems may lead to Molock's undoing. She thought about the meaning of those words. Not only wondering *how* it would lead to Molock's undoing, but also the fact that Valian was pondering an idea, a plan. He was contemplating, which was something Haley was led to believe fairies weren't capable of doing. Was Valian *learning?* Was he learning from *her?* Was she giving something to *him? Teaching* him?

The thought was appealing. She played out scenarios in her mind as she stirred.

"Egg's please . . . four," Hilda commanded. Four eggs came flying out of cold storage, cracked themselves over the bowl, and the shells deposited themselves into the trash. "The trash is full. Goodbye, trash," Hilda said.

Haley watched as the trash magically disappeared.

"You're awfully quiet this morning. What's on your mind?" Hilda asked, watching Haley.

"Oh, I was just thinking about yesterday," she answered.

"Yes, it was quite a day for all of you."

"Are the fairies still asleep?" Haley asked.

"No, the guardians took them to the infirmary at the palace."

"Infirmary? You have an infirmary? I don't understand. I thought that everyone here was able to heal themselves," Haley said, confused.

"Not in *every* way," Hilda replied. "The fairies that went to the infirmary are able to heal themselves physically, but they need more than physical help. They need mental and spiritual healing. They must be closely monitored and the physicians will administer to them, for their sense and reason. The doctors will apply guidance, counsel, and instruction for as long as it takes."

"So, it's a sort of psychiatric hospital?" Haley asked.

"Yes, that's it, exactly," Hilda replied.

"So everyone can heal themselves physically but not mentally."

"No, we also have several hospitals for physical injuries."

Haley looked at Hilda, she was confused. Hilda stopped what she was doing and faced Haley.

"Only the Manwan race has the healing gene as far as we know. None of the other fairy cultures have that ability, nor do any of the other creatures that live here, that we know of. Oh, they can use potions and elixirs, incantations, and magic, but they cannot heal themselves the way Manwans can."

Haley was silent. Hilda began mixing again and telling various ingredients to add themselves.

"What about Zeb and Sarah? Are they gone too?" she asked.

"Yes. Valian, Sersha, and Henry took them to the infirmary just before sunrise. They wanted to give Zeb and Sarah some privacy as well as therapy. Zeb has caused a lot of heartache. The families of the captives have been deeply affected. I don't believe any of them bear ill will toward him, but their hearts have been wounded."

Haley shook her head. "But this is a place of peace and harmony."

"That is true, but we have feelings and emotions, too. While not quite as intense as those of humans, we are not perfect nor immune to anger and hurt. We choose to try not to harbor such things. They pollute and corrupt, defiling nature's way. Those that reside in Roan practice things which keep us clean and pure. That which is immoral does not easily influence us. Sadly, other realms aren't so fortunate."

They worked on in silence. Haley had much to ponder. She was continually surprised by the way of life here. She learned something new every day about the fairies and their way of living and thinking. She spent the next several hours helping Hilda mix and bake. They made cookies, cakes, and pastries of many varieties, enjoying one another's company, laughing and joking most of the morning.

Henry arrived, of course, just before lunch. He was alone and Haley was impressed he was able to navigate the route by himself.

"They let me go alone, because it was still light out," he confessed. "Sersha and Valian will come to get us later on tonight. There's going to be a celebration in our honor after dark!" he said, excitedly.

Haley smiled at him. She could understand his excitement and felt like that herself, yet she didn't see what the big deal was. *We accomplished our mission together. Everyone played a part,* she thought. She wished to convey that message to the queen before the celebration started.

They sat down to a quiet lunch, the three of them. Henry had fun telling the dishes to wash themselves and telling the lamps and candles to light on their own.

"This is *so* cool!" he said, enthusiastically.

They settled down in front of the fireplace. Hilda told the wood to light and threw a handful of dust into the flames. The flickering light began to turn colors. Not just the usual reds and yellows but silver, gold, purple, and pink then colorful bursts of glitter began to pop in the flames like fireworks on the fourth of July. The smoke plumes reflected the same colors and if one had been outside, they would have seen their brilliance rise from the chimney. Suddenly, the fire began to crackle loudly and the twins looked on in wonder. The flames began to dance across the inside of the hearth. They looked closely and could see tiny little heads, arms, and legs dancing around the burning logs. Haley began to laugh with delight as the fire joined hands and danced together. Some did a jig while others were doing the tango.

"What are they?!" Henry exclaimed, looking on in awe and amusement.

"They are a type of flame fairy," Hilda said, delighting in their expressions.

"Like the flame fairies that clean up the leaf litter and dead foliage?" Haley asked.

"What are you talking about, Haley?" Henry asked.

"Yes," Hilda replied. "They're cousins."

Haley explained her sailing trip with Sersha to Henry, telling him about the creatures they had seen.

"Holy Toledo!" he exclaimed. "Wish I could have been there!"

"You will," Haley answered. "Maybe Sersha will take us on another excursion soon."

"A good share of those creatures will be at the celebration tonight," Hilda piped in. "A good deal *more* will be there, but you will have to look close to see them. Some can disappear before your eyes and some can change their form. There are creatures that can turn themselves into plants and make themselves appear as fairies," Hilda continued. "They can't stay that way though."

The twins looked at each other, full of expectation. They could hardly wait until dark. Henry suggested they leave for the celebration without Sersha and Valian.

"No!" Hilda interrupted, with a stern look. "It's too dangerous. There are things out there that will eat other creatures, including *you*. Besides, you don't know where it's being held."

"It's not going to be at the palace?" Haley asked.

"No, it will be held in a special place in the outskirts," Hilda answered.

"Oh cool," said Henry. "I like the outskirts."

"It's not on this side of the city though," Hilda added, trying to dispel the idea from his mind.

"Creatures that eat other creatures?" Haley asked, shocked.

"Well, it's not that they are malicious or bad tempered, it's just in their nature. They eat what they eat. Have you ever heard of a bulwark?" Hilda asked.

"Yes," Haley answered. "I saw them in Bella's Blossom Shop. What about them?"

"Well, one of their functions and the reason they are so popular is because they eat just about anything. They are good guard flowers, especially the kind that wander property borders. Just about everyone I know has one."

"What about you?" Henry asked. "Do you have one?"

"Yes, I have several."

"You do?" Haley asked, startled. "I didn't see any when Henry was learning to fly."

"I have the gloaming variety. They only come out at dusk. I keep them in my greenhouse. They are protected from the light by two way glass."

"Two way glass?" Henry asked.

"You can see into the room from the outside, but from inside you can't see out," Hilda explained.

"That's weird," said Henry. "We have glass like that at home. You can see out, but not in."

"That's weird," Hilda said. The twins laughed.

"Can we go see the—"

The soft gong went off and the twin's ran to the door. Valian and Sersha were waiting on the stoop. They came in and sat down.

"We'll leave shortly," said Sersha, seeing the anxious looks on their faces.

Hilda brought out mugs of rainbow dew and they visited for a few minutes.

"Will you need any help with all those goodies?" Sersha asked.

"No, I'll use my postern," she replied.

"All right, everybody ready?" Sersha teased, looking at the twins with a mischievous smile.

"Yes! Let's go!" Henry exclaimed, eagerly.

"What's a postern?" Haley asked, as they took off.

"It's a doorway," Sersha answered. "It's like the portals we use, like the one you came through, except posterns on our side don't lead to the other side, they lead to other places in our world."

"Cool," Henry responded. "Where are they?"

"Well, just about everybody has one."

"I know!" Haley shouted. "The pictures! They're in the pictures!"

"Yes," Valian replied, amazed. "How did you know?" "When we were first in the palace, I thought I could see the leaves in the trees moving."

Valian smiled. "You're pretty sharp," he said softly.

Haley turned red but smiled back.

The sun was almost down. The group took off. The twins followed behind, taking in all the sights. They flew over the city making their way to the outskirts.

It was a beautiful night, warm with just a hint of a breeze. As they drew nearer to their destination, they could hear the faint sounds of a gathering. Voices carried on the wind. They had flown further than the twins expected. Out of the city and into the darkening countryside, over hills and valleys. The voices got louder as they came up over the edge of a dense wood.

Before them was a lit up dell. Bonfires were roaring everywhere. There were, surprisingly, quite a few homes out here. Lanterns were strung throughout branches of the trees. They reminded Haley of the Chinese type, round and made of paper. The trees here were as tall as the ones in Roan. Steps wound their way from the top of the trees, round and round, with torches lighting the way to the bottom. There were lanterns everywhere and balloons were tied to the large decks overlooking the forest floor. Almost every home displayed them.

On the ground, there were many quaint little cottages, half of which were hidden from view by bushes, small trees, and ivy. Big patches of sunflowers and climbing roses also made the cottages hard to spot. If it weren't for the torches, lanterns, and the fact that every home was lit up, Haley didn't think she would have known they were there.

Fairies were flying everywhere and she could hear the beat of drums. They landed in the center of the village. It was a huge open area and the largest bonfire of all was merrily crackling. It was a spectacular sight. There were makeshift open tents which housed the food. Stone hearths smoked with sizzling meat. Many tents contained long picnic style tables accompanied by comfortable looking couches.

Fairies milled around setting things up, adding balloons, lanterns, and moving chairs, what really caught the twins' attention were the gatherings around the bonfires. There was music and singing. Strange creatures danced around the fire pits, chanting and laughing. Many flipped through the air like acrobats, making Haley laugh.

Sersha pointed out pixies, wood nymphs, tree sprites, and brownies. There were even a few mermaids with their heads poking out of the nearby ponds, singing and giggling as they watched the festivities. The twins were dazzled.

Sersha and Valian led them to an enclosed tent where they met up with Lilia, relaxing on a soft couch. Inside, they were surprised to be able to see through the walls as if they were invisible.

"Good evening," said Lilia. "We honor you tonight." She was as glorious as ever, dressed in a scarlet gown and a simple crown of gold. "Let us announce your arrival," she said.

She waved her hand and the door opened. Four husky guardians appeared out of nowhere to escort her to the largest tent. Haley was startled by their size and muscular stature.

"Don't worry," Sersha whispered, seeing the look on Haley's face. "We're well protected, even though we're on the ground. The entire dell is surrounded by walking bulwarks. They've been enchanted to stay at the borders."

Haley felt much better.

They followed the queen into the large tent. Lilia waved her hand through the air. A deep sound of a horn echoed through the dell, long and low. Everyone stopped what they were doing and gathered around the tent. There were dozens of different varieties of creatures, young and old. All together there were at least a thousand in attendance.

"May I have your attention, please?" Lilia spoke, her voice amplified somehow. "Welcome to all!"

The crowd cheered.

"We are here to pay tribute to four of our citizens, two of which are newcomers. They have worked together to steal away the evil one's prize and rescued those that were in bondage!"

There was more cheering and clapping from the crowd. Lilia held up her hand for silence.

"Not many of you know them. First, may I introduce the mastermind behind this feat and the rescuer of the fairies, Haley Miles! Haley, please step forward and be recognized," Lilia shouted over the cheers and clapping.

Haley stepped forward, her face turning red with embarrassment, she curtsied.

Motioning her hand toward Henry, the queen continued, "And, may I introduce Haley's twin brother, Henry. He cut down many boar trolls with a bow and arrow!"

Loud cheers went up for Henry. Those were the most dangerous of the troll species and everyone clapped louder because of that fact. Henry stepped forward and took a small bow.

"And you already know these next two. They have served us well over the years, our two chief guardians, Sersha and Valian!"

More cheering and clapping went up for their own. Lilia lifted her hand once again for quiet.

"This is not just a celebration for their victory, but also a pre-coronation."

The crowd grew silent.

"For their courage and bravery, and expertise in the way of battle, Henry and Haley . . . " she said, motioning toward them. "If they accept, they shall join the guardian band."

Loud cheers echoed through the dell. The twins were taken by surprise. They stood with their mouths gaping, at a loss for words. After more applause, the queen raised her hand one more time.

"Let the celebration begin!" she shouted.

Everyone cheered and dispersed. Some went back to the bonfire, but the majority went into the food tents. A few others gathered around Henry and Haley, clapping them on the back and congratulating them, especially Sersha and Valian. They were beaming.

"Isn't it wonderful?" Sersha said to Haley. "Mom told me last night!" she exclaimed with excitement.

Haley was dumbfounded.

"Wow," Haley replied, "I never dreamed . . . "

"Isn't it cool?" Henry said, excitedly, as he and Valian walked through the crowd toward her.

"Wow," Haley said again, smiling. "I don't know anything about being a—"

"We'll teach you!" Sersha interrupted, with a big grin.

Suddenly, Haley's thoughts dwelt on her parents. "What about our parents? Will we ever be able to see them again? Will they remember us?" she asked, looking at Sersha. "Of course, you will see them again. You still have plenty of time to get back. Their memories will be restored and you can return home whenever you want."

Haley breathed a sigh of relief. "Can we think about it first?"

"Certainly. You two talk about it and we'll abide by your decision. Come on! Let's join in the fun!" Sersha said excitedly, putting her arm around Haley's shoulders, leading her back into the crowd.

They went to the bonfire and had a fabulous time, dancing around and flying through the air; they did somersaults, cartwheels, and flips. Someone threw some dust into the fire, soon joined by fire fairies that danced and danced.

Haley did several cartwheels high in the air and stopped suddenly. Looking up in the sky, she saw a falling star.

"I saw a falling star!" she called out to Sersha, who was doing a twirl with Valian. They stopped and looked toward the night sky. Soon another falling star went streaking by, then another.

"It's a meteor shower!" Valian called out to her, zipping past Sersha and up to Haley. They hovered in the sky, watching the wonderful display of natural fireworks. Valian took Haley's hand and pulled her higher into the air. They hovered over the treetops, hand in hand. "You are just as captivating as those stars," he whispered to her.

Haley turned. She looked into his pale, blue eyes and whispered back. "Thank you, Valian," she smiled, they settled onto the highest branch, watching the sky. A short time later they heard the familiar chiming, announcing the main course was ready. "I suppose we should go," she said, softly.

"Yes, they're probably wondering what happened to us."

They flew hand in hand over to the food tent. Sersha saw them coming and smiled when she saw them holding hands.

Everyone stuffed themselves. There were so many different dishes of goodies, it was hard to know what to choose. Plates were loaded down and seconds dished out. Valian and Haley joined Sersha and Henry at a comfy sofa under one of the many tents. They sat, chatted and ate then ate some more. Henry went back for thirds.

It was a joyous evening. Many people went back to the bonfires to dance and sing. There was also magic. A few witches flew in from twenty realms away. They celebrated long into the night as the moon slowly made its way across the sky. The witches fascinated Haley. They were clad in various types of clothes, most of which reminded her of a movie she saw years ago called *Hocus Pocus*. They wore black pointed hats and their brooms were long and sturdy. Each woman wore a cape, black on the outside with various colors on the inside. The witches sat at the next table beside them, Haley found she couldn't take her eyes off them. Most of them were beautiful but, some of them looked the part of witches portrayed as wicked and evil. Hilda came strolling up to the table with a tray of goodies.

"Hilda!" Haley cried. "It's good to see you!"

"Here," said Hilda, holding out the tray. "I made these especially for you and Henry."

Haley took one of the small squares and took a bite.

"Mmm," she said. "This is delicious. What is it?"

"It's an old family recipe passed down from generation to generation. It's full of secret ingredients."

"Tastes like a brownie," Henry piped in.

"A very special brownie," Hilda added, as she walked over to the witches table and sat down.

Haley felt a little envious of Hilda, who sat with the witches. She wished she could sit with them. She had always been interested in witches and planned on being a witch last Halloween, if she hadn't found Sarah's wedding dress.

"She knows them?" she asked Sersha.

"They're her relatives," Sersha replied

"Relatives?" Haley asked. "Hilda is a witch?"

"Well yes, she is one of the rune clan. I thought you knew that."

"No."

"But you called her Broom Hilda."

"You know about her?"

"Where do you think the idea of Broom Hilda came from?"

"I-I just thought it was made up," said Haley, surprised.

"Don't you remember when I told you about fairy tales being true?"

"Yes, but I didn't realize that had anything to do with witches," Haley said, looking over at the witches table. "Could I meet them?" she asked, hopefully.

"Sure, come on," Sersha answered, cheerfully, getting up from the table. Haley followed her. "Everyone, this is Haley, she's been dying to meet you."

Haley shook hands as Sersha named them all. When they got halfway down the table, Haley was especially drawn to one witch in particular.

Sersha called her Tilly. She looked like she was in her early forties. Her hair was pitch black and her green cape accentuated her emerald, green eyes. She had a pretty face and long fingernails painted red, which she was tapping on the table.

Haley was ecstatic about meeting them all and wanted to sit and listen to them talk. She thought they must have many exciting tales to tell.

Tilly didn't say much but listened as the others chattered loudly. She kept looking over at Haley, which made her a bit fidgety. She wondered what the witch was thinking. Haley saw movement from Tilly's lap; she saw, with astonishment, a black cat. It stood up, stretched, and curled back onto her lap. *Wow,* she thought.

The stories about witches and black cats are really true. She continued to listen in on several different conversations.

"Eye of newt . . . frog entrails with one part scorpion blood . . . "

Laughter rose up from the other end of the table, witches were slapping the top and leaning back in fits of laughter. Haley could have sat there for hours listening. Abruptly, Tilly, who had been watching her, stood up.

"It is time," she said. The others looked up at Tilly then at the moon.

"Oh, my goodness, how time flies," said one witch with a nose that stuck out at least two inches, with a big wart on it.

"My, it's getting late," said a short plump witch.

"We have to fly," Tilly said to Haley, with a strange stare. "It was a pleasure to meet you. We'll have to have you for dinner sometime," she said, with just a hint of a smile in the corner of her mouth.

They mounted their brooms. With a glance back at Haley, Tilly took off like a shot, streaking across the sky at incredible speed, with the other witches hot on her trail.

"Wow," Haley said aloud. She walked back over to the table by the others. "They are incredible," she breathed with a sigh.

"Yeah, they're great," Sersha responded. "You've got to be careful with witches, though."

"What do you mean?" Haley asked, curiously.

"You never can tell what a witch will do. They can be very mischievous." Sersha had Haley's complete attention. "There are many different clans.

Most are friendly, but some of the witch realms have been corrupted by Molock's evil influence. You'll want to steer clear of them."

"Where do they live? Do they ever come to Roan?" Henry asked, completely fascinated.

"They live in the outer realms. As far as we know, they have never been spotted near Roan, but they can fly just as fast the rune clan, it's rumored they only travel at night. They join the night creatures and God only knows what they do out there. I've heard of rituals, spells, and even sacrifices."

That last statement gave Haley shivers up and down her back. She hoped she'd never run into any of the bad witches.

"Let's go wear off this food," Sersha said, looking over at Henry, getting up.

She and Henry flew over toward the bonfires. Valian stood next to Haley watching them go.

"Don't worry about the witches," he said, looking into Haley's eyes. "I won't let anything happen to you," he said, with a smile that melted her heart. "Come on!" he shouted, grabbing her hand.

They joined the others in song and dance, then gathered together in a circle around the fire and sat down. Some of the elder fairies told ghost stories that could curl the hair of the younger ones. Luckily, the children already left for the night, exhausted and happy.

The moon was almost out of sight and everyone began leaving. They silently flew home with fond memories of the evening. Haley broke the silence a couple miles from the palace.

"Where were Sarah and the girls tonight?" she asked.

"They stayed back at the palace," Valian answered. "They wanted to be with Zeb and Sarah said she didn't much feel like celebrating."

"How long will it be before we know what's going to happen with Zeb?" she asked.

"It shouldn't be long. He should be in the last stage now. With any luck he'll be awake by tomorrow evening," Valian replied. "He is heavily guarded, so if there's trouble, it will be handled swiftly."

"I hope he gets better," said Haley. "Sarah loves him so much and the girls are always talking about their father."

"He is loved by many. That's what he needs most of all to get through this. He is a strong, kind-hearted man. I believe he will be whole again." Valian sounded so sure of himself; Haley had no doubt Zeb would be all right.

Chapter Thirteen

JOURNEY'S END

Haley and Henry arrived at the palace and went to their separate quarters. Haley ran a hot bubble bath and soaked for a good long time. She thought about everything that happened to her and Henry since they moved into old man Johnson's place. It seemed like a lifetime ago.

She wondered if she really wanted to stay and become a guardian. She missed her parents, but she loved it here. It was a fun and wondrous place. She wondered what it would be like going back, living out her life on the other side after all that happened. She decided she would take her time in making any decision.

Henry would want to stay. He craved adventure as much as she did and she found it difficult thinking about leaving Valian. She had grown quite fond of him. He made her feel beautiful and special. With a happy sigh, she got out of the tub, put her nightgown on, and climbed into her soft down-filled bed. Haley drifted off into a peaceful sleep where she dreamed of flying hand in hand with Valian.

Back at the celebration grounds, the last few fairies and creatures dispersed, going home. No one saw the towering dark shadow lurking beyond the tree line. They didn't hear the snickering, nor did they feel the eyes looking greedily out at them. For hours, the shadow watched each movement, studying every creature. Eyes followed those that departed with great interest. The shadow looked down. Dangling from its long thin finger, a sparkling ruby swung back and forth, on a silver chain.

Haley awoke refreshed. She slept the deepest she ever had. Someone came in and opened the drapes, revealing a bright sunny day. She jumped out of bed and dressed quickly. Down in the great ballroom she found Henry eating a late breakfast.

"Hey, sleepy head, I thought you'd never get up," he said.

"What time did you get up?" she asked suspiciously.

"Ten minutes ago," he confessed, with a laugh.

"Where is everybody?" she asked.

"You haven't heard?"

She shook her head.

"Zeb is awake and everyone went to the infirmary to see him."

"Is he all right?"

"Haven't heard yet," he mumbled through a mouth full of food.

"Well, come on! Let's go!" she exclaimed.

Just then, Sersha and Valian landed in one of the column-terraced doorways. The smiles on their faces told the story, but Haley had to hear it.

"Is he all right?" she asked.

"Yes!" Sersha said with joy.

"When did he wake up? Did he remember anything? How are Sarah and the girls?" A flood of questions came streaming from the twins.

"Take it easy. One question at a time!" Valian laughed.

"Let's sit down. I'm starving," said Sersha. "We'll tell you all about it."

Breakfast was brought in and through mouthfuls of food, Sersha began telling them what happened.

"Well," she began. "I got up a couple of hours ago, when word came that Zeb was awake. I woke Valian and we went to the infirmary to see him. Sarah was there and she was ecstatic. She was sleeping at his bedside when he woke up. She felt a kiss on her hand and woke to see him sitting up in bed. She said when he smiled at her, she knew he was going to be all right. Then, he asked her for a sandwich," Sersha said, laughing. "He doesn't remember anything after entering the evil realm. His mind is a complete blank. He doesn't remember any of the things he did after Molock had him under its control and we don't want to tell him. Zeb would be devastated if he knew all the terrible things he did. He doesn't need to hear about it now. It's frustrating enough for him that he can't remember. When he found out where he was, he asked Sarah how she got here. Sarah told him about you two and how you came through the portal and agreed to help search. She told him, you two found him, which is sort of the truth."

"Can we go see him after we eat?" Haley asked, hopefully.

"Yes," said Valian. "He is asking to meet you."

The twins were excited and rushed through breakfast.

They followed Valian and Sersha through a labyrinth of rooms, hallways, and corridors outside across several terraces to a building on the far side of the palace. Haley saw a sign that read "INFIRMARY" as they entered. Inside, it was buzzing with activity. Nurses hurried from bed to bed, attending to patients in the waiting area.

Some creatures Haley recognized as being ones Sersha pointed out at the celebration. Others she'd never seen before. Several small dwarves were gathered around another dwarf, who was babbling senselessly, holding his head and moaning. She heard the word "spider" as they passed by.

A nurse came up, wanting to know who was sick and was quite relieved when they announced they were there to visit. She led them to an escalator and told them to go to the third floor and see the head nurse. They found the head nurse, she led them to a room painted a warm, pale yellow. When they walked in, Sarah looked up.

"Haley! Henry!" she exclaimed, running to them. She hugged them both and then hugged Sersha and Valian, then back to the twins again.

"Oh, isn't it wonderful?!" she cried, pulling Haley toward the bed.

Lying on the bed was a thin but cleaned up Zeb. He had color back in his cheeks, but he was considerably weaker. Sarah introduced the twins and Zeb was all smiles. "I want to thank you for what you did," he said, beginning to tear up. "I am so grateful to have my wife and children back safe and sound."

"Oh, hey," Henry blurted out, full of grins. "We were glad to do it. It was fun!"

Everyone laughed.

"We've heard so much about you," Haley told him. "We live in the house you built . . . well on the grounds where your house stood, anyway."

"I know," said Zeb. "They told me."

"We have so much to talk about," Haley said, taking a deep breath. "I don't know where to start."

"We'll have plenty of time to talk," said Zeb. "That is, if you're going to stay."

Everyone got quiet. Haley looked at Henry.

"Have you thought about it?" she asked him.

He shook his head yes. "What do you want to do?"

Henry looked around the room at all his new friends. He looked back at Haley.

"I'd love to stay, if you want to."

She sighed. "Well, I'd love to stay too, but I don't think I'm ready to give up my life on the other side just yet. I'd miss my parents and I just-I can't explain it. I know I will want to come back and stay, but just not yet."

They all looked sad but nodded their heads in understanding. Zeb closed his eyes. He still looked quite tired.

"Come," said Valian. "He needs his rest."

"We'll come back and visit later!" Haley called over her shoulder as they went out the door. Back outside, she turned to the others. "I want to make this my home," she said, looking at them all. "But first, I need to be with my parents for a while. I am going to want to tell them about all of you and this place. I want them to continue to be a part of my life. Then we'll come back to stay. I also have some things I'd like to bring back with me."

Everyone nodded. They decided to leave the next morning. Everyone went back to the palace.

Lilia was out on the large terrace having tea and they joined her. "It's a beautiful day, don't you think?" the queen said, breathing in deeply. "Ah . . . smell the roses. Well, have you two decided what you're going to do?" she asked, studying the twins.

"We'd like to stay," Haley replied, smiling. "But after spending some time with our parents."

"Wonderful. I understand it isn't easy leaving your parents and the life you're used to living. You take as much time as you need. In the meantime, we'll get to work on your home."

"Our home?" Haley asked.

"You'll need a place to live when you return. Have you thought of where you'd like to put it?"

"I-I didn't realize-I mean, I thought we would be staying here," said Haley.

The thought of having her own home was exciting. Her first place. She dreamed for a long time about when she would leave home and be out on her own, in her own place.

"I-well, I—"

"Of course, you haven't seen even one tenth of the city. You can have it built wherever you want," interrupted the queen. "Why don't you and Sersha go sailing today and pick out a spot."

"What about me?" Henry asked. "Do I get my own place, too?"

Haley never gave it a thought. She always assumed she and Henry would be together.

"Do you want your own place?" Lilia asked.

"Well sure," he replied, looking at Haley. "Could we be close to each other?"

Haley grinned at him. "Wherever you'd like."

"Cool."

The twins were excited.

"I really like the outskirts where Hilda lives," said Haley.

"Can we look there first?"

"Sure!" Sersha answered. "You want to go now?"

"Yes," the twins answered together.

Sersha looked at Valian. "You want to come along?"

"I'd love to," he answered, with a smile. Haley smiled back.

They flew off the terrace together, south toward the outskirts. They spent most of the afternoon soaring over the treetops, in search of the perfect place. Haley finally chose a pretty little spot on the edge of the forest, a little hollow backed by the trees. On the left were a dozen or so young birch. On the right, one of the many brooks ran by with small-tiered waterfalls gently tumbling into the outskirts. Willow trees, maples, and oaks lined the bank. Haley would have a good-sized front yard; ample space would surround her little cottage. She could envision flower gardens and several trellises for climbing roses.

Henry always wanted a tree house. Living off the ground appealed to him and he chose a huge oak on the edge of the forest.

"What do you want your home to be built out of?" Valian asked Haley. "Wood, stone, logs, brick?"

Haley thought a moment. She decided on a complete stone structure with a large fireplace.

Henry chose to build with wood. It seemed practical since he'd be living in a tree.

With their locations picked out, the four flew back to Roan.

Haley wanted to visit Zeb before dinner. He was feeling better when they arrived. A different nurse was on duty, a friendly blonde fairy who encouraged visitors.

They sat talking for hours about their home and all the changes that took place in the last two hundred years or so. Susan and Rose were there and were especially interested in dolls that could walk and talk, as well as televisions. They found it difficult to comprehend.

Sarah and Zeb were fascinated by the talk of cars, airplanes, radios, and refrigerators.

"What wonders!" Sarah exclaimed. It kind of scared her to think such progress had been made in such a short period of time. She looked at Zeb. "I don't think I want to go back."

He looked at his lovely wife. "I know how you feel, darling. Listening to everything Haley and Henry have told us . . . it wouldn't be like home anymore. All of our friends are gone, our home has changed completely, and we don't really belong there."

Zeb looked at Sersha and Valian.

"Would we be able to stay?" Sarah asked.

"We would love to have you stay," Sersha said, with a big smile.

Everyone in the room grinned.

"As soon as you are well enough, we'll make arrangements to build you a home, too."

Zeb was beginning to look tired and he closed his eyes.

"I think it's time we said good night," said Sersha. "We'll see you when we get back," said Haley.

They crossed the open courtyards leading back to the palace. Haley was busy thinking about the trip home.

"We'll have to go back and get our winter gear," she said to Henry.

"Oh, yeah, I forgot about that," he replied.

"Your things have already been brought to the palace," said Sersha. "We'll take you to the portal that comes out just inside your courtyard."

"What?" the twins echoed.

"Yes, there is an entrance right beside the oak tree."

"You mean all this time we could have-we had an entrance right in front of our noses?" Henry asked in disbelief. "Indeed," said Valian. "Zeb discovered that entrance when he dug his first cistern well. That's how we met him. However, that entrance he tried to seal by filling in the cistern. It didn't work of course, but he thought it did. When he first entered our side, we made friends, and while he was here, he discovered several other entrances. He left by a different portal every time he visited."

"Wow," Henry exclaimed. "That's how he was able to make the map."

"Yes," Sersha replied. "He found many entrances. I think he was worried about his children accidentally walking through the entrance in your yard, so he thought by filling in the cistern he would close it up. What he didn't understand is, the glittering towers don't always appear like clockwork. That particular entrance appears at random. It is this portal in which you will return home."

The twins were pleased. They wouldn't have to go trampling through the snowy countryside to get home.

"What about our wings?" Haley suddenly remembered. "How are we going to hide our wings?"

"I can't help you there," said Sersha, "but my mother can. She is the only one that has the ability to bestow a shroud. You can take care of that just before you leave in the morning."

"Great," Haley breathed a sigh of relief. "We don't need to freak out our parents."

The four went back to the palace and enjoyed a quiet dinner with Lilia before bed. They talked about the twins becoming guardians and their new homes. Haley had a difficult time falling asleep. She kept having strange dreams and they woke her up several times. She couldn't remember what the dreams were about, but they left an uneasy feeling in the pit of her stomach. She finally fell into a deep sleep a couple hours before dawn.

Her steward knocked on the door to wake her. She climbed out of bed, still incredibly tired, remembering today was the day they were going back home victorious. They'd completed what they set out to do. She felt proud of herself and Henry. Maybe they would fit in here in fairy world. She was excited about going home and bringing back a few things when they decided to return.

She met the others in the great hall for breakfast. As she entered, Haley spotted their winter gear on a table by one of the terrace archways. Henry looked as though he didn't sleep well either, but it hadn't affected his appetite.

Sarah was already at the Infirmary, but Susan and Rose were there, having a delightful meal. The twins ate silently, thinking about leaving.

"Well, I suppose we should get going, huh?" she stated, looking at Henry.

"Yeah, I suppose," he replied.

It seemed as if the excitement had worn off about going home. Everyone could sense their lack of enthusiasm. Haley kept wondering if they would really be able to come back. She prayed it wasn't a crazy, wonderful dream.

Lilia took the twins into a small room off the great hall.

"I am going to shroud your wings now."

She picked up a small box, opened it, and took out two small gems on chains.

"After a lot of thought, I am presenting you with your given gems."

She put one of the chains around Haley's neck. It was a delicate, creamy white pearl on a silver chain.

"Haley, this pearl is a representation of the gift you already hold. You have demonstrated a natural ability to see. You have dreams and intuition. Pearls are born when the moon is full. It is a result of reflection. The silver chain which encompasses it also has many of the same properties. Silver is formed when the beam of a full moon casts its radiance on the veins of obsidian rock. Obsidian can't absorb light of any kind. It repels light and causes the rock to bleed. Silver is the end result. The combination of the pearl and silver will compliment your gift."

Haley looked at the necklace. It was beautiful. She wished she could see what Lilia saw. To her, it just looked like a pearl on a silver chain.

"Thank you, your majesty," she said, with a quick bend of the knee.

"And for you, Sir Henry." Lilia put a gold chain around his neck bearing a small emerald and explained, "The emerald represents the core of the earth. It is growth and bounty. It is strength. Gold illuminates light. It represents intelligence and understanding, an incredibly wonderful gift you already possess."

Henry looked at the queen as if she'd lost her mind.

"Intelligence?" he repeated. Nobody ever called him intelligent. He grinned at Haley, who grinned back.

"Gold," Lilia continued, "Is created in much the same way as silver. When the sun shines on the obsidian rock, its inability to absorb the light causes gold to trickle from its surface. Small pools of gold and silver are found scattered throughout many different realms. New pools are being discovered all the time, which means veins of obsidian are spreading."

"What is this obsidian?" Henry asked. "Valian found Zeb wearing obsidian rock on a chain around his neck. When he saw it, he yanked it off him and hit it with his sword. Is it a bad rock or something?"

"Well . . . " Lilia began, "Why don't I explain it when you get back?"

She cast her hand before the twins and announced they were ready. Henry and Haley looked at each other. They were surprised at not being able to see each other's wings.

"Wow," said Henry. "How did you do that?"

She smiled and ushered them toward the door.

"Make sure you keep your given gems hidden from view and don't take them off. You'll need them," she said, as they joined the others.

"Well, it's time to go," said Haley.

Everyone hugged and the twins put on their winter clothes and boots.

"Where you going?" Susan asked.

"We're going home to see our parents," Haley said, struggling with a snowshoe.

"You're coming back, aren't you?" she asked, hugging Haley around the waist.

"Of course, we are," she answered, smiling down at the pretty little girl. "And I'll be bringing a surprise back for the both of you."

Rose and Susan began jumping up and down yelling, "YAY! YAY!"

"Are you ready?" Sersha asked.

"Ready as I'll ever be," answered Henry, rising into the air, moving toward the terrace arch.

Valian, Sersha, and Haley followed, soon they were flying across the city. A short time later, they landed in a large mushroom field beyond the borders of the outskirts. The mushrooms towered above their heads like giant redwood trees. Before them, a sparkling tower swirled like glitter in a blender.

"It's time to change your size," Valian said. A second later with a snap of color, everyone grew.

"What a rush!" Henry said, laughing.

Everyone hugged one last time. Valian looked into Haley's eyes.

"Be careful," he said with concern, and kissed her hand. "Farewell, milady. Don't be too long," he said, with a worried look.

Haley smiled and turned to go. She and Henry took each other by the hand and with a last look behind them, turned and vanished into the glittering tower.

The twins expected they would travel upward, opposite of the way they entered fairy world, however, they swirled and twirled downward. It wasn't long before they could see a tiny speck come into view, which grew bigger and bigger. They felt themselves gently pushed, as if a large warm hand was placed on their heads. Haley popped out first. She began to giggle. When Henry came through, Haley continued to laugh.

"What's so funny?" he asked.

"I'll bet that's what it feels like when a chicken lays an egg."

He smiled. "Incredible," Henry remarked.

They stood in the middle of their courtyard, next to the huge oak tree with their mouths hanging open. The courtyard was full of sunshine and blooming flowers. It was spring.

"Holy cow," said Henry. "I can't believe it! We were only gone a few days!" he exclaimed.

"Time is different in fairy world, remember? Sersha said a hundred years here, is just a moment in time on the other side."

"It just doesn't make sense to me. The sun came up and set the same way. I just don't get it."

"Maybe we're not meant to. Some things just can't be explained, like most of the stuff in fairy world."

Henry nodded. "Hey, we'd better get this winter stuff off," he said.

They stored their gear in the courtyard shed. "Henry! Haley!" called a voice. Carol opened the arched, courtyard door to the estate and stuck her head out. "There you are! Where have you two been? Out exploring again? Estelle has been cooking and baking all day for your father's party. Everything's ready, now get in here. He'll be home any minute."

"Okay, Mom! Be right there!" yelled Henry.

Carol went back inside. The twins looked at each other in amazement.

"She didn't realize anything," Haley said, softly.

"Cool. We even got out of school for the whole season."

"Yeah, I wonder how that was explained away. Sersha must have done something to the whole school because if we didn't show up for classes, the school surely would have called wondering where we were," said Haley.

"Yeah," Henry agreed. "Well, come on, let's go. I didn't realize it was Dad's birthday already," he said, laughing.

As they walked through the foyer, Henry spotted their pictures back on the wall. Everything looked the same as before they left. They entered the kitchen. Estelle turned from the sink and gave them a knowing, yet welcoming look. Carol walked past them with a chocolate cake.

"Can you two help carry this food into the parlor?" she asked, going through the door.

As soon as she was gone, the twins ran and gave Estelle a hug.

"Welcome home," she whispered. "It's so good to have you back again. How was your adventure?" she asked.

The twins both began talking at once.

"Shhh . . . I don't need the entire story right now. Was it fun?"

The twins were all smiles and nodded their heads as Carol came back in.

"Well? What are you waiting for?" she asked, slightly irritated.

"Sorry, Mom," said Haley, picking up a dish. She gave Carol a peck on the cheek as she left the room. Carol smiled and shook her head.

The parlor was completely decorated. There were balloons, and streamers hung everywhere. Presents were piled on a table in the corner.

Haley glanced down at them. "From Haley", "From Henry" could be read on the tags. Haley looked up confused. Estelle was standing in the doorway with a tray of lemonade and glasses. She gave Haley a wink and a smile. Haley smiled back.

Paul came home a half an hour later and they had a wonderful secret homecoming and birthday party. It was good to be home again.

Haley watched her parents throughout the evening and knew she couldn't leave. The only way that would be possible was if she and Henry told them the entire story. How that would be taken was anyone's guess.

The twins enjoyed the evening, then dismissed themselves around eleven to go to bed. Estelle retired hours earlier, so they didn't have a chance to tell her everything that happened. They climbed the tower stairs and went to their rooms. Haley sat down on the bed and looked around. It was such a lovely, feminine room. A soft rap came on the door.

"Come in," she said, expecting to see Henry, but it was Estelle.

"Oh, hi," said Haley. "I thought you were asleep."

"No, not at all," said Estelle. "Who could sleep with you two back and for how long?" Haley looked up, questioningly.

"I saw the gem you are wearing when you bent over in the parlor. I knew then that you would be going back," she said with soft, sad smile. "So, tell me what happened."

Haley and Estelle sat on the bed. Haley told her the whole story from start to finish. When she was done, Estelle was beaming.

"I knew it," she said. "I knew it. I knew you were destined for something great. I could see it the moment I met you. You are a very special young woman, Haley. I see a great and wondrous future in store for you."

Haley smiled at the rosy-cheeked little woman sitting beside her.

"It sounds like this young man, this Valian, has taken a fancy to you."

Haley blushed. "I like him a lot. I only wish I could talk to mom about him, about everything that's happened."

Estelle nodded. "You will when the time is right. Well, my dear, I wish you all the best. And don't worry about your parents. They will be well taken care of when you decide to leave. I've grown to love them like family. I'd best be off to bed now," she said, getting up to leave. "You sleep well and don't worry about a thing."

She wondered if Estelle lived with the fairies at one time. If she had, why had she chosen a life here when she could live in such splendor on the other side. She thought about Susan and Rose with their excitement upon hearing about walking, talking dolls. She smiled at the thought. She would go to town tomorrow and pick some up for them.

The next morning, the twins took the money from their allowance they'd been saving forever and hiked into town. They talked about their parents and Estelle's visit to Haley the night before. As they rounded the bend in the road, Owens Country Store came into view. They both stopped. A shiny Cadillac stood in the parking lot. They looked at each other, trying to decide if they wanted to go in.

"It's probably just Mrs. Seers, grocery shopping," said Haley.

"Let's sneak in the back door," whispered Henry. "There's no bell on that door. Maybe we will be able to hear something about Ike."

Haley nodded in agreement. They quickly ran into the forest that bordered the back of the store. Using the trees for cover, they made their way to the back door and snuck inside.

Luckily, it was an old fashioned store that didn't have mirrors at the end of each aisle. Quietly, they made their way down the farthest aisle and peeked around the end. They both held their breath.

Ike, Sr. was standing only ten feet away with his back toward them. He was examining a display of binoculars on the long counter. After a moment, he turned toward the aisle they were hiding in. Haley put her hand up to her mouth to keep from making a sound. She looked at Henry with fright in her eyes. Around Ike, Sr.'s neck was a large, jagged piece of obsidian. Haley began to tremble slightly and Henry held her arm at her side to keep her from knocking something off the shelves they were standing next to.

Old Clara Owens was behind the counter, she walked down to where Ike, Sr. was standing. "Find anythin' interestin'?" she asked.

"Yes," Ike replied. "I would like to buy a couple pairs of these," he said, looking up at Clara. "I'll take the best you've got."

"Goin' bird watchin'?" Clara chuckled.

"No," Ike said, with a cold look. He changed somehow. Haley couldn't quite put her finger on it. He seemed to have grown taller and maybe a bit skinnier than when she first met him.

Clara shrugged her shoulders and then spotted the black rock hanging around his neck.

"Say, that's an unusual looking necklace," she said, leaning over the edge of the counter a bit.

Ike slowly looked up from the binoculars he was holding. "Thank you," he said, in an odd voice.

Clara reached across to touch the black rock. "What is it?"

Before she could grab the stone, Ike, Sr. took a step back. Clara looked at him, somewhat startled.

"It's black onyx," Ike, Sr. said almost defensively. "Oh," Clara responded, still slightly disturbed by his reaction. "Well, these are the best we got," she said, handing him another pair of binoculars.

"I'll take them," he responded and walked down to the cash register.

The twins took the opportunity to quickly sneak back out the rear door and ran into the forest.

"Oh, my gosh!" Haley blurted out, panting. "Did you see what was around his neck? Obsidian rock!"

"Yes!" Henry replied. "He has either had that rock for a long time or he's found a way to get back into fairy world!"

"We've got to warn Sersha!" Haley called over her shoulder as she hurried toward the road.

They ran a short distance through the forest and crossed the road out of sight from the store. Once on the other side, they climbed up a small embankment and hid.

They poked their heads up to watch. They could see the parking lot, but most of the store was hidden by the bend in the road. A short time later, they saw Ike, Sr. get into the Cadillac and back out.

He drove toward them slower than normal and Haley was scared he might have seen them. He drove by, slowing almost to a halt. The twins were ready to run but he didn't stop. He sped up and disappeared around the next bend.

They got up and took off running toward home. There was a bridge they would have to cross, which was part of the Seers' long driveway. The creek was wide there and the water moved fast. When they got to the bridge, they considered whether Ike, Sr. had already gone by. They stood waiting. A flock of crows took roost in a tree behind them and they had a difficult time hearing anything else. Haley strained her ears to hear the sound of an approaching vehicle but couldn't hear a thing. Suddenly, the crows got quiet. They didn't make a sound. A car was coming down the gravel road and they shrunk back, hiding behind an area of bushes leading up to the water's edge.

The Cadillac came around the corner and the crows took off, cawing, then flew away. It made the hair stand up on the back of Henry's neck. Ike, Sr. slowly crossed the bridge and drove up the winding path to his house. As soon as he was gone, they ran across the bridge and through the woods.

Haley was ticked off because she didn't get to buy the dolls for the girls. She was even more upset when she remembered she didn't have Sarah's ruby necklace. Up in Henry's room, she asked, "How are we ever going to see when we can use the portal in the courtyard, when I don't have the necklace?"

She was worried and scared they wouldn't be able to return to fairy world. How did Ike, Sr. get his hands on obsidian stone? How did he find his way to the other side? What exactly *was* obsidian rock? What kind of properties did it have? She and Henry discussed those questions and couldn't come up with any answers. All they knew was that obsidian stone was bad. Also, the chain it hung from was made of silver, they both knew its properties and what it enhanced in its wearer.

The sun began to set and they went through dinner silent, deep in thought. Estelle could see something was wrong but couldn't ask them about it with Paul and Carol sitting there. She would have to wait until later in the evening when Paul was in his study and Carol was busy with her painting.

After dinner, Haley volunteered to help Estelle wash the dishes, which surprised Carol and made Henry roll his eyes. He detested doing the dishes but helped them clear the table.

Carol gave her children a peck on the cheek and went into her studio. Paul was busy with the evening paper and walked into his study, closing the door.

At once, the twins were telling Estelle about Ike, Sr.

"I had my suspicions about him when he came and introduced himself to your mom that day. He didn't come across the way he portrayed himself. And then, the day you left, he came again."

"Yeah! I remember!" exclaimed Henry. "We were just leaving when we saw his car pull in the driveway! What did he want?"

"He came to see your parents. He said he was doing some research, because he was planning on writing an article for the Moyie Springs newspaper. He said he was looking for any old literature about Zeb Bonner and his family. That Bonner had made a map of his journey west and it would be very helpful."

The twins looked at each other, knowing the other's thoughts.

"He was looking for the map," Estelle continued. "He asked whether either of you were at home, I told him you were out exploring. Then he took off, like he suddenly remembered he had forgotten to do something. It worried me and I hoped you two were okay. When you didn't come back after a few days, I assumed you had made it to the other side all right."

The twins went wearily up to bed. They decided they would go out to the courtyard portal in the morning and see if they'd be lucky enough to get through. Not more than an hour after they went to bed, one of the windows in Haley's room swung open with a crash, sending glass flying all over the place. Haley bolted out of bed in alarm. Before her, Sersha stood, trembling all over. She looked horrible. She was scratched up, bleeding on her arms, and she had a gash below her right eye. One of her wings was bent over, hanging like a snapped branch.

"You have . . . to come back . . . trouble . . . Valian . . . please come . . ." Sersha collapsed.

Author's Note

I had the honor of visiting the real Bonners Ferry in Idaho at the end of September 2011 when I was halfway done with *A New Kind of Battle.* I found it to be a fascinating, wonderful place, full of history and warm-hearted people. It was exactly the way I imagined it would be.

Sitting down with seven residents who were born and raised in Bonners Ferry was an unexpected pleasure. The stories they had to tell were nothing short of spellbinding. We met at the Northside School, built in 1912, which is now a charming bed and breakfast.

During our visit together, the group spoke about the Hawkins House, a large log house used as a restaurant. Mary Hawkins was a teacher at the South Side School and later became the second superintendent. I also discovered a man named Edward L. Bonner actually constructed a ferry to cross the Kootenai River and became the founder of Bonners Ferry. Thanks go out to my wonderful hosts: Howard Kent, Pat Meeker-Stewart, Judy Meeker-Shearer, Ruth Miller, Eunice Dinning, LaDonna Dinning, and a special thank you to Kelly Meeker-Hinthorn who put it all together.

About the Author

Elizabeth Rymer Patterson, a spellbinding author from Florida, invites readers on an enchanting journey into the magical realms of the *Bonners' Fairy* series. With a childhood love for fairy tales and a passion for nature, Elizabeth's storytelling seamlessly blends fantasy and reality. Her tales transport readers to whimsical landscapes where fairies dance, and magic intertwines with everyday life. Join Elizabeth on a magical adventure through the pages of her *Bonners' Fairy* books, where ordinary moments transform into extraordinary wonders.

Bonner's Fairy Series

Book One
The Legend Begins

Book Two
A New Kind of Battle

Book Three
Mischief and Mayhem

Book Four
Sailing Toward Destiny

Book Five
Secrets and Spies

Book Six
Caroline Belle and the Curse of a Blue Moon
(To be released in 2025)

Resources

211

Website

https://www.bonnersfairy.com

Facebook

www.facebook.com/BonnersFairy